Puffin Books

Editor: Kaye Webb

PS 224

20p

We Couldn't Leave Dinah

Although Mick and Caroline Templeton went to school in England they spent their holidays on Clerinel, a little Franco-British island in the English Channel. Their home, their family, their friends, and above all their ponies were there, and war and the threat of invasion seemed very remote.

So when the Germans suddenly pounced on the island, Mick and Caroline were horrified to be stranded on the quay in the confusion of evacuation. Helplessly they watched their father and brother steaming away, while they heard for the first time the tramp of German soldiers. Alone in an enemy-occupied country they went into hiding, and decided to stay and try to sabotage the enemy's invasion plans. Every day they stayed the risk of discovery grew greater, but their courage and enterprise increased.

This is a vivid and compelling book. Even if the atmosphere of a country at war may be unfamiliar to boys and girls reading about it twenty-five years afterwards, the combination of adventure and pony lore and the really breath-taking excitement of the children's adventures are timeless in their appeal.

We Couldn't Leave Dinah was awarded the Carnegie Medal for 'the most outstanding book published in 1941', and we are very glad to have it in our Puffin library.

Cover design by Elisabeth Grant

Mary Treadgold

We Couldn't Leave Dinah

Illustrated by Elisabeth Grant

Penguin Books
in association with Jonathan Cape

Penguin Books Ltd, Harmondsworth, Middlesex,
England
Penguin Books Inc., 3300 Clipper Mill Road,
Baltimore, Md 21211, U.S.A.
Penguin Books Australia Ltd, Ringwood, Victoria,
Australia

First published by Jonathan Cape 1941
Published in Puffin Books 1964
Reprinted 1967

Copyright © Mary Treadgold, 1941

Made and printed in Great Britain by
C. Nicholls & Company Ltd

Set in Monotype Baskerville

With love to my Father and Mother,
Jack and Hilda Treadgold

Contents

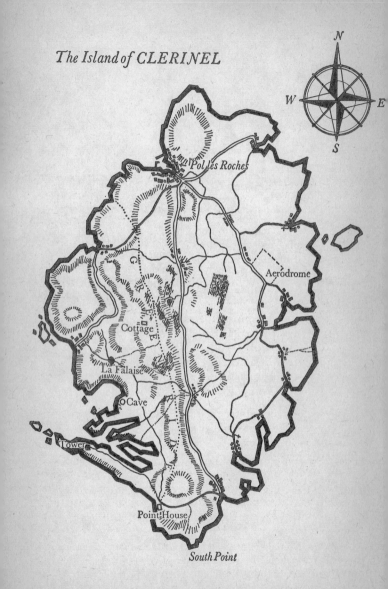

The Island of CLERINEL

N
W E
S

Pol les Roches

Aerodrome

Cottage

La Falaise

Cave

Tower

Point House

South Point

Chapter 1

It May Never Happen!

Caroline decided afterwards that the worst moment of the whole affair was when she met Thomas on the front doorstep. There were other terrible moments to follow, moments when you passionately desired an earthquake or tidal wave to blot you out straightaway to save any more trouble. But no crisis however frightful or prolonged compared with the moment of meeting Thomas on the door-step.

The day had begun quite well, more or less like all the other days in those last lovely weeks of the summer holidays. Caroline had begun it by hanging perilously out of her bedroom window with her striped pyjama coat flapping in the light early morning wind.

'Dinah! Din-AH!'

How very loud your voice, even at its lowest, sounded when everybody else was still asleep.

'Dinah! Din-AH!'

Caroline dropped her note half a tone as a concession to a slumbering houseful of people, and cocked an ear in the direction of the stable. *Stamp-stamp.* That was Punch's hooves restlessly beating against the partition. *Stamp-stamp.* That was Bellman imitating Punch. Caroline's ears were keen. There was not even an answering whinny from her own beloved Dinah. Caroline kicked out of her pyjamas in disgust. She seized a sponge, dabbed ineffectually at herself, and dived into a blue pullover and a pair of aged jodhpurs, smacked her hair twice with a hairbrush, and shot out of the room. She whistled across the landing with every tooth still rattling from the knocking she had given her head the night before in this effort to wake at six o'clock.

She paused for a split second half-way down the stairs and

listened, wobbling on one toe. The snores undoubtedly proceeded from Mick's room. She giggled to herself and stored the fact for future reference.

> Yah-o-o, yoh-o-o,
> Playing on de old banjo,

she hummed as she sped across the large silent hall. The maids had not yet flung back the old-fashioned French shutters that guarded the windows of all the larger houses on the island, but the sun was already slanting through the slats with the specks of yesterday's dust delicately running up and down its beams. In the ghostly light Caroline carefully drew back the bolts of the front door. She opened the door noiselessly and slipped out.

> Dere I see old Father Jim
> Playing on de old banjo –

Gosh, what a gorgeous morning! About the most super morning of all the super mornings of the most super holidays they'd ever had. Well, almost the most super holidays – Caroline hastily thrust that disquieting and obtrusive shadow back into the hinterland of her mind by telling a sleeping world all over again about Father Jim's banjo-o. She ran round the house to the stable on the grass for the pure pleasure of feeling the dew soak through her gym-shoes in little fountains.

'Din-AH,' hissed Caroline urgently at the stable-door. She was rewarded by a prompt snuffling noise and the appearance round the stall of Dinah's dark, graceful head, her blaze looking quite startlingly white in the dim light of the stable. Punch and Bellman, as befitted the property of other owners, very properly continued their stamping with no apparent interest in Caroline's arrival.

'No, I'm not going to take you out right away,' Caroline said severely. 'The Meeting's not till ten and this time you're going to arrive spick-and-span if I die. I've not got up at six just to play with you.'

She remembered with a shudder the last meeting of the Pony Club when Dinah had arrived woefully unspick-and-span, and the Pony Club President, Peter Beaumarchais, had raised one eloquent eyebrow like Miss Biddle, Caroline's form mistress, when she had found an untidy desk. She led Dinah out of her stall and fastened her between pillar ropes in the wide doorway. Dinah sniffed the morning air, nodding her head up and down pleasurably. Caroline produced a grubby lump of sugar out of her pocket, ran a critical eye over Dinah's points, compared her to her advantage with the two ponies belonging to her brothers, sucked her teeth like Petit-Jean, the stable-boy, and went off to fetch the brushes.

Though perfect in Templeton eyes the Templetons' ponies would have taken no prizes at Olympia. They were, with their broad withers and short sturdy legs, admirably suited to the rather rough riding the island offered.

Mick's Punch was a bright little chestnut, as stocky and well-knit as his fourteen-year-old owner. Mick's parents were apt to say – in the absence of the children – that the two were not unalike in temperament, both being slow and dependable with occasional disconcerting displays of sheer cantankerousness.

Caroline's Dinah put up slightly more show of aristocracy than Punch. She had been shipped over to Clerinel from England in her salad days, and her rather higher action and general appearance suggested a strain of thoroughbred somewhere in her pedigree. She was the colour of rich treacle toffee, about thirteen and a half hands, and not so at home on the moors and unmade roads as Punch or Thomas's pony, Bellman. That last worthy was far and away the least patrician of the party. Up to the time when Thomas had been promoted to a pony of his own after a long and humiliating phase of Punch and a leading-rein, Bellman had been merely the Lawn-Mower Pony under the ridiculous name of Tiny. Luckily Mr Templeton's acquisition of a motor mower to cope with the daisies on the lawn had coincided with Thomas's sixth birthday. There was no money to buy Thomas a pony, so Tiny, fat as a barrel and with as much vivacity as a feather-bed, was hastily clipped, provided with saddle and bridle, and led round to the front door on the birthday morn. Thomas gravely received the gift with no outward signs of recognition. He rechristened Tiny on the spot 'Bellman' from *John Peel*, though it transpired later that he had no idea whether the Bellman of the song was horse, hound, or huntsman. After this début Bellman's previous incarnation behind the mower was never mentioned, although Mick and Caroline sometimes wondered privately which of the two modes of life Bellman himself secretly preferred.

Caroline returned with an armful of brushes and combs and soft cloths, and the next half-hour or so was spent profitably both for herself and Dinah. She emerged at last from under Dinah's belly and squinted hideously at her handiwork. Dinah softly nuzzled her shoulder. Her coat gleamed like an advertisement for boot polish. Caroline nodded in satisfaction. 'Umm, umm,' she murmured. 'You'll do now, Dinah. You'll pass all right now.' She took a look from the off side. She was entranced at the spectacular results of her labours. 'That'll learn 'em,' she said to herself. 'Golly, I wish there were shows on Clerinel. You'd wipe the floor with the whole boiling.'

The sunlight was warming her skin through the blue pullover. She leaned up against the doorpost with one arm round Dinah's smooth neck. She felt relaxed and pleasantly lazy. Her eyes grew dreamy as she pictured herself in immaculate riding kit, leading a spirited, blue-rosetted Dinah round the ring with the judge stepping eagerly forward to shake hands. 'Never, Miss Templeton,' he would say, 'never have I seen a horse take that gate better. . . .' By the time Caroline had set the scene definitely at Olympia with her odious London cousins, Hubert and Penelope, goggling from the ringside, the distant *ting-tong* of the breakfast bell had floated across the stable-yard. Caroline began to come to, her face still remaining vacant with pleasant imaginings.

'Breakfast, mademoiselle Caroline.' Petit-Jean, in his blue jersey and long blue trousers, loomed up beside her. Nobody had ever persuaded Petit-Jean into the breeches proper to his profession. 'Ummmmm,' murmured Caroline, staring with screwed-up, knowledgeable eye at an imaginary saddle-sore near Dinah's withers.

'Breakfast, mademoiselle Caroline.' Petit-Jean was gently insistent. Dinah lazily swished her tail at a fancied fly. Caroline collected up the brushes, handed them over to Petit-Jean, wiped her hands hard down her jodhpurs, led Dinah back into her stall and stepped out again into the bright sunlight.

> Yah-o-o, yoh-o-o,
> Playing on de old banjo.

She came suddenly to life again as a whiff of fried bacon drifted across the stable-yard. She tore round the house, singing in a tuneless roar. On the front-door steps she could see her younger brother planted, gazing in the direction of the stable. In his butcher-blue linen knickers with his short red legs set firmly astride, Thomas looked as solid as Gibraltar. He was obviously waiting for her.

'Yah-o-o, yoh-o-o,' Caroline yelled with ghastly Red Indian fervour and bore down upon him, ignorant that the beauty of the brightest day was in one moment to be blackened out for her as though it had never been. There was a brief scuffle and a mêlée of arms and legs. Thomas spun round on his axis with suspicious readiness and allowed his small behind to be jovially smacked to an accompaniment of earsplitting shrieks. He emerged headfirst from under his sister's arm and the cause of his unwonted placidity immediately transpired. Caroline always remembered the next moment with a shiver of horror. Timing his thrust with the exquisite precision of a veteran actor and with the barely-disguised relish with which most of us enjoy imparting bad news, he said slowly and unctuously, 'Ole Hitler's goin' to take this island.' He then wriggled round under Caroline's arm like the flamingo in *Alice in Wonderland* and stared up into his sister's face.

He was disappointed. Nothing happened at all. He had expected her to scream and stamp both her feet. But Caroline was standing, still as a stone. Her inside rose up, heaved round and subsided into its proper place. 'Be quiet,' said Caroline fiercely to her inside. She felt sick with that nausea that attacks you when you have for some time been thrusting a haunting shadow away from yourself, and quite suddenly it comes back, no longer a shadow but an awful reality. She swallowed hard. The aroma of bacon suddenly sickened her. It was the most frightful moment of her life, worse than seeing Mick off to school or dreaming that Daddy had lost all his money and that she had to sell Dinah.

But not for Thomas the pleasure of seeing his wounding arrow find its mark. Dismay unexpectedly found relief in sheer downright bad-temper. 'Bunk,' said Caroline – and shook him till his face turned as scarlet as his fat little legs. 'Bunk, bunk, bunk,' she repeated furiously – and shook him until he crowed dizzily. Then she marched indoors with a breathless Thomas trailing dismally after her and panting with the monotony of a small gramophone, 'Isn't bunk. Ole Hitler *is* goin' to take this island. Isn't bunk. Ole Hitler *is* goin' to take this island,' all the way into the dining-room.

'Shut up, Thomas. Though I'm afraid it isn't entirely bunk. Hello, Caroline. Come and get on with your breakfast, both of you. Thomas, if you're going to rush off like that another time you might at least eat what you've got impaled on your fork before you go.' Mr Templeton, tall and looking more like a soldier than an ex-journalist, helped himself to some more toast as his family tumbled into the sunlit dining-room. On the far side of the table Mick's dark head could be seen buried inside the *Clerinel Gazette*. Thomas and Caroline slid into their places, and Thomas tucked a dinner-napkin carefully inside his white jersey.

Viewed round the Point House breakfast-table this morning, the Templetons did not obviously proclaim that they were all members of the same family. Mick and Thomas shared the same square build with their father, but whereas Mr Templeton was tall, Mick at fourteen and Thomas at seven were both small for their ages. Caroline, who was a long and leggy creature, already overtopped Mick, although she was a year younger. She and Mick had the dark colouring of their mother. Thomas took after his grandfather with his flaming mop of red curls, but Mick's short, straight dark thatch and Caroline's stumpy pigtails and their rather pallid clear skins told the observer that they were brother and sister.

Mick and Caroline up to a year ago had been educated together at a co-educational school in the West of England. They had both thrived at Herrinways where a discerning headmaster had discovered quite early Mick's absorption in animals and birds, and had turned the slow, thorough, patient little boy loose every afternoon with a thermos and his own field-glasses. At the same time he had directed the sister's devastating energy to the games-field and her vivid imagination to the excellent school library.

But all that, as Caroline would poetically sigh, was 'sweet yesteryear'. Mick had now been wafted off to his public-school where, though he disguised it even from Caroline, he was profoundly bored. St Dorothy's in Cornwall had taken Caroline to its bosom. She was riotously happy there, although her one fear, apart from the one that had shadowed these holidays, was of losing Mick in the hurly-burly of their respective school lives. Rapturously as she adored St Dorothy's, Caroline lived through each day for the increasing nearness of the holidays, when she and Mick, muffled in their all-disguising school uniforms, would meet on the pier at Plymouth for the Clerinel boat. The first days of the holidays were always passed for Caroline in an agony of watchfulness lest Mick's dependence upon her company should have diminished during the past weeks of separation. The first week she alternately spent in a delirium of happiness or a frenzy of despair that sent her sniffing under the hydrangea bushes in the garden. Mother was the only person who understood at these dire times, and Mother – alas, cruel fate – was for the time being inaccessible. She had gone to visit an aunt in Africa whom the children had never seen but who had brought Mother up when she was a little girl. War, after many false alarms, had come, and Mother was staying until she could get a safe passage home.

At the time of this story Daddy was living alone on Clerinel with Thomas, except for the holidays when Mick and Caroline noisily descended upon him.

'I've been afraid for some time it might happen, in fact ever since the fall of France and Germany took over the Channel Islands.' Daddy's voice momentarily died in a

15

mouthful of toast and marmalade. 'I didn't want to spoil your holidays by mentioning it, though. But I was afraid the position of Clerinel, so short a flip from the English coast, would be too great a temptation to Hitler. There's no doubt that those inlets where you children bathe would make excellent bases for his submarines to blockade the Channel.'

'Daddy.' Caroline's voice was imploring. This was the nightmare that had almost spoilt the holidays for her ever since she had first imagined it in the dormitory at St Dorothy's, after Jersey and Guernsey had passed into Nazi hands. 'Daddy, Hitler won't be coming today, will he?'

Mr Templeton laid down his cup and stared at her. Mick grinned and Thomas looked frightened.

'Good heavens, Caroline. Even Hitler doesn't move at that rate. Oh, I forgot. Of course you were over in the stable with Dinah when the paper arrived. No, my dear. The whole thing's only a suggestion of the Press. Germany hasn't so much as threatened or denied her intentions of taking over the island. It's only in the air. There's no need for either of you really to worry about it. It may never happen.'

'Bet you it does.' Mick's voice was gloomy. He tilted his chair backwards and forwards. 'Clerinel's just about Hitler's mark. You think how he'd eat up the airport with his beastly bombers. I don't suppose we'd defend it any more than we did the Channel Islands, do you, Daddy?' He surveyed the remainder of his breakfast with distaste. The Templetons' appetites were apt to abate under pressure of catastrophe. There was a pause. Mr Templeton went on unconcernedly with his breakfast while Caroline waited, hoping that somebody else would say what was weighing on her mind.

'Daddy' – her voice sounded parched in her own ears – 'we shan't have to leave Clerinel, shall we? I mean, not *leave* Clerinel. We could stay here and – and not interfere with them, couldn't we?'

There. It was out. The whole core of the haunting fear now lay out in the daylight for the whole family to see. Caroline felt dried up inside as she looked at Daddy, and from Daddy to Mick for reassurance. But Mick was also eyeing Daddy anxiously.

'Well,' said Daddy drily, 'you can stay if you want to, Caroline. But I warn you you'll spend the remainder of the war in an internment camp if you do. To begin with, the Nazis will almost certainly commandeer this house for some official, and, secondly, do remember you aren't, strictly speaking, a native of this island. You're English – enemy. And enemies are put under lock and key. You'd really better come with us, you know. You don't want to spend your youth sitting in chokey in Pol les Roches with a German bayonet threatening your tummy.' He picked up the little pile of letters by his plate and started to open them.

Caroline could bear it no longer. Her bacon tasted like sand and she felt she might burst at any moment. She pushed her chair back and went over to the window. Mick was still sitting, gazing glumly into space and drumming softly with his heels on the wooden floor. Thomas had disappeared on his own ploys.

She pushed the window further open and leaned out. Clerinel at its very loveliest lay before her, enchanted as a dream-island in the mists of early September. Woods and the low, rounded hills laden with thyme and heather encircled the house, and fell gently away down, down in a widening sweep until far below in the basin of mist they met the sea. Caroline could hear the slow thunder of the hidden surf upon their own piece of the shore. The garden shelved away in a series of terraces almost from under the dining-room window. The wind was blowing the mist away, and she knew that she would soon be able to peer down to where the garden ended in a little wild combe that ran down to the beach and the rickety boat-house. Caroline felt sick all over again at the thought of a fat German officer strutting down the little combe where they used to run in their bathing things, where they galloped the ponies before sedately walking them over the sandy ridge and on to the shore, where Mother and Daddy strolled in the summer evenings.

What Daddy and Mick said was appallingly true. Clerinel could scarcely have escaped the unpleasantly roving eye of the Führer seeking further establishments for attack against England. Its position in the Channel was ideal. It lay west of the Channel Islands and near enough to the French coast to render communications easy – and it was near enough to the south-west peninsula of England to be in an advantageous position for launching an air attack against that area. The heavy bombers with their fighter escorts would be over their targets within a comparatively few moments of departure. In the broken coastline to the north-west of the Templetons' house, where the sea ran inland in long deep inlets, the U-boats could stealthily slip like ugly sharks under the overhanging cliffs. Caroline shuddered at the sinister picture. 'They could even hide food for an invading army up those inlets,' she said to herself. 'Oh, we can't go, we can't, we can't.'

The Templeton family had lived on Clerinel ever since the children's grandfather had returned thither in his old age. Sinclair Templeton as a young man had taken his wife for a fishing holiday in the unexploited group of Anglo-French islands of which Clerinel was the largest. Neither of the two older children had cared particularly for the portly old gentleman who had tweaked their ears and dug their ribs like an Edwardian buck, but both agreed that Grandfather had known a good thing in islands.

After his month's relaxation on Clerinel he had returned reluctantly to his spats and top-hat in the hot City where, as he afterwards told a small Mick and Caroline, pennies lay on the pavements of Throgmorton Street. As he picked them up in the busy, noisy City he would dream sentimentally of that island beyond the railway and the sea, and hear again the beating of its waters. He had gone back, old and moneyed. Close to where, thirty years before, he had rocked uncomfortably in a small boat while Grandmamma sat under a pink sunshade on the shore, old Mr Templeton bought his land and built the square, spacious Point House. It lay, solid and serene, sheltered from the worst gales but open, always open, to the salt tang of the sea. There, where the long low uplands ran down to the white sands and the gulls swooped and screamed across the breakwater, he had lived until gentle, mousy little Grandmamma had died and he had followed her a year later. There the younger Templeton generation had been brought up. They had stabled their ponies where Grandfather had kept his dog-cart. Their boat was drawn up in the cove where Grandmamma had sketched the pleasant landscape. They picnicked and bathed on the beaches, rode over the hills, laughed and cried and squabbled in the terraced garden, and raced shouting down the windswept corridors of the house. At the end of the holidays, clutching their suitcases, they were packed back to school, where each dreamed secretly of that far-distant island until the claims of school overrode all else.

'We shall go potty – nuts – bats!' Caroline turned away from the window, her face set in long mournful lines. Even her pigtails drooped dejectedly. 'And what about the ponies? Oh, Daddy, what about Dinah? We couldn't leave Dinah.'

'Pull yourself together, Caroline.' Daddy looked up from his letters and spoke bracingly. 'It hasn't happened yet. Dinah? No, of course we couldn't take the ponies. They'd be perfectly all right. Petit-Jean would be here. But I'm not going to have you spoiling the rest of the holidays like this for yourself and everybody else. Even Thomas appears to have been quite unnerved.' He glanced through the window at where a small, disconsolate figure could be seen delicately watering an invisible plant with a red watering-can.

'Come along, pull yourself together,' he repeated. 'I wish to goodness the *Clerinel Gazette* had never mentioned the wretched business. Now then, what are you people doing today? Didn't I hear something about a meeting of the Pony Club?'

The wilting countenances of his two eldest offspring brightened imperceptibly.

'It's at ten o'clock,' Mick uttered in dirge-like tones.

'To discuss the new headquarters,' Caroline added like a death-knell.

'Very nice too,' said Daddy crisply. 'But what's gone wrong with the old ones? I rather liked that hut in the Lawrences' garden.'

'Mr Lawrence wants to use it as a potting-shed. His old

one blew down in the gale last month. In any case we were pretty sick of it,' said Mick with a shade more animation.

'And it's not really big enough now there are sixteen of us and with all the Junior Members. We can't have decent picnics there and there's nowhere to picket the ponies or keep anything,' put in Caroline.

'Ambitious children!' said Daddy, as he collected his letters into his pocket. 'I suppose a mere grown-up mayn't inquire the whereabouts of the new headquarters – or don't you know yourselves yet?'

'Oh, we know – or at least we think we know. That's what the meeting's about. We're going to inspect them. But we aren't telling till we're sure,' said Caroline in one breath.

'It's nowhere where it oughtn't to be,' added her brother hastily. 'You'll be shown it all right, Daddy. Probably on Anniversary Day.'

'Heavens, I'd forgotten that was on us again.' Daddy paused, aghast at the flight of time. 'Well, it's nothing to do with the Templeton family this year, thank the Lord. Never shall I forget the state of this house after last year's Pony Club celebrations when you were President, Mick. I suppose Peter Beaumarchais' father is the lucky parent-host this year.'

'He probably considers it a great honour,' said Caroline stiffly. 'We don't like to force our people into doing anything they don't want to do. Besides, the house wasn't in any state at all last year. And what there was we tidied up ourselves, me and Thomas and Mick. I definitely remember sweeping the mud up from the drawing-room myself and scraping up those crumbs that got trodden in.'

'And I cleared up that lemonade Alison upset on the sofa,' said Mick offendedly.

'And we wiped up that ice that got spilled ourselves, and when the peculiar-looking cousin of the Lindsays knocked over your Chinese vase I picked up the bits and wiped the papers on your desk.' Caroline's voice swelled on a rising crescendo of self-righteousness.

'All right. All right.' Mr Templeton's voice shook with

laughter. 'I didn't mean it. You know I dote on all Pony Club Anniversaries. The moment when that inspiring lemonade cup goes the round is the high-water mark of my life. You're riding to your meeting, aren't you? I thought Dinah looked very spruce this morning, Caroline. I saw her out of the window while I was shaving. Mick'll have his work cut out if Punch is going to rise to those heights.'

Caroline beamed. Mick rose from his seat with a do-or-die expression. Mr Templeton departed to his study, satisfied that at any rate for the moment he had managed to deflect his family's attention from the possible disasters heralded by the *Clerinel Gazette*.

Chapter 2

The Pony Club Meets

'Whoop-eeee!'

'Here they come! Oi, buck up there!'

'Come on then, you Templetons!'

'We've been waiting *ages* for you!'

'Whatever *have* you been up to?'

'Hello, Caroline! Hello, Dinah!'

'Hello!' 'Hello!' 'Hello!'

'Sorry,' yelled Caroline. She came tearing along the beach, hair flying and eyes streaming in the salt wind, sand scattering under Dinah's hooves in all directions. 'Woof!' Dinah splashed joyfully through a shallow creek and the water flew up in a shower over her jodhpurs. 'We had an awful do.' The light wind carried her words out to sea. 'Mick forgot to test his girth. Beastly thing turned over. I came on.'

A further thundering of hooves along the shore, and Mick lying across Punch's neck bore down on the crowd, waving aloft a spiked walking stick with a trailer of gleaming brown seaweed waving like a banner on it. 'Poof!' The tent-pegger drew up breathless. 'Sorry, everyone!' he jerked out.

The Pony Club surged forward in a body. Ponies and riders jostled together, flank pressed flank, irons clinked, tails flicked:

'Whoa there! Steady now!'

'Steady on, Gay Girl!'

'Steady, Robin! Good boy, good boy!'

'Keep off there! Dash it, *can't* you keep off?'

'Dinah, *will* you stop fidgeting?'

'I say, Alison, I jumped our four-bar.'

'Di-*nah*!'

'How d'you like this new saddle?'

'Bet you knocked it down.'

'Jolly nice piece of leather.'

'That girth still looks slack to me.'

'Pepper!'

'Robin!'

'Gay Girl!'

'Whoa there!'

'Steady, steady, girl!'

'SHUT UP, EVERYBODY, SHUT UP.'

Peter Beaumarchais, the Pony Club President, with great difficulty made himself heard over the din and clatter. He detached himself from the seething crowd and rode out on to the sand. A tall, dark boy with a thin, clever face, he surveyed the excited members with the same air of authority with which he managed his lively little grey, Pepper.

When the Pony Club had been started for the English residents on Clerinel some years ago, it had been fully intended by well-meaning parents that it should be run on the lines of the Pony Clubs in England and supervised by a grown-up. No parent had ever quite discovered how the plans had miscarried. Sufficient to say that the Clerinel Pony Club speedily developed an independent character that would have caused any Secretary of a more conventional English Pony Club to have handed in an angry resignation. Further, but not quite so speedily, adult authority was 'faded out' and replaced by a series of juvenile Presidents annually elected. These retained their authority by various disciplinarian methods and resigned their office the day after the Anniversary Celebrations, when the reigning President's parents entertained the entire Pony Club to a party, the nature of which was left to the discretion of the President himself. Peter Beaumarchais' election had followed Mick's year in office. He was Mick's closest friend, was nearly a year older than Mick, and had considerable dignity and poise, partly, so the others said, because he was French on his father's side. Pam Lawrence was overheard to say to Alison Lindsay that Peter's election gave a great air to the Club – at which Caroline was mightily offended for Mick's sake.

'Will you all kindly shut up? Now then, Mick, what do you think of it? It would be a nice change from having Headquarters right inland, wouldn't it?' Peter peremptorily recalled the Pony Club to business. He waved his stick towards the cliffs behind them. The whole Club promptly turned its ponies round, back to the sea, and sat gazing open-mouthed at where Peter was pointing. Everyone waited for the pronouncement of the late President.

Mick trotted Punch over to Peter, and narrowed his eyes in a considering manner up at the cliff. His stubbly hair was blown stiffly upright by the wind and even his eyebrows seemed to stand on end.

'You can't see it very well from where you and Peter are. I call that an advantage, don't you? We don't want people to be able to find it easily.'

Alison Lindsay sounded a trifle anxious. The suggestion for the new Headquarters had emanated from her and she was feeling the responsibility heavy. There was a murmur of approval from the Club.

'I shouldn't think you could see it from anywhere except from the sea. And that ledge in front would be nice for sitting on. Besides,' Mick's voice was pleased, 'they'll never be able to climb the path up to it.' From which cryptic utterance the members of the Clerinel Pony Club deduced that their poor decrepit old parents would never manage the ascent to search out their offspring.

'Well, let's go and have a closer look before we decide anything.' Peter touched Pepper with his heels and led the way up the winding cliff path.

Caroline edged Dinah fourth into the long cavalcade, cutting shamelessly across fat Rosemary Ellis's light bay, Mascot, and earning a plaintive, 'Ow, you pig,' from Rosemary. As the string of ponies wound and twisted up the grass-bordered sandy track, she leaned back at her ease in the saddle. The spray Dinah's hooves had dashed up in that glorious gallop along the beach still tasted salt on her lips. Her cheeks stung and glowed where the wind had buffeted them. Her whole body felt light and pliable and beautifully aired. She sang noiselessly to herself as Dinah walked springily up behind Richard Penfold's Robin. You couldn't really believe in awful things like Hitler when you were out in sun and wind and sea-spray and with people as absolutely marvellous as the Pony Club. It was frightfully silly to have got all worked up at breakfast – Caroline blushed at the recollection – anybody else's family would probably have laughed themselves sick. She expanded with sudden rapturous affection for Daddy and Mick and Thomas, in fact for the whole Pony Club – for Peter and Nicholas and Alison, for Richard and Pam, for Kit and for everybody, even fat Rosemary although she was pretty feeble. She turned in the saddle and bestowed a crocodilian grin upon the startled Rosemary, as, with a last scramble of her trim little legs, Dinah made her way over the top of the cliff on to the heather-covered turf and stood still as a stone with the wind blowing through her stiff mane.

The Pony Club picketed its ponies in the small coppice of silver-birches well away from the edge, busily criticizing each other's methods the while. Then, staggering a little as it regained its land-legs, it processed again in single file down to the ledge Mick had commented upon and which it had passed half-way up the cliff path. The sixteen Senior Members ranged themselves in a line with their backs to the shore, and surveyed in silence what was perhaps the most original headquarters any Pony Club had ever been lucky enough to possess.

At the back of the ledge, which, as Mick had indicated, was wide enough to accommodate the whole Club, Seniors and Juniors, a large, spacious cave, with a smaller cave beside it, receded far back into the sandstone cliff. High-arched, deep-recessed, level-floored with natural sandstone shelves, it was a pearl among caves. Each child mentally reviewed it from the standpoint of its parents. It was dry. It was safe.

Nicholas Lindsay broke the admiring silence. 'It's the very place,' he said and stepped inside.

'It's absolutely It,' breathed Caroline to Pam. She hopped on one foot with happiness.

'We rather banked on everybody liking it,' began Peter apologetically as he followed Nicholas into the Cave. 'Pam and I collected up most of our stuff from the shed yesterday and brought it over in the trap.'

The Club gave a squeak of excitement at the sight of its property piled in the middle of the Cave floor. Stacks of old *Horse and Hound*, the Club china, the ancient carpet filched from the Templetons' attic, the old deal table contributed by Richard Penfold's mother, the three-legged stools bought out of Club subscriptions, bundles of cutlery, old passe-partouted pictures of Grand National winners – all lay in a drunken heap waiting to be sorted. The Club, by this time, had rushed inside and was fingering its perquisites as though it had never seen them before.

But Peter had more to show them. He was already half out of the Cave and shouting to them to follow. 'Pam and I've had a bit of an idea about the little cave.'

He led the way up to two new iron staples firmly fixed in the back wall of the smaller, shallower cave.

'Oooh,' Alison interrupted him with a shriek, her round face glowing. 'Ponies!'

'Ponies?' There was a stir among the members, now almost satiated with the delights of the new Headquarters.

'Tell them, Peter,' Pam besought him, her mouth creased into a grin at the sensation Peter had caused.

'Well, we thought it might be possible to stable a couple of ponies here when we've fixed up a partition and a barrier at the entrance. We thought we might be able to arrange to sleep here sometime, if you all like the idea.' He paused rather diffidently and looked round the circle. There was no doubt at all about the Pony Club's response:

'Sleep here? *Sleep* here?'

'Pee-ter, what a wizard idea!'

'Gosh! I say, gosh!'

'Would they ever let us?'

'Could we bathe by moonlight?'

'Jolly good idea! I say, super idea!'

'Good old Peter! Good work! I *say*!'

The Pony Club was beside itself with excitement. It jumped about and whacked its thighs with its sticks. Sleep at Headquarters! Have tea there, supper there, breakfast there, wake up there, take off one's clothes there!

'I say, should we wear pyjamas?'

'What about bedding?'

'I suppose Mummy *would* say yes . . .'

'Shut *up*,' yelled Peter. 'It was really Pam's idea –'

'Good work, Pam –'

'Shut *up*. I thought we might do it after my party on Anniversary Day. Shut *up*, Caroline. Richard, if you can't pipe down you'll simply have to go and sit on the beach. No, I've not decided what the Party's going to be and if I had I wouldn't tell you. You can jolly well wait for your invitations. But we thought we could cart bedding here in the trap and on two ponies. Use saddle-bags or something. We'll make a list of what we need. Oh, golly – I clean forgot.' He paused and took a deep breath. 'Members of the Clerinel Pony Club,' he shouted in a stentorian official voice, 'is it your pleasure that we adopt these quarters as our permanent club premises?'

'*Rather*!'

'Aye, aye! Aye, aye!'

'All right. Shut *up*. Pam, put it down in the minute book. Alison, quick, that bottle of raspberryade at the top of the china crate.'

He waved the pink bottle high over his head.

'Don't waste any,' shrieked Caroline, dashing forward with the old spoutless milk-jug. 'Go ahead, Peter. I'll catch the drips.'

Peter brought the raspberryade bottle down with a crash on the rock, while Caroline carefully guided the jug as the liquid ran in a frothy pink cascade down the rock-face.

'I declare this to be the new and permanent Headquarters of the Clerinel Pony Club. Caroline, is there enough for everybody to have a sip?'

'I'm sure I don't know what the Juniors will say to being left out of all this,' sighed a careworn elder sister, as Caroline proffered her the few remaining drops. The rest of the Pony Club had subsided exhaustedly on to the ledge.

'Thomas'll be furious. We left him watering the garden.' Caroline seized the jug and tilted it back into her own mouth. She felt madly happy again. The awful watery depression of breakfast had completely evaporated. The sheer normality of everybody else and the excitement of the raspberryade ceremony had reassured her and made her feel snug and secure again. She was, in fact, as overblown as a barrage balloon with elation – and it took her in a manner we all know to our cost. With the recklessness of a braggart bravado she suddenly felt she could afford to flaunt and mock at her earlier fears. Before she could stop herself she was giggling to fat Rosemary, 'What price now Hitler pinching Clerinel?'

Before the words were fairly out of her mouth she could have murdered herself.

'What say?'

Rosemary's eyes were popping out of her head. 'Hitler pinch Clerinel?' Her high-pitched voice squeaked like a startled rat.

'Sssh. Don't say anything,' implored Caroline frantic-ally, horror-stricken at her own monstrous betrayal of herself. How silly it all sounded!

'Whatever *are* you talking about?' She writhed as the rat's squeak relentlessly dominated the somewhat lethargic conversation of the now recumbent Pony Club. 'PINCH CLERINEL?'

There was a sudden dreadful silence, and Caroline prayed for an earthquake. Puce in the face she threw an agonized look of entreaty at Mick, who answered with one of complete disgust but nevertheless entered the arena.

'Daddy said so. It was in the *Gazette* and he showed it to us. Daddy was a journalist,' Mick announced in pugilistic tones as though this statement clinched the whole argument.

The Pony Club stirred uneasily and murmured. The draught was being let in badly on its enjoyment. Someone voiced the one unspoken thought:

'But what would happen to US?' Unlike its elders, the

Pony Club took no pains to conceal its frank egotism.

'Rot.' Richard Penfold's father was editor of the *Clerinel Post*, stern rival to the *Gazette*. His scornful voice rose over the buzz of conversation. 'Father said that article in the *Gazette* was *rot*. He said who'd want Clerinel.'

The Pony Club breathed again. The scions of the opposing camps glared belligerently at one another. But Caroline, aghast at the disturbance she had created, was scarcely listening. She was watching Peter. Peter, who by virtue of his years acted as arbitrator in all disputes, was not even listening to this most serious difference of opinion. Peter was sitting on the rock at the far end of the ledge. He was looking at them as though he had never seen any of them before in his life. He looked old. His face was pinched and his eyes bleak like a winter's day. For an awful moment Caroline felt that she was looking at the face of a stranger. She had never seen Peter like this before. She scrambled desperately to her feet and stumbled across feet and sticks and prostrate bodies to the rock. It suddenly became terribly important that Peter should stop looking like that.

'Peter, you don't think it will happen, do you? You don't think the Germans will come, do you?'

The Pony Club was sitting upright now, its eyes fixed on the President's face. Peter grinned suddenly. Caroline was pawing at his breeches like an importunate puppy. Then his face clouded again. He turned his face away and looked out to sea.

'No, of course I don't think it will happen,' he said rather crossly – and his tone carried complete conviction.

*

And so the days went on, long lazy days of picnics and sailing, tennis, and riding. Summer determined not to die without a struggle, and in mid September, only a week before Peter's Anniversary Party, gave them a last display of incredibly warm, halcyon days, when the Templetons once more plunged joyfully back into summer shorts and Aertex shirts. Every morning detachments of the Pony Club met at the Cave to sweep and dust and pin up and unpack. It was soon quite obvious that on the day of the Celebrations the new Headquarters would be in fit state to receive, if necessary, the Queen of England, let alone critical parents with noses raised like porpoises to detect damp.

The furnishing of the Club premises and speculation and argument concerning the probable character of the Beaumarchais' party had, Mr Templeton was thankful to note, driven out all thoughts of ensuing trouble on the island. There was actually nothing to keep it there. The whole topic simply died down as though extinguished by a candle-snuffer. No more alarming leaders appeared in the newspapers, and Hitler made no pronouncements whatsoever upon the subject. The children were not to know that the Clerinel Press was now severely censored from London. Nor, if the island Guard was quietly augmented during these days and certain preparations made in town and village all over the island, did any news of it reach the Point House junior members. Nor, again, if Mr Templeton put through a good many expensive calls to his Fleet Street friends and kept three suitcases packed under his bed, did he see fit to say anything to his family. What time Mick and Caroline did not spend in the stable or careering round the paddock or sailing their boat *Daydream* was passed at the new Headquarters. They appeared to be incapable of discussing anything but the new premises, to the extent that Mr Templeton had not the least difficulty in making a shrewd guess at their whereabouts.

'We may not be as frantically County as that foul Pony Club of Hubert and Penelope's,' Mick said, 'but we've got tons more exciting quarters.'

He was lounging in a deck-chair on the terrace in front of the house, watching for the evening appearance of the postman on the white road at the bottom of the drive.

'Hubert and Penelope'd loathe the Cave.' Caroline sniffed disapprovingly. She was sitting cross-legged on the grass in a tangle of saddlery rubbing Dinah's bridle energetically with soft soap. 'Do you remember how rude they were about my jodhpurs? I know perfectly well they aren't up to much, but I don't need to have that pop-eyed Penelope tell me how awful she thought I looked, and Hubert laughing behind my back when he thought I wasn't looking. His ears stick out quite revoltingly anyway so he can't talk. They're an absolutely sickening pair.'

Caroline lashed herself into a fury and scrubbed away at the martingale as though she were soaping Hubert's ears flat to his head.

'Thomas's ears stick out,' murmured Mick sleepily from the deck-chair. Thomas was weeding busily in a neighbouring bed.

'Not very far out.' Daddy had come up, laden with writing pad and pencil, in time to hear the last remark. 'Thomas, I saw Jeanne putting a jug of barley-water out on the window ledge – if someone were kind enough to go and fetch it. Caroline, I don't know anything about these domestic matters, but I'm sure Mummy would have something to say about the lack of buttons upon that cuff. Hubert and Penelope may be unpleasant little prigs – though I suppose I ought not to say that about my own nephew and niece – but they did manage to turn themselves out well in their riding things when they stayed here that time.'

Mick snorted derisively and sat up to see if Thomas was in sight with the barley-water.

'Oh,' said Caroline in outraged tones. 'Daddy, how can you? Why, Penelope always wants to wear her best things. Why, Daddy, she even –'

'Well, I thought they looked very neat at whichever Anniversary Party it was they did go to with you.' Daddy leaned back in his deck-chair and looked reflectively at the landscape, calm and lovely where sea and hills were transmuted to flaming gold in the evening sun.

'Richard Penfold's. And anyway we all look neat at an Anniversary Party,' said Caroline virtuously. 'It was the one where the Penfolds had that marvellous treasure-hunt. D'you remember, Mick? And that little beast Penelope pinched that clue from under my nose in the Martello Tower –'

'I hope the Beaumarchais won't start you treasure-hunting all over the island in defence areas. You'll be picked off with rifles by the island Guard if you begin bucketing about near the Tower these days.' Mr Templeton tactfully changed the subject.

'Peter's frightfully late with his invitations, whatever the party's going to be. Mine were out long before this last year,' Mick said smugly, as he craned his neck to see if the postman was in sight.

'Well, you had me to help you,' retorted Caroline, hot in defence of Peter. 'I wish it could be another treasure-hunt this year,' she went on as she polished Dinah's throat-latch off with a soft cloth. 'Some of those clues were awfully clever and it was fun riding over the whole island.'

'I'd *much* rather it was a circus – a really e-normous circus.' Thomas had clattered back, dangerously balancing the barley-water on one dirty palm.

'Whoopee! Post.' Caroline shot to her feet, fell over the gear, and departed with a rocket-like motion to meet old Henri as he came paddling up the drive, a blue-bloused bent figure.

'I almost dread your Mother coming back,' Daddy said uneasily as he watched the flying form of his daughter clear a flower-bed. 'She'll have a fit when Caroline descends upon her like a young giraffe. Still, I suppose we can't actually stop her growing.'

'Here we are at last.' Caroline bore down upon them, triumphantly waving a large square envelope. 'Mick, you open it,' she offered generously, prancing noisily round the deck-chairs. Thomas had carefully put down his glass and was standing expectantly on one leg like an anxious stork. 'Get on with it,' she added, 'or I shall bust.'

Concealing his excitement, the ex-President raised himself to a sitting position and languidly stretched out a hand for the envelope. 'Now let's see what Peter can do,' he said in offensively patronizing tones, conscious of his own highly successful gymkhana last year. He ripped the large envelope open, drew out the white invitation card and slowly turned it the right way up. The children closed round it.

'O golly!'
'Cripes!'

'He's gone potty!'

They stared unbelievingly at one another and simultaneously bent over the card again. Mick held it up to the light as though some invisible writing might appear. Caroline seized it and turned it over, in the hope that further explanation might be inscribed on the back.

'He's gone barmy,' said Mick at last in awed tones. At this juncture, Mr Templeton reached for the invitation, read it, and began to laugh. It read:

Monsieur Beaumarchais and Peter have the honour to invite Michael, Caroline, and Thomas Templeton to a Carnival at La Falaise on 23 September at 3.0 p.m.

Underneath in the left-hand corner was printed in small Gothic lettering the magic word 'Ponies'. So far so good. Daddy's eye passed again to the right-hand corner. 'Fancy-Dress with Masks.'

'We couldn't,' moaned Caroline. 'We couldn't *possibly* go in fancy-dress.' Frightful recollections assailed her of those dreadful childhood parties they had attended with Hubert and Penelope, when she and Mick in agonies of self-consciousness had squirmed their way, dressed as elf and fairy, into a crowd of equally self-conscious sprites and pixies and pierrots and clowns. Those awful Marches Past! The clapping, uncomprehending Mothers and Nannies! Hubert and Penelope smirking as the Babes in the Wood! Ugh! Anathema were dressing-up and charades to the elder Templeton children after Hubert and Penelope's fancy-dress parties.

'It's even worse it being with the ponies. Dinah'd hate it. You shouldn't be expected to make fools of horses.' Caroline looked tragically round her family. After so much anticipation the disappointment was keen.

'We can't possibly go. Peter must have gone quite off it. He knows we loathe anything like that,' said Mick gruffly.

'I expect it's his awful father's idea. Mick, I bet it's his father.' M. Beaumarchais, who bore a close resemblance to an English caricature of a French parent, was not popular with the Templetons.

At this crisis a small insistent monotone made itself heard above the stricken groans of the elders. 'Could I go as a brigand? Could I go as a brigand?' Thomas, his eyes wide with excitement, was tugging at Caroline's arm.

'Goodness, I don't know, Thomas,' wailed his sister. 'We probably aren't going at all.'

The corners of Thomas's mouth turned down, and Mr Templeton, suddenly inspired, struck in hastily.

'I should think you'd make a very good brigand, Thomas. Er – Caroline, didn't you tell me you were reading the *Idylls of the King* last term? Why don't you think out some sort of get-up and go to the party as one of the characters from that?' He watched her shrewdly, believing that the appeal to her imagination would override her distaste for fancy-dress. He went on quickly before Caroline had time to speak. 'You could turn out the old piece-box in the attic. I know there's a jewelled belt off one of Mummy's evening dresses there, because I saw it sticking out of the box myself only the other day.' Caroline eyed him doubtfully. 'You could go as Elaine, the Lily Maid of Astolat,' finished Daddy craftily, hoping that Mick would not elect to greet this suggestion with a mocking guffaw.

Caroline's features imperceptibly relaxed. Elaine. She'd always loved Elaine, so beautiful, so wronged. It might not be so bad being Elaine with a jewelled belt. After all Elaine wasn't like being a fairy or an elf. She could use the old blue velvet curtains that used to be in the drawing-room for a costume, and make long sweeping plaits of wool. Concealing her enthusiasm, she looked at Daddy and nodded slowly. She was not going to capitulate too easily to the Beaumarchais' unfortunate invitation.

'Now there's only Mick left. We shall have to find something for him.' Mr Templeton was determinedly cheerful.

'I'm not going,' said Mick distantly, gazing stonily into space.

'O Daddy. O Mick. O Daddy, make him go –' wailed Caroline, the last shreds of pretence departing before this fresh crisis.

'Wait a moment, Caroline. Mick, you'll be masked, you know. Nobody will recognize you.'

'I'm not going.'

'Daddy, if Mick doesn't go I won't.'

'Wait a moment. Mick, why don't you borrow Petit-Jean's jersey and trousers and wear your sea-boots, and go as one of the island fishermen? Then you would feel at home and it would be a most suitable garb to ride Punch in.'

Silence. Mick continued to gaze sternly with Napoleonic mien out to sea.

'O Mick, say you will. Do say you will. You'll miss You Know What after the party if you don't –'

'You'd look almost as you do when you're in your own boat, Mick.'

Pause.

'Mmmm. I'll see. I might. It depends. But I don't think so.'

'Caroline.' Daddy beckoned his daughter aside. Thomas was rushing up and down, shouting about pieces of eight and the Jolly Roger. 'Caroline,' he spoke under his breath, 'in the right-hand drawer of my bureau you'll find some sheets of the best note-paper. If I were you I should nip indoors and get your acceptance written.'

Chapter 3

Carnival Parade

For the next few days the children saw very little of each other. Mick, as always towards the end of the summer holidays, disappeared for three days' fishing with two aged fishermen, the le Mesurier brothers, who lived in Pol les Roches, the only large town on the island. He departed every morning at dawn, and reappeared at supper-time with sunburned countenance and abnormal appetite.

Caroline sat about under piles of velvet curtain and ancient tarnished evening-dresses, inexpertly cobbling under Jeanne's tuition with large crooked stitches. In the kitchen Jeanne muttered to Marie, the little housemaid, that it was a pity Mademoiselle's fine school in England did not teach Mademoiselle how to *sew*.

Two days before Peter's party Caroline and Thomas tried their hands at making masks out of brown paper and stiffening them inside with paste. But the finished results slid about on their faces and skated round behind their ears so persistently that they clawed them off, staggering about the room with laughter, and had to persuade Daddy to drive them into Pol les Roches that afternoon. The drapers where the English residents bought their Guy Fawkes materials managed to unearth a boxful of proper silk Venetian masks. Mr Templeton bought his family one each, and then took Caroline and Thomas to tea and ices by the band on the pier. So, as Caroline told Mick that evening, good could come out of evil, even Peter's carnival.

The Templetons did not see anything during these few days of either Peter or the other members of the Pony Club. There was no time, with all the sewing to be done and with Mick away all day, to ride further afield than was strictly necessary to exercise the ponies. Besides, the Cave had been spring-cleaned up to such a standard of perfection that to polish or sweep any more would have been merely to gild the lily. There was nothing left for the reluctant Pony Club to do but await the Anniversary Celebrations with patience. Caroline had run into Alison Lindsay in Pol les Roches the afternoon they had driven in to buy the masks. Alison had agreed at the top of her loud, cheerful voice that fancy-dress parties were pretty lousy and that it probably was Peter's awful father who was responsible.

On the evening before the party, when Caroline was desperately tacking together Elaine's tinsel bodice, Mick strolled out into the garden to report that Peter had rung up about the night they were all going to spend in the Cave. He didn't want them to bring sleeping-bags after all, as he was busy cutting piles and piles of heather and transporting it in sacks in the trap.

'You didn't say anything about us not liking fancy-dress, did you?' asked Caroline anxiously. She held no great opinion of her brother's tact.

'Never even thought about it,' Mick replied airily. The unspoken loyalty that exists between the members of his sex prevented him from complaining to Caroline that Peter's manner down the telephone had been offhand to the point of rudeness. Mick simply could not make out what had come over Peter these days, but was not prepared to open up a discussion on the subject. He shrugged his shoulders behind Caroline's back and wandered off to the stable, leaving Caroline to her needlework.

Though she would have been flayed alive before she told her brother, Caroline was secretly quite elated at her prospective translation before the homely Pony Club into the Lily Maid of Astolat. When Mick had safely departed with his fishing tackle, she locked her bedroom door and floated up and down the room in the half-finished costume with long black tacking threads trailing behind. The school dancing-shoes with gold pom-poms, the royal-blue velvet kirtle, flowing so regally in folds to the floor, the belt that flashed round her waist like the jewels from a thousand diadems, enraptured her imagination. She wished she dared suggest that Mick should come as Sir Lancelot. She tied on the two darning-wool plaits over her own stubby pigtails and peered through the window at Petit-Jean lethargically sweeping the stable-yard, with a die-away expression that spoke sorrowfully of a Lancelot tarrying all too long upon the road. Oh, Elaine was going to be a grand success, thought Caroline, filled with kindly pity for the impoverished imaginations that would appear as commonplace clowns and fairies.

It was on the afternoon of the party, when the three children, mounted respectively on Punch, Dinah, and Tiny-Bellman, assembled for a final inspection by Mr Templeton, that things began to go wrong.

The fault lay entirely with the weather. It was really swelteringly hot. The sea was hidden by a drifting heat-mist, the hills shimmered in the torrid sunlight, and the grass almost crackled when you walked on it. It was so stifling and airless that you knew the whole lovely summer simply must sooner or later collapse in a thunderstorm. In their heavy fancy-dresses, Caroline and Mick wilted in the saddle at the thought of a three-mile ride along a hot smoking road.

Daddy was quite apologetic as he walked round them, shortening Thomas's stirrups and straightening the fold of Caroline's kirtle. 'I wouldn't have suggested these costumes for the world if I'd thought it would be a day like this,' he said and mopped his brow. Even he seemed limp and distracted with the heat. He was not coming to the party after all, as some proofs had apparently turned up which must be corrected by return of post. He looked worried and seemed unusually fussed about what exactly they were going to do and where they were going to be.

At last they were off, walking the ponies slowly down the drive and turning for a last wave to Daddy before rounding the corner. By the time they had gone half a mile nobody felt in the least like a party. Mick sat Punch with the martyred air of one nobly restraining the inevitable 'I told you so'. Caroline was consumed with remorse at having goaded her brother into fancy-dress. Even Thomas who, as a jolly little brigand in sleeveless shirt, corked moustache and scarlet cap, was the coolest of the three whined when Mick shouted at him to keep Bellman going. The ponies, maddened by the flies, bounced and minced in the most infuriating manner. Caroline, who had not bargained for the difficulties of riding astride in a sweeping velvet skirt, had much ado not to fall off. Mick's high-necked jersey clung to his back and neck and wrists until he was nearly demented with its prickly heat. Their masks slipped and slithered on their noses. Mick's rubber sea-boots squeaked irritatingly against the hot leather of his saddle. The sun-hat Daddy had insisted Caroline should wear until she reached La Falaise kept tilting over her eyes. The sun beat relentlessly down on the dusty road. Worst of all, the nearer they got to their destination the acuter became the attack of self-consciousness that descended with devastating suddenness upon the two older children.

'Oh lord!' Mick broke the silence of a mile and a half of jogging torment, 'let's go home. It's too awful. We shall peg out if we don't get into some shade soon. Let's turn back, for goodness' sake.'

Caroline wearily pushed back the clinging woollen plaits from her damp forehead and opened her mouth to give eager assent. Every garment she had on seemed to be pasted against her skin. Her mouth was dry with thirst. The prospect of returning to the Point House with its cool, shaded rooms seemed like Elysium. In after years she and Mick were often to wonder how different the course of events would have been if the three of them had turned back upon that grilling September afternoon and never gone to Peter Beaumarchais' carnival.

But it was not to be! At that very moment when so much – though they did not know it – depended upon their decision, there was a clatter of hooves behind them, and a cowboy and a gipsy waving a tambourine came cantering up. It was too late!

'Hello, Mick. Hello, Caroline. Hello, Thomas.'

It was not particularly difficult to recognize beneath the

gipsy's mask Pam Lawrence's cherubic face, and no mask or ten-gallon hat on earth could have disguised Richard Penfold's barn-door mouth. Nor did Pam and Richard appear to have much trouble in identifying the Templetons. 'Seems kind of pointless, doesn't it?' Richard said in flat tones, with an astonished look at Caroline's sun-hat. All five jogged on without enthusiasm towards La Falaise.

The grey seventeenth-century house which the Beaumarchais' had bought some six years before was most inappropriately named. It lay in a deep hollow of the hills about half a mile inland. Whereas the Templetons' home on South Point had been built open to the sea on the one side, La Falaise was completely enclosed by the hills that rose between it and the sea.

Not a breath of air stirred the heavy trees shadowing the lawn, as the five riders joined the crowds already swarming through the gates and round the marquee. The party was in full swing. Caroline edged Dinah into the shade of a large Spanish chestnut and looked about her. Half the island seemed to be present at the Pony Club Anniversary. People were milling past her, greeting friends and chattering to one another. Parents and relations were patting the noses of the horses, Pony Club members and their guests were sedately walking their ponies round and round the lawn. The whole scene was gay with colour from the fancy-dresses of the younger guests. Fairies, gipsies, clowns, cowboys, peasants, every conceivable disguise – they pressed round the marquee where already pink ices were being passed from hand to hand.

Caroline's head was aching with a knocking, throbbing pain. It was worse even than she had anticipated! What on earth were the Beaumarchais' thinking of? The whole party was on a far more elaborate scale than most Pony Club celebrations, and nothing like such fun. She could see nobody whom she knew, and nobody was taking any notice of the Lily Maid. Mick seemed to have disappeared completely. Thomas had been early wafted off with various of his small cronies. She smoothed out the already crumpled programme that had been handed to her at the gate. Oh dear! There was to be a Paper-Chase for the second item. The thought of galloping across miles of hot countryside made her feel quite ill. And – horror of horrors – the Paper-Chase was to be preceded by that most dreaded item of their nursery parties, a Fancy-Dress Parade.

'I won't,' said Caroline, clenching her teeth. She looked wildly round for Mick's support. People were still coming in through the gate, smart, cool, with parasols and sunglasses. Already the parade was beginning to line up under the direction of M. Beaumarchais. He was running fussily to and fro, a small spare man, with yellow wrinkled face and black moustache, pairing riders off according to their costume. Thomas was already at the end of the column with another chubby little brigand. And there was Mick – Caroline nearly mustered a giggle – the picture of dignified disgust, with fat Rosemary in the peasant costume worn by all the women of the island.

'There's no one in any kind of get-up like mine,' panicked Caroline. 'I know he'll make me go by myself at the end of the line.' She ran a despairing hand through her hair. Even as she raised her arm the worst happened! The tacking threads none too securely fastening tinsel bodice to velvet kirtle slowly and remorselessly parted company. Elaine was falling to pieces!

'I should stage a bolt if I were you.' Caroline swivelled round in the saddle as the whisper sounded at her shoulder. The masked rider on the little grey pony grinned. He was dressed in a pirate's costume and sat his horse as though he had grown up on it.

'O Peter,' groaned the distraught Lady of Astolat. 'What shall I do? I can't possibly go into the Parade with my vest showing.'

'Do what I say,' retorted Peter the Pirate, moving Pepper away. 'Fake a bolt.' He raised his hand in a half-salute and rode off to join the Parade.

Caroline gradually edged Dinah round to face the steep woodland path that led out of the garden and up on to the cliffs. Out of the corner of her eye she could see the Pol les Roches band getting ready for the March Past. She pressed her knees into the warm leather to hold Dinah in readiness while she warily watched the conductor's baton. Would M. Beaumarchais chivvy her into the Parade before the band struck up?

Crash bang! Tor-*e*-ador, oh Tor-or-*e*-ador! Trombones, trumpets, cornets, and drums blared into *Carmen*. The procession hesitated and then jogged sheepishly forward. Away shot Caroline up the path, releasing Dinah like an arrow, her hasty departure from the festivities unnoticed save by one startled Papa.

Tor-*e*-ador, oh Tor-or-*e*-ador! She could hear the strains dying away in the hollow below her. Caroline's spirits rapidly lightened. Dinah galloped on and on up the winding path, emitting little snorts of satisfaction.

Whizz! Caroline viciously kicked off the gold pom-pommed shoes. Swish! She tore off the kirtle, now suspended by a safety-pin in the rear, and hurled it over a bush as she fled past. Off went the plaits, off the many-jewelled belt. At the top of the path where the wood opened on to the hills, the Lady Elaine emerged, regrettably clad only in tinsel bodice and gym-knickers.

Sunlight dazzled her eyes. Fresh air swept up from the sea. After the hot damp hollow Caroline felt a sense of release. The headache miraculously vanished, and the cross tetchy feeling disappeared as if somebody had smoothed it out with a cool hand. She turned Dinah seawards and cantered happily along to a little green combe which ran gently down between two high ridges to the beach. She had the good sense to follow the trail of torn paper that proclaimed the path of the coming Paper-Chase. The trail, she noticed, cut straight across the top of the combe.

'If I sit just down there by those bushes,' she decided as Dinah slowed to a trot, 'I can see the Paper-Chase go across the top and join in with them, and then nobody will ever know what I've been up to.'

She tethered Dinah down the little combe by the gorse-bushes, and lay down in the shadow of a rowan tree with scarlet shining berries. She lay flat on her back and stared up at the pale-blue sky and then shut her eyes.

It was very airless again down the combe. The afternoon was beginning to draw in. Shadows were creeping like long fingers down the sides of the hills. The sun was dimmed by heavy banks of clouds promising the long-awaited thunderstorm. The sea was oily and the waves fell sluggishly along the beach. To the south in the next cove was the Cave, already filled with mounds of heather for the evening excursion. She sat up with knees to chin. Beyond the cove she could see the long narrow neck of land running out into the sea upon which was built the old nineteenth-century Martello Tower. The Tower was now a munition dump, one of the island's most strategic points. Daddy said that it could be held for weeks by quite a small body of men. She wondered if the four or five men in the uniform of the island Guard who were lounging about outside the Tower could see her perched in her gym-knickers on the slope of the combe, and decided that they couldn't. Five minutes. Ten minutes. Caroline wondered if the storm could possibly hold out until after tonight's excitement. She was not sure that she would care for being in the Cave in a bad thunderstorm.

Fifteen minutes. The Paper-Chase would be along the top of the combe any moment now. Caroline was just going to reach for Dinah's bridle, when she heard the slow *cloppety-clop* of hooves coming along the cliff path above her. Surely the Paper-Chase couldn't be coming from the direction of the sea? She dropped flat on her tummy, regardless of the fierce gorse prickles. This was different from riding among a lot of people in fancy-dress. Being caught by strangers in your gym-knickers was like those awful dreams where you streak down Piccadilly in pyjamas.

She peered up at the path which wound horizontally along the side of the combe. Then suddenly her eyes nearly jumped out of her head. With scarcely a sound, with scarcely the disturbance of a stone, round a shoulder of the hill and going towards the top of the combe came a silent column of riders. Who on earth? What on earth? Caroline lay transfixed. They passed across her line of vision like a company of ghosts – Caroline realized with a shock that every rider was in fancy dress, and every one was masked! Cavaliers and priests, ragged jesters and knights, they filed noiselessly up the still combe. The leader was in gay Elizabethan dress with a jaunty blue feather topping a round bullet-head and thick neck. Was there *another* carnival on Clerinel? The procession disappeared over the ridge at the head of the combe. Then, before Caroline had time to meditate upon this mysterious occurrence, distant shouts from the woods above La Falaise told her that the Paper-Chase had begun. Vigorously brushing the prickles off her knickers, she galloped up the combe just in time to be swept into the tail-end of the crowd as it precipitated itself across the head of the combe.

The trail almost immediately doubled back on itself behind La Falaise. It was obviously making for the coastline, but it took a great sweep inland to avoid the long sea inlet that lay between the series of small coves where the Cave was and the headland with the Tower. Dinah, refreshed by her graze, shamelessly took a short cut and tore past the last stragglers, ears flattened to her head.

'Ooh, Carry-line, where's your skirt gone?' squeaked Rosemary Ellis as Caroline shot past. 'Where d'you think?' Caroline flung back at her. She was beginning to feel bad-tempered all over again. It really was a sickening Paper-Chase, with everybody bundling along like sacks of potatoes. She drew rein slightly and looked round for her brothers. Pig, oh pig! A young man, on a grey not unlike Peter's Pepper, had dashed past her, almost brushing her from the saddle. Caroline angrily controlled Dinah and glowered after him and the half-dozen riders who poured in his wake. Then she stared, almost dropping the snaffle in her astonishment. How – queer! Over the first rider's head, impudently careening in the breeze created by their passage, waved a blue feather. How very, very odd!

The Beaumarchais had evidently managed to obtain permission for their guests to ride through the Tower enclosure, for the trail of torn paper streamed like Lux flakes along the side of the sea inlet. The island Guards, who knew them all personally, waved their rifles as they thundered past

They had withdrawn from the barbed-wire gate at the neck of the headland, but Caroline noticed that the trail turned off well short of the inner enclosure where the Guard lounged with fixed bayonets at the entrance.

The ponies raced down the slope on the south side and opened out on the sandy shore, going in the direction of South Point. Caroline could see the line of paper stretching across the cove and then showing white on the cliff-path at the far side.

As the stream passed her, she looked back for the young man with the blue feather who had fallen behind at the entrance to the Tower. She was so cross that she felt like stopping him and telling him what she thought of his manners. But there was nobody behind her at all. The landscape was silent and quite empty – except for one stocky little pony laboriously picking its way down the slope. It was mounted by a small, huddled figure with a scarlet cap rakishly askew.

Caroline waited for Thomas and Bellman to bump to a standstill beside her. It was plain that the latter was prepared to go on strike at any moment. He planted his four feet firmly in the sand and braced himself against any attempt that might be made to induce him to move them. Thomas appeared a very hot and dusty small brigand. The cork moustache was smudged across his cheeks and his scarf hung in limp folds. Bellman's reins were bunched anyhow in his hands. He looked pathetically up at his sister.

'I don't like this party,' he said on a forlorn note that tore at Caroline's heartstrings. Bellman's ears drooped in sympathy.

'I got a headick,' he went on dejectedly. 'Don't want to go back to the party, Caroline.' He gave her an imploring glance.

'Oh dear,' said Caroline. 'What an awful day this is.'

It seemed to be getting closer and closer. Her clothes were sticking to her with a damp persistency. The sky was darkening to an angry orange and the clouds were gathering more threateningly over the sea. Caroline looked across the cove. The last stragglers were disappearing over the top of the far cliff. It was too late now for either of them to catch up with the Paper-Chase. She turned her attention to poor, tired Thomas.

'I wish Mummy was home,' Thomas was saying shakily. His face was red and screwed-up. Caroline looked more closely at him. He must be feeling pretty frightful, she thought, to say that about Mother out loud, even though they were always, all three of them, thinking it. She came to a hasty decision.

'Look here,' she leaned over and patted the little red cap gently, 'I tell you what, Thomas. You go along home and tell Daddy what's happened. It's not very far from here, and you can go quite slowly and be home for a late tea.'

Thomas's mouth quivered, but his eyes brightened.

'Do you think I could?' he said in a more hopeful voice. 'Would it be rude?'

'No, of course it wouldn't,' said Caroline briskly. 'I'll say you felt sick if anyone asks. Off you go.'

Thomas gave a little sigh of relief. 'Orright,' he said, and tugged at Bellman's reins. Bellman, sensing a return to the stable, condescended to lift one hoof daintily out of the sand. Thomas gave a further jerk to the snaffle, and the pair meandered off across the beach in the direction of the Point House.

Caroline watched them out of sight. Then she turned Dinah and made for La Falaise by the quickest way across the cliffs. With any luck she was going to arrive back on the lawn only just in the wake of the Paper-Chase. And was she going to say something about gate-crashers! She glowed with fury at the recollection of the blue-feathered gentleman. Gate-crashers! There was nothing else he and his friends could be. She was sure they hadn't been there at the beginning and she'd never clapped eyes on any of them before, masks or no masks. Coo, she'd show them.

She reached the beginning of the wood and trotted wearily down the path between the trees to the lawn, past the gold pom-pommed shoes and the blue skirt festooned over a hawthorn bush. Whew! It was stifling. The warm, damp air from the hollow rose to envelop her like a blanket as she descended. 'I shall die if there aren't any ices left,' she moaned to herself, as she switched with a bracken stalk at the tormenting flies.

Between the trees she could see the crowd swarming round the marquee on the lawn below. She peered through the overhanging boughs. There was no sign of Blue Feather among the guests. The flies buzzed incessantly round her head. The bites were already swelling up and itching to distraction. One stocking was laddered to the ankle by an errant bramble. Perspiring, mosquito-bitten, dishevelled, with the tinsel blouse hanging damply round her neck, she posted painfully down the last bend of the path and emerged on to the lawn.

Hello! Caroline blinked. Surely that was their old Ford parked by the gate! All thought of Blue Feather and ices gone, she cast her eye round. Daddy must have finished his proofs after all. Poor old Thomas! He would be fed up when he found Daddy had come to the party after all. She swung herself gingerly out of the saddle and prepared to lead Dinah to find Daddy.

'Caroline.'

Daddy was behind her, gripping her shoulder. At his side stood a white-faced silent Mick.

'Thank God you've come,' said Daddy briefly. 'Where's Thomas?'

'Why? What?' Caroline stammered.

'Quick. Where's Thomas?' She had never seen Daddy look like this before.

'G-gone home.' Caroline got the words out somehow. Her heart was beating like a trip-hammer and she held tight to Dinah's bridle.

'Right. I'll go back and collect him. Hand Dinah and Punch over to the Beaumarchais' groom. Let me think a minute. Yes. Find Mr Lawrence and tell him you're both to go to Pol les Roches with him. He's over there getting Pam and Mrs Lawrence away. Thomas and I'll meet you on the boat by the gangway. It's the *Island Queen*. That quite clear, both of you?'

There was a terrifying urgency in Daddy's voice. Mick nodded. Caroline at last found tongue.

'Boat?' she said, and swallowed hard. 'What's happened? Daddy, what's happened?'

But there was no time apparently for explanations. 'I had a call from London,' Mr Templeton said tersely over his shoulder. 'Mick'll tell you about it. Don't kick up a show whatever you do, Caroline. Lawrence and I want you children clear before the panic starts. Oh lord, that's torn it –'

HONK HONK! HONK HONK!

Mick and Caroline switched round. A large grey official-looking car was tearing up the drive, hooting raucously as the crowd scattered. A man with a megaphone was standing up beside the driver. He was shouting one sentence over and over again. It rose over the lighthearted chatter and the flaring band music.

'The Nazis are coming! The Nazis are coming!'

As the car tore past the children Mick seized Caroline's arm. Together they stumbled across the lawn to the Lawrences' Alvis where it was parked by the gates. At the same instant there was a flash followed by a deafening crash. The long-expected thunderstorm chose this dramatic moment to break in a torrential deluge of rain over Clerinel.

Chapter 4

Last Boat

'If we could only scream and wake up –' Caroline poked her head tortoise-wise over the top of Mrs Lawrence's dressing-case. She spoke in an undertone so that the Lawrences in the front seat should not hear her. The sound of her own voice after the long silent drive quite startled her.

It was like a dream-journey through a green underworld twilight, she thought, as the car flashed round another bend. The mud flung up from the wet road spattered the window. The pile of suitcases swayed almost over on top of her, and she pushed them back towards Mick's corner with her shoulder. Through the streaming glass she snatched a glimpse of black hurrying figures on the road, their heads bent against the storm.

'Don't think. Don't think,' Caroline urged herself desperately. If you stopped for a second to think what was really happening to you, the aching tears would outwit your efforts to keep them behind your eyes. 'This time you can't wake up,' she went on arguing to herself. This time you couldn't pinch yourself or scream for Mother or wait for the bright sunlight to chase the terrors back beyond the borders of sleep. This nightmare dragged on and on in a dreadful confusion of tearing wind and flapping leaves and rain, distraught people running about with white, distracted faces, and cars starting up and disappearing into the storm.

'I think it's lifting slightly,' she heard Pam's father say as they whirled down on to the coast road. She peered once more through the misted pane. An angry white-flecked sea was lashing at the sand-dunes. Sand was driving in great slants across the road in front of the car, and the black clouds were lying almost across the very roof. On the bend of the hill, wading through the swirling rivulets of rainwater, they passed more pitiful little groups of refugees, shawls over heads, sodden bundles on their shoulders. They were gone like dream-figures, and the road stretched before them empty.

'They look so frightened, Bill.' Mrs Lawrence spoke in low, horrified tones.

'They may well,' answered Bill Lawrence grimly as he changed gear with a rasp. The road wound precipitously up between towering banks of rock and heather. The Alvis chugged her way on to the open moors again. Drenched acres of brown dying heather stretched as far as the eye could see. Far away along the cliff-line Caroline saw the gulls beating their way home against the storm. Mr Lawrence raised his voice as a gust of wind blew into the car. 'You'd look frightened if you didn't know what was going to happen to you. We know, and Mick and Caroline know, that we've all of us got every chance of getting away. But half these poor wretches may never get near the boats at all. This isn't a proper orderly evacuation. It's all far too unpremeditated for my liking.'

'But what do you think will happen?' Pam, wedged sideways between her father and mother, sounded alarmed. 'When will the Nazis come? Will they come tonight? D'you think they'll come by boat or what?'

'Heaven knows, Pam. I don't,' responded her father, lighting a cigarette with one hand. 'The whole thing may be only one of these mad scares and we shall find we've all been evacuated for nothing. As for how they'll come I should think they'll come by every conceivable way, short of coming up through the earth. Boat certainly. Troop-carrying aeroplanes –'

But Caroline had stopped listening. Evacuated for nothing! She clutched at a wild hope. Perhaps they'd all turn round in mid-Channel and come steaming back again. Perhaps there was just a faint chance of seeing the Point House and the ponies again after all. She dared not think of the dreadful moment when the Beaumarchais' groom had come up and led Dinah and Punch away. Mick had just turned and walked very quickly into the house so that he shouldn't see Punch's tail flickering away round the corner. Caroline wondered if the groom would ride the ponies home that night. It was a mercy Petit-Jean was there to look after them. Before she could stop herself she had given a little sorrowful snort. The ponies were gone, everything was gone, and Mick hunched in his corner seemed lost to her for ever down the dark corridors of this nightmare. He hadn't even spoken to her since Daddy had left them to go and pick up Thomas. She gave Mick a tentative prod through a hole in the mound of cases.

'What is it?'

'You do think, don't you, they'll look after the ponies all right?' Caroline whispered, in dire need of some speedy consolation.

'I don't know. How should I know?' Mick in his misery was irritable. Then with evident compunction: 'Yes, of course they will. They'll be all right, Caroline.'

'What else? Go on, Daddy.' In Pam's ebullient nature alarm had quickly given place to a demand for the sensational. She was gazing up at her father with round blue eyes.

'Well, there's a good chance of Fifth Column work – treachery by people already living on the island who have got German sympathies, you know.'

Pam was paying no attention. She had wriggled round and was looking at the pair at the back, her fair hair bobbing round her face as the Alvis bumped over the rough road.

'Gosh, you two are snowed under!' she commented. Then she giggled. 'I say, d'you realize it was tonight we were all supposed to be sleeping in the Cave? It would have been pretty damp, wouldn't it? Oh, goodness, Mummy, you weren't meant to hear that. I clean forgot.' She clapped her hand to her mouth and screwed round to look up at her mother.

Mrs Lawrence smiled wryly. 'Darling, I really don't think it matters much now,' she said. She turned her head so that Pam could not see her face. Then she went on in cheerful tones, 'It sounds a most attractive programme. Were Mick and Caroline to be there too?'

'You know,' Pam's father cut in, 'you youngsters will have to keep in touch with one another. We mustn't let the Pony Club be downed by Hitler. Those of you who are in London will have to get together and try and arrange rides in the Row and meetings at each other's houses, or wherever you are staying.'

The Row! Hubert and Penelope! Mick and Caroline simultaneously peeped at each other through the mound of suitcases and hastily looked away again. Of all important things they'd entirely forgotten to ask Daddy where he was evacuating them to. But of course there was, there could be only one place. Hubert and Penelope and Aunt Marcia.

Recollections flooded Caroline of dreary duty-visits to the tall sombre house in Eaton Square, of Penelope's dreadful, toothy-smiled governess, Miss Timpson, of Hubert's adenoided voice like a fog on Monday morning, of Aunt Marcia hearty and weatherbeaten in hideous tweeds – the whole personnel of that singularly uninspiring household processed through her memory and passed into a vista of eternal rides on rocking-horse hacks in the Row. Oh, well, everything was just about as frightful as it could be. Even if the ship sank beneath them in mid-ocean it couldn't be any worse, Caroline reflected as she sank into a comfortable wallow of self-pity.

'We're going to be in London for some time at any rate.' Mr Lawrence was determined to cheer the sagging spirits of his rear-seat passengers. 'And I know the Lindsays are staying with relatives in Chelsea. You won't have your President, of course, as the Beaumarchais are remaining at La Falaise. The Penfolds won't be in town either, for I heard Richard say they were all going to Somerset. But I believe, Pam, you'll be able to raise enough to have some fun in exile.'

That's all he knows, brooded Caroline darkly. Fat lot of fun there'll be with Hubert and Penelope trying to boss everybody. How *could* he talk about the Row? Had he ever *seen* the Row? Had he ever *seen* the bag-of-bone horses which were all they'd ever be given to ride? Oh, Dinah, Dinah! Caroline's resentment rose like the mercury in the nursery thermometer. She was determined not to be cheered by the rosy prospect that Mr Lawrence was envisaging for the Clerinel refugees. She stared balefully out through the streaming window.

They were nearing the big cross-roads above Pol les Roches. The open country had given place to the untidy scattering of stucco bungalows that indicated the proximity of the parent town, and the road was sprinkled with a steady stream of the bungalows' inhabitants all making for Pol les Roches and the boats. The Alvis threaded its way in and out, its tyres none too certain on the wet, shining surface.

'Not much farther now.' Mr Lawrence accelerated as the crowd momentarily thinned out. 'We shall just do it in daylight if we don't run into a traffic jam beyond the cross-roads.' He raised his voice so that the pair at the back could hear. 'Mick, what arrangements exactly did you make with your father? We all went off in such a rush that I didn't quite gather what his plan was.'

Mick leaned forward. In the gathering darkness his face looked white and tired. 'He said go on board –'

'And wait near the gangway till he and Thomas got there,' Caroline struck in. These awful makeshift arrangements with everybody trying to meet everybody else were all part of the nightmare. She would have given the world to have seen Daddy and Thomas drop through the car-roof so that they couldn't lose each other again.

'That sounds clear enough,' said Mr Lawrence, relieved that he had not got to add the two elder Templetons to his own troubles on this pleasure-cruise. 'Do you think you can cope with yourselves the moment we get to the harbour? Because I must do something about the car. We shan't be allowed to take it on board, and I'm not particularly keen to make a present of it to Germany. I rather think I know a little garage down by the quay where it won't be ferreted out very easily.'

'Oh, we'll be quite all right –' Mick answered quickly

for himself and Caroline. The prospect of being once more responsible for his own actions made him feel less helpless than when he and Caroline were handed about from grown-up to grown-up like parcels.

A sudden jolt interrupted him as Mr Lawrence braked in a hurry. They had nearly bumped into a solid jam of cars and lorries drawn up behind the lights at the cross-roads. They stretched well across the width of the road, presenting an impassable barrier. The Alvis's engine ticked over furiously.

'This,' said Mr Lawrence, no longer listening to Mick, 'This is the one thing I hoped we'd avoid.'

The four roads that radiated from the roundabout in front of them had been made some ten years ago and covered the whole island. Clerinel relied entirely upon these few, atrociously kept lines of communication. For the rest a network of lanes and tracks served villages and odd houses lying beyond and outside them. There was not, except on fête and market days, any traffic worth speaking of on these big main roads. You could hack along on their grass verges as they wound through the hills for miles without meeting more than a farm waggon, delivery van, or occasional private car. Even Mr and Mrs Lawrence therefore gazed open-mouthed at the spectacle now presented to them.

In every road converging upon the roundabout, cars, vans, lorries, motor-bikes, every conceivable vehicle, were wedged in inextricable confusion. Drivers were yelling and hooting like maniacs, pedestrians scurrying in and out between tail-light and radiator, cyclists wobbling a passage to the next lorry, policemen shouting, and the traffic-lights flickering through their rotation with no appreciable speed-up in the block. Mr Lawrence edged the nose of the Alvis in between a large furniture van containing half the population of a village near South Point and an enormous farm-waggon loaded with eight shouting black-browed children, hen-coops, pigs and sheep with nets thrown over their struggles, and so many earth-crusted implements that it looked as though a whole farm were being bodily evacuated.

Already, as far as Caroline could see back along the road, a line of cars was drawn up behind the Alvis. A cyclist was balancing himself with one grimy hand spread against their side-window. A motor-bike klaxon sounded by a furious-looking young man screeched on the other side. Children stumbled and fell against their mudguards; wheelbarrows, prams, handcarts, scraped the bumpers.

'It's all right,' Mr Lawrence said soothingly. 'I'd allowed for all this. It merely means we shall embark in black-out instead of more comfortably in the daylight.'

'But they can't all get on the boat, can they?' asked Pam, looking distressfully at the stream of people. 'Will there be other boats?'

'Oh, there'll be boats going until the Nazis actually arrive. They'll be all right,' replied her father briefly, somewhat in contradiction of his earlier words. Even as he spoke the car in front crawled forward a few inches and he accelerated. An old woman, with a hen squawking and fluttering in her arms, skipped nimbly out of the way.

'Caroline, I expect your father's somewhere down there with Thomas. It'll be touch and go who gets to the boat first.'

Caroline peered down the road that led out towards South Point as they slowly circled the roundabout, but it was too dark now to distinguish any one car.

Night was bringing with it a new terror to the island of Clerinel. Under wings of darkness the enemy that threatened its quiet shores could so stealthily slip among the inhabitants. There seemed to be a new urgency in the air as the Alvis moved forward, downhill into the little town. To Caroline's too-vivid imagination, the people were more determinedly pushing their way down the cobbled street as the last comforting traces of daylight were put out by the dark houses on either side. Their feet seemed to patter more frenziedly by the car windows. You could almost hear their low hurried breathing as they streamed past in the darkness.

Suddenly Pam gave a little shriek. 'Look, look, there's

55

Alison!' They strained forward. At the back window of the car in front Alison's snub-nosed features could just be distinguished pressed against the glass. A hand waved feverishly as a van forced its way between the two cars.

The gesture warmed Caroline. 'It means there are still people we know alive,' she consoled herself, and the dreadful feeling of being alive alone in a world of strangers packed up and departed.

Then quite suddenly everything went well. As though Alison's waving hand had been a signal the street flattened out, the bumping cobbles became large smooth paving-stones, the gaunt narrow houses disappeared, the block of cars moved forward quicker, quicker, and a whiff of salt wind and tar rushed into the car. The Alvis accelerated for the last time, pulled out of the line, swung round to the left, ran cautiously along a little way, and stopped. They had reached the harbour.

'Hop out, you two, quickly.' Mr Lawrence leaned back and pressed the catch on Caroline's side. 'I can't stop here. We'll be with you almost at once. There's the boat over there.'

'Bag for us. Get places for us with you.' Pam popped her head out of the window as Mick and Caroline with cramped and aching limbs fell out of the car into the enveloping night.

'Straight to the boat, mind.'

'Don't speak to anyone.'

'Cheerio, see you later.'

The chorus of well-intentioned instructions became fainter and fainter as the car-door slammed and the Alvis slid slowly forward into the velvety darkness, leaving the two Templetons standing staring after its disappearing tail-light.

Neither spoke for a minute. A cold wind blew suddenly and swiftly across their shoulders. A flurry of raindrops beat on their faces. Invisible in the black-out, the crowd surged and pressed past them like an unseen army.

'Mick.'

Caroline clutched unashamedly at her brother's arm. She

could see nothing in the darkness. She could only feel people running all round her. She dared not move an inch farther into the night. Complete panic threatened to engulf her.

'Mick – I can't see you –'

'All right. It's all right. I'm here,' said Mick from the darkness beside her. It was the second demand Caroline had made upon him that evening. He would have been quite surprised by the new protective feeling he was experiencing if he had had time to think about it. However, feeling suddenly very old and responsible, he took Caroline's hand. Its cold fingers threaded gratefully between his. He strained his eyes into the darkness, where the harbour buildings were gradually taking shape as he became used to the black-out. Yes, there she was, the good old *Island Queen*. He could just recognize the familiar squat funnels and the low, rather clumsy build of the little ship that carried them across the Channel to school each term.

'It's all right,' he repeated and gave her shoulder a gentle thump. 'Come on. Let's go and find Daddy. He may have gone on board already.'

Still clinging to each other, Mick and Caroline turned and moved along with the crowd which was flowing steadily towards the gangway of the *Island Queen*. The black bulk loomed high above them as they inched their way along, Caroline at every step falling over the peasant skirt she had borrowed from Rosemary before they left La Falaise. Everything seemed curiously silent on board, as though the black-out had suppressed all the noises people generally made when travelling. The boat was moving imperceptibly with the tide. They could see the row of unlighted portholes, and Mick even distinguished the word 'Queen' painted on a lifebelt.

The crowd filed in orderly fashion past the policemen and dock officials at the foot of the gangway. At the head it was sent right and left along the deck to find what space it could. Already dim forms were lying on the boards, huddled against bundles and suitcases. The one shaded electric bulb above a companion-way threw a half-light over the crowd round the head of the gangway. Officials, porters, sailors were hurrying to and fro in their anxiety to get away as quickly as possible.

'We shall never find him in all this,' whispered Caroline despairingly, after some ten minutes of being nearly suffocated in the jam.

'Oh yes, we shall.' Mick spoke in equally subdued but firm tones. He was not going to let Caroline know how worried he felt. He was sure Daddy had not realized that there would be so many people. The children had been pushed right away from the gangway as they thrust their way on board. Mick stood on tiptoe to get a better view. Surely Daddy and Thomas must be coming along soon!

'I'm sure he's had a car-smash or Thomas never got home or they've been struck by lightning – ' Caroline's imagination was rapidly getting the upper hand of her common sense.

'O Mick, *do* do something,' she urged half-sobbing. 'Where can they be?' She shook Mick's arm in her anxiety. The deck-space was nearly gone, and still the crowd swarmed up the gangway, and still no Daddy and Thomas appeared. Soon they would say the *Island Queen* was full and they would all sail away to England and Daddy and Thomas would be left on Clerinel. 'Mick, you *must* do something.'

'They're probably below.' Mick sounded far more reassuring than he felt.

'But he *said* at the top of the gangway,' Caroline insisted. 'I know something awful's happened. I know he wouldn't go below. Truly he wouldn't. Oooh, what's that? –' She buried her head panic-stricken in Mick's jersey as the night was suddenly rent by a deafening shriek from a ship's siren. It screamed twice, its long wail echoing and re-echoing across the darkened town.

But Mick this time curiously made no move to comfort her. He had jerked his head up and was listening intently. 'That's odd,' he was saying in puzzled tones. 'That's awfully odd.' He put out his hand to a passing sailor who was staggering under a load of luggage. 'Whose siren's that?' he demanded peremptorily.

'*Island Queen*'s. Alongside. Sailing now.' The sailor trudged on down the deck.

'Come on, quick.' Mick seized the essentials of the situation in one movement of his usually slow-working mind. With a dazed Caroline falling after him he forced a passage down the gangway. 'Come on. We've *got* to get there.'

They pushed and shoved, elbows out and heads down, desperation casting manners to the winds. At every yard they were driven back by the people still pressing on to the boat. Mick dragged and pushed Caroline along, gripping her shoulder as they fought a passage along the quay.

'Mick, what is it? What's happened?' Caroline's breath came in great gulping jerks.

'Wrong ship. Sister ship. We were on the *Queen of Clerinel*. Never saw *Island Queen* alongside,' panted Mick, diving between two laden peasants and pulling Caroline after him.

Wheee-eee-eee! Another bellow broke from the *Island Queen*, and Mick pulled up short, with Caroline precipitating herself over his feet. The bellow was farther away!

'She's moving. She's gone,' sobbed Caroline, clinging round Mick's ankles with desperate hands.

Mick stood horror-stricken, gazing out into the darkness while with one hand he automatically hauled his sister to her feet. The laboured motion of a ship's engine came clearly across the harbour; he heard the slow churning of water many feet below, and the swish of ropes and rattle of chains on the quayside. The *Island Queen* with her precious cargo of refugees was slipping quietly away to the open sea.

At that instant a car came racing down the cobbled street at the back of the harbour with its headlights blazing. At the bottom of the steep hill where the street opened upon the quay it swung round as the Alvis had done. Before it drew up its headlights described a flashing arc of light towards the slowly moving *Island Queen*. 'Put out those lights,' roared a dozen official voices. Out snapped the lights, but not before they had swept the *Island Queen* from bows to stern and shown her for the last time to Pol les Roches lovely and remote as she went on her forthfaring.

In that moment between the stopping of the car and the extinguishing of the lights they had rested on the stern and illuminated the deck. On the quayside where they clutched each other the eyes of Mick and Caroline widened and became fixed. There, leaning over the rails, looking anxiously towards where the *Queen of Clerinel* still lay berthed, stood Daddy muffled in his greatcoat, and behind him Thomas and Petit-Jean and a girl whom Mick thought was Marie.

Before Mick could shout the light was extinguished by the driver of the car. There was a silence. Then over the water came a last distant bellow from the *Island Queen*, as though she were calling hope and encouragement to the sister ship who had still to find the sea.

Mick pulled himself together. 'Well, that's that,' he said. 'We'd better get back to the *Queen of Clerinel*. After all she *is* going to England, and judging by the way Daddy was looking at her he guessed we'd be on her. Even if she doesn't land us at the same port as Daddy, we can borrow money off the purser and wire Aunt Marcia the moment we get ashore.' He screwed his eyes up to see how Caroline was standing up to this disaster.

Caroline had cheered up quite visibly now that she knew that her family was not lying in the local mortuary, blackened by lightning or mutilated by a head-on collision. The more recent episode of the *Island Queen* had made her forget for the moment how awful everything was. After all, they would eventually all land together in England, and everybody seemed to be managing very nicely even if things had got a bit muddled. She and Mick were acquitting themselves quite creditably and both were showing the common sense that their respective schools were always dinning into them. As they turned to make their way back to their original boat she felt quite lighthearted, considering everything, and was already composing the saga of adventure that would be recounted to the Upper Fourth on the first night of term.

Alas, alas! Poor Caroline! Fate had one more catastrophic surprise to divulge that night. No sooner had she and Mick set one foot before the other upon the return journey to the *Queen of Clerinel* than she, no whit less vociferous than her sister, let out a couple of ear-piercing bellows.

'Quick!' screamed Caroline, and she and Mick simultaneously broke into a shuffling run. At that very moment it seemed as though that part of Pol les Roches not evacuated with the *Island Queen* converged upon the *Queen of Clerinel*. Would-be evacuees fought and shrieked and scrambled. They changed their minds and decided not to evacuate, they changed them again and rushed back. Women screamed and wept, children wailed, the men tore and fought up the gangway, while the officials fell back helplessly before the onslaught. The police threatened a baton charge and the ship's siren bellowed again and again, the hoarse voice rising above the uproar on the quay. And on the edge of the mob Mick and Caroline danced impotently up and down, unable to move forward one inch.

'STAND AWAY THERE. STAND AWAY.'

'Let us through. Please let us through.' Mick's voice spent itself like a little whistle against the burly backs in front. Nobody took the smallest notice of the two children.

The same last raucous bellow, the same rattling of chains, the same churning of the water. The *Queen of Clerinel* moved down the harbour waters to follow her sister ship. As the last note of the siren died in the darkness across the harbour, a great sigh went up from the crowd on the quay, and a silence fell so deep that you could hear the water lapping at the slippery quayside steps.

On the fringe of the crowd, completely paralysed by this latest development, Mick and Caroline stood, their mouths open and their eyes starting like those of young hares from their heads. Around them the crowd was beginning very

slowly to disperse. Wives and children had gone off to safety, and there was nothing more to do but go home and wait for what might come. The steady tramp-tramp of passing sea-boots beat on the children's ears. The crowd was thinning into little groups talking in low voices. Mick and Caroline still stood, quite unable to cope with the situation. Then slowly through Mick's numbed brain there trickled like waterdrops a remembrance of what Pam's father had said about there being other boats that would sail until the Nazis arrived. He nudged Caroline who was still standing motionless beside him.

'S'all right,' he began for the third time that evening. But the words were struck from his lips. His jaw dropped. In the distance, coming nearer and nearer from the direction of France, was the low droning of a heavy aeroplane. Every man on the quayside stopped dead in his tracks as the drone grew to a roar and the roar to the thunder of an express train. Hidden in the night sky, the first great troop-carrying aeroplane swept over Pol les Roches to the airfield on the east side of the island.

The sound died in the distance and the people on the quayside came to life. 'The Nazis! The Nazis! They're here! They've come!' In a minute the children were left standing on a deserted quayside, with the rain pouring down upon them and the roar of the Nazi troop-carriers in their ears.

Chapter 5

Back to the Point

'Well,' said Caroline calmly, 'now what do we do?' She shook herself as she spoke, and the raindrops pattered off her neck on to the paving-stones with little plops.

It was ten minutes since the last plane had streaked over their heads, and they were still standing in the middle of the empty quay with their thick garments smelling like a couple of wet dogs in the rain. Silence had descended upon Pol les Roches. The tall shuttered houses bordering the quay showed no glimmer of life. No citizen was going to stand on his doorstep to listen to the invader pass across his roof-top. No searchlights or guns were sweeping the sky to hunt the enemy away from Clerinel. No soldiers ran along the harbour to guard its entry. The rain was actually stopping by degrees and the wind had already slackened to a night breeze. The only sound, it seemed to the children, in the whole of Pol les Roches was the creak and groan of the fishing smacks as they rocked in the harbour basin.

Caroline put out a wet clammy hand through the black-out and dragged at Mick's jersey. 'Oi,' she said, 'wake up. What do we do now? We can't stand here all night.'

Now that calamity had fastened itself so completely upon the Templeton family, she felt suddenly as cool and collected as though somebody had obligingly turned the shower-bath upon her. Efficiency positively inflated her. She felt more than capable of dealing with the whole Nazi invasion, Hitler included. She gave Mick another poke where he stood dreaming.

Mick emerged slowly from his trance, blinking his eyes like one awakened out of slumber. With the air of a seer making some world-shaking pronouncement he turned towards his sister. 'My goodness,' he said, 'I *am* hungry. Have we anything to eat on us anywhere?' He looked hopefully at Caroline who was plunging about in the pockets of her voluminous skirt.

'I thought when I sat down in the car it was on something pretty hard,' she said. 'It's worked round almost to the back.' She produced a small narrow object, and examined it closely. 'That pig Rosemary,' she commented. 'No wonder she's got those awful spots!' She broke the marzipan bar in half and handed one piece to Mick. 'You'll have to make it do,' she admonished him. 'That's all there is. Have you any money on you?'

'Not a sou.' Mick bit hard on the marzipan bar. 'It's all in my tie-drawer at home. Look here, we'd better clear out right away, because the whole town'll be in Nazi hands by dawn. Those planes will have landed enough men at the airport to march down and take possession without any trouble.'

'I suppose we'd better trek for home – no, I'm sorry there isn't any more marzipan – it won't be much catch without Daddy and Marie and Jeanne, but I don't see what else we can do.' Caroline spoke doubtfully.

'At any rate there'll be food there,' said Mick simply. His void had scarcely been affected by the Clarnico bar.

'As a matter of fact,' Caroline interrupted, 'we've simply *got* to get home as quickly as we can. Do you realize that if Petit-Jean decided to evacuate with the family at the last moment there's nobody to feed the ponies? It was your talking about food that reminded me.'

'I must say,' Mick remarked thoughtfully, as they turned to make their way off the quay, 'I don't quite know even when we do get home what we're going to do next.'

'Oh, that's all right,' replied Caroline airily. 'Something'll turn up. You'll see. Daddy'll come and fetch us off before long.'

Mick frowned in the darkness, realizing that his sister was too elated at her own calmness in the situation to take in fully all its implications. 'Look,' he said rather crushingly, 'pull yourself together. It's no good talking like that about Daddy coming to get us off. Daddy can't get us off. To begin with, he doesn't know we aren't on the *Queen of Clerinel*. If the Lawrences got on to his boat they'll tell him we're safe on the other, and if they got on to our boat when we'd disembarked then he'll think we're safe with them. He'll be expecting us to turn up at Aunt Marcia's, and he won't do anything until we don't.' He looked apprehensively at Caroline's outline, expecting that this brutal summary of a difficult situation would prick her display of self-confidence like a bubble. But Caroline in this mood was not so easily daunted. She was standing on the pavingstones with her hands on her hips, calmly waiting for him to finish speaking.

'All right,' she said. 'But when he does find out then he'll get us taken off. He can't just leave us to be interned, can he?'

'My good girl!' Mick was fairly frothing with impatience at this feminine obtuseness. 'What's he going to get us off *in*? The *Ark Royal*? Do for heaven's sake remember we're on enemy territory. We *can't* be got off.'

'All right. All right. Keep your hair on. I know what I shall do anyway.'

'What?' Sceptical voice from Mick.

'Go and tell the Beaumarchais what's happened. Peter and his father'll do something about us.'

There was a pause. Even Caroline was slightly startled at herself for suddenly producing this brilliant idea as out of a hat.

'Do you know,' Mick said slowly, 'I think that's a pretty good scheme.'

Caroline warmed to him. 'Come on then,' she said eagerly, and took his arm affectionately. 'Let's get home right away. We can have breakfast and then ride over to La Falaise, when we've seen to the ponies. It'll be frantic fun surprising them just when they're thinking they won't see us again until the war's over. Mick, d'you know, I rather like having adventures. I think we're getting on rather well, don't you? I mean, it's not many families have to plan their lives for themselves like us, is it? I mean – ow, leggo my shoulder! *Mick, what is it?*'

Mick was digging his fingers into his sister's collar-bone, in an effort to stem this frightful spate of boastful garrulity. 'Shut up and listen,' he hissed.

Tramp. Tramp. Tramp. Tramp.

Caroline froze slowly to the spot. Her hair rose on end and a cold shiver coursed down her spine. Her legs threatened to melt into the paving-stones. Mick was listening, his hand still pressing into her shoulder. *Tramp. Tramp.* Far away up the street, but approaching the quayside where they stood transfixed in the darkness, came the wavering light of an electric torch carried by an owner obviously uncertain of his way. Caroline's braggart confidence ebbed into the gutter. *Tramp. Tramp.* Whoever it was feared no man. There was nothing furtive about this night-walker who traversed the quayside of Pol les Roches near midnight.

> Muss i' denn, muss i' denn,
> Vom Städtlein hinaus –

Even at this moment of crisis Caroline mentally saluted the little tune the nursery musical-box had tinkled to them so often. Suggestive of gaily-painted Bavarian villages and dancing boys and girls in the fairy-land of Southern Germany, the song sounded queerly out of place on an empty quayside on a soaking wet night.

> Und du, mein Schatz, bleibst hier.

Tramp. Tramp. The singer was matching the rhythm of his step to that of his song. Mick and Caroline stood motionless. A dark figure loomed up a few yards away and passed them, still singing softly the little old song.

> Wenn ich komm, wenn ich komm,
> Wenn ich wieder, wieder komm.

The figure walked down to the edge of the quay and stood there, evidently looking out at the harbour mouth. There was the sound of a match striking and a spurt of flame as a cigarette was lit. Caroline frowned. Where, oh where had she seen that head, that thick neck before? Somewhere –

somebody – quite lately – her brain, tired out with excitement, refused to make the effort. It was unimportant anyway and – the figure by the quay-edge moved suddenly and, in defiance of all black-out regulations, waved its torch once, twice, in sweeping circles over its head. Flash! Flash!

Flick! Flick!

From beyond the bar a red light answered the torch. The figure turned away and walked slowly along the edge.

'Looking for the steps,' murmured Mick.

The glowing cigarette end started to descend lower and lower until it finally disappeared from sight below the edge of the quay as the smoker went down the quay steps. At the same time the children's pricked ears caught a low *throb-throb* coming from the direction of the harbour mouth. Something was clearly going to happen!

The tide was too low for the children to see even the outline of the small craft that was stealthily nosing its way into the harbour. Three or four minutes passed. Caroline changed her weight from one leg to the other to ease her cold and aching limbs. The mysterious signaller had evidently done his job properly, for the next thing they heard was the muffled bump of a fender against stone and the scrape of a painter passing through the iron ring on the wall. A low murmur of voices and some general commotion from the little craft drifted up to the listeners.

All at once the fitful glimmer of the torch began to waver its way up over the ground level. Mick pressed Caroline's hand. 'Make for the houses,' he breathed. There was not a moment to waste. One man with one torch might miss the pair where they stood, but a body of men all possibly armed with torches could scarcely fail to throw them into relief against the light. Caroline by sheer will-power induced her paralysed limbs to creep into the dark shadow of the houses at the back of the quay.

They need not have moved with such caution. The landing-party, whoever it was, was far too concerned with getting itself disembarked to bother about any strange flickering shadows in doorways. As the children shrank back into the old porch the last man evidently came ashore. They heard an indistinguishable order given in low tones, the chugging of the engine as it restarted, and the shuffling of many pairs of boots on the quayside as their owners formed themselves into some kind of column. Another order, and the column was marching quietly but with perfect precision across the quay to the street. At their head was the man with the torch. He was holding it down so that the light made an uncertain circle on the wet ground. Where the quayside joined the street he stepped smartly aside, and the children saw countless pairs of boots tread briskly across the misty pool of light as the column swung past him.

It evidently was not part of the plan that he should accompany the landing party, for the last man, whom Mick thought must be the officer in command, stopped by him in the little illuminated circle. A muted conversation followed. The signaller was obviously giving directions to the leader who did not know the town, for he pointed up the street with his torch. He swung it up and then casually held it pointed back against his own chest, so that the light should not be seen while he was talking. The circle shifted slightly, and moved up his tunic, illuminating the buttons and collar-badges.

Caroline, ensconced in the doorway, gave a little gasp. That was who it was then! This second time she recognized the identity of that thick neck and bull head. The yellow circle was playing on the heavy jowl of Blue Feather. She was certain, absolutely, that it was Blue Feather.

*

'Oh, I do wish I knew what to make of it,' said Caroline for the twentieth time, in yearning tones.

She and Mick were sitting side by side with their feet straight out in front of them. The scene was laid behind a bush off the road down which they had sped in the Lawrences' Alvis only the evening before. 'And I little thought,' Caroline had complained, 'that I should be walking every yard of the way back with torn and bleeding feet.' Under the circumstances this last exaggeration was pardonable. Nobody looks their best in a cold grey dawn after a wet night hidden in a doorway watching boatload after boatload of enemy troops invade one's home. Neither Templeton presented a pretty picture as they reclined under the gorsebush. Whey-faced with lack of sleep and with generous smears of mud upon their persons they looked, in fact, quite deplorable messes. Caroline's pigtails hung in limp straight dangles, Mick's thatch was plastered in lank streaks flatly across his forehead. Their feet were covered in white dust, their blue clothes were stiff and heavy with rainwater and caked with mud, their hands and nails were black with dirt. Wisps of grass and burrs, collected from their many halts along the road, adhered in diverse places. Above this distressing display two blear-eyed, exhausted countenances stared wearily upon the dawn-world.

'It's just as well Mummy can't see you now,' said Mick, looking critically at his sister's pea-green visage.

'I can't help it,' returned Caroline miserably. 'You're jolly lucky not to have a tummy that goes back on you in emergencies, Mick,' she added with an envious look at Mick's stalwart seaworthy form. The last remnants of her self-importance had trickled away like sawdust, as she had huddled shivering for some two hours against Mick's shoulder in the draughty doorway down on the quay. Ever since they had crawled out of Pol les Roches in the small hours, she had lurched along behind Mick with frequent lamentable retirements behind the hedge. 'And,' she added pathetically, 'I've not really had enough to be sick *on*, if you get me.' She gave a gusty sigh and lay down on her back to let the cool early morning breeze blow across her face.

'I do wish I knew about that Blue Feather man,' she reiterated. 'It's all very well for you to keep on saying it's plain enough that he's a Nazi officer signalling the landing-parties ashore while the others arrived by plane, but that doesn't explain a bit what he was doing in fancy-dress –'

'I don't believe it's the same man at all, or else you dreamed all that about him being at the Carnival. I never saw anybody with a blue feather there anyway.' Mick was getting weary to his bones of Blue Feather. He took off his waterlogged boots to ease his feet.

'Oh, it is; I didn't,' Caroline sat upright, bursting with indignation. 'I did see him, and he wasn't at the party so that's why you didn't see him. I've told you over and over again. You are beastly, Mick. And I've an awful feeling, too, that he's going to enter our lives. You know how you do get a feeling like that. Just a feeling. That we're going to be absolutely *haunted* by Blue Feather.' She looked tragically across at Mick.

'Bunk,' said that gentleman, wriggling his toes. 'What you need is some food inside you – same as me. It's a pity you're feeling dicky because I was hoping you'd cook bacon and eggs when we got home.' Caroline turned a glazed eye upon him. 'I could do with fried bread too,' he went on wistfully, adding, 'What, not again?' in shocked tones as Caroline fled round to the other side of the bush.

'We'd better be getting on, or we shall be running into those hell-hounds coming down from the aerodrome. Besides, there are the ponies to be fed.' He got up stiffly as Caroline, swallowing hard, emerged.

'This is an adventure, isn't it?' he observed without much enthusiasm as they plodded along the empty road.

Caroline was understood to comment tartly that being stranded on an enemy-occupied island, with a Mystery Man popping round every corner, was an adventure she could dispense with. 'It's just like a story I read about the last war, where two girls got left behind in Belgium when the Germans invaded it. I thought they were frightfully silly, always rescuing each other in funny long skirts and terrific buns of hair. But I didn't think that kind of thing ever really happened,' she ended on the querulous note of one whom life has wantonly betrayed.

'It's such a frightfully silly thing to have happened,' remarked Mick gloomily. 'It's not as though we'd done anything terrifically noble in staying on the island. It's just a stupid, idiotic accident that's going to be a beastly nuisance for everybody. Daddy'll enjoy arriving at Aunt

Marcia's and saying, "Oh, we left Caroline and Michael behind," won't he? And us parading about our own island in fancy dress like a pair of scarecrows. The whole thing's so frightfully *silly*. It's not exciting like real book-adventure.' Mick sounded thoroughly disgusted with the whole tiresome affair. He scuffled angrily along the road.

'Just think how the Arthur Ransome children would dote on it.' Caroline swished at a nettle with a bracken-stalk.

'And the Locketts,' contributed Mick, kicking at a stone in the path with vicious boot.

Followed a profound silence while each child brooded upon those fascinating, incredible spirits of the nursery bookshelf, each the irresistible magnet of adventure.

'It's getting too light to go much farther on this road,' Mick observed at last. 'We shall only run into the soldiers, and even if we do look like islanders it might be awkward.'

'Cut 'cross country,' suggested Caroline. 'We can get on to the Green Ride from here.'

Mick nodded, cast a mysterious glance round the empty landscape like a stage conspirator, and dived through the hedge with Caroline tumbling after him.

The sun was just coming up over the line of hills to the east and the golden light of a still autumn morning beginning to flood fields and woods. The thunderstorm of the previous night had cleared the atmosphere without breaking up the weather or, at any rate, without doing more than hasten the transition from summer to autumn. For the first time the early morning held that clear, slightly crisp freshness that suggests the slow falling of leaves upon damp earth and the curling smoke of bonfires – all the rich insignia of autumn. Mick led the way at the double across a cornfield recently harvested, and plunged on the far side down a bank tightly fenced with boughs into a wood, deep with moss and leaf mould.

'Left,' murmured Caroline, her voice hushed by the quietness of woods no world-terror had yet disturbed. 'I know this bit. Thomas and Mummy and I picnicked here once.' She pushed past Mick, dragging her long skirt across the trailing brambles, and marched ahead down a path between the tall beech-trees. Now that she was leading Mick the responsibility acted as an astringent. She forgot she felt sick and skipped so nimbly over the little running rivulets left by the storm that Mick had to break into a stiff trot to keep up. At a fork on the far side of the second clearing, she unhesitatingly picked on the left branch and followed it to the far edge of the wood, where it unexpectedly became a rutted farm-track leading into a farmyard.

After the horror of their rain-washed night, it was quite reassuring to spy a little pink-washed grey-shuttered house by a duck-splash, with smoke coming out of the chimneys and an elderly rosy-cheeked woman carrying a pail of milk across the yard. The peace of this sunny morning, the cosy farmyard life going on just as usual made the excitements of last night's escapades seem like a fantastic fairy-tale. Caroline, peeping from behind a tumbledown gate, was assailed with a longing to go up and knock on the old door and ask to be allowed to sit by the kitchen fire and drink a glass of the milk she had seen frothing over the pail. This little farm at the edge of the wood in the heart of the island seemed so snug, so secure. She made vigorous pantomime signs to Mick, but he shook his head. There were the ponies waiting to be fed at home. Caroline sighed and followed Mick through the hedge on the other side of the farm-track.

Across two more fields bearing in the direction of the sea, down into a hollow yellow with broom, and up again through a coppice that shelved so steeply that the muscles in the calves ached – Mick now knew his whereabouts. When the woodland emerged on the open hillside in a riot of bracken, he blinked in the sudden daylight and set off like a homeward-trotting pony with Caroline hard behind him.

The sun was now well up in the pure blue sky. The dew on the cropped turf twinkled in the light. Gossamer spider webs swung delicately on the bracken stalks. Mick paused a moment, shading his eyes to locate a familiar landmark of the Pony Club. There it was – the twisted chimney of the old ruined cottage half-way up the next slope. The children's feet made grey trails as they ran across the wet grass and up the hillside. The cottage had been derelict now for many a year. Foxgloves bobbed and bowed round the cracked doorstep, nettle poked its angry head in through the old broken window-frames. A small weasel dancing about the threshold darted away to safety among the loose stones by the path as Mick and Caroline came dashing up. At the doorstep they paused for breath, while the bryony clinging to the crumbling doorpost beat gently against their faces.

Mick took another bearing with professional eye between the jutting headland and a twisted rowan. 'There,' he said briefly, and off they set again to the far side of the clearing. They searched carefully along the fringe of bracken until they found the large white boulder set in place with much labour a year back by Richard Penfold and Nicholas Lindsay, with Caroline and Peter holding their ponies for them as they staggered up the hill with their burden.

About a hundred and fifty years before, when the practice of smuggling had reached its romantic height, the smugglers, with the incriminating cargoes that had been landed round the rocky coast of Clerinel, had made their own secret ways to the inlets from house and hamlet across the cliffs. Horse and rider were long since dust, grass and bracken grew high over the winding track that pursued its zigzag course over the hills. Occasionally a stray fisherman returning home or a courting couple pushing their way absently through the bracken had stumbled upon traces of the old road. But until the Pony Club under the presidency of Nicholas had accidentally lighted upon it during a drag-hunt it had been among the ancient and forgotten things of an earlier age. On the large-scale survey maps it was still indicated by a series of dots, but nobody had ever felt moved to unearth the hidden path from beneath the bracken and heather until Caroline had suggested that the Pony Club should track it down. The work had entailed days of lying flat on one's tummy, wriggling a way through the undergrowth, slowly marking the old worn ruts with stones carried up into the hills in Mrs Lawrence's gardening trug.

It seemed odd to be running down the Green Ride in the

early morning without the others. Almost every moment Caroline, trotting behind Mick's blue jersey, expected to hear the thud of the ponies' hooves and hear the shouts of greeting. 'I feel just like a ghost returning to its ancient habitation,' she said to herself. It was almost unbelievable that everything was not just as usual, that Daddy and Thomas were not going to be discovered at breakfast in the Point House, that Pam and Alison and Kit and Richard and the others would not be waiting for them after breakfast, ready for a gallop on the moors.

They crossed the path that led across to La Falaise which had been the old Seigneurie of the island, where the 'smuggling Seigneur' had tippled his way to death so many years ago. At any rate, Caroline comforted herself, Peter is still at La Falaise and we can go straight over there as soon as we've had breakfast and seen to the ponies. Peter won't be changed, thank goodness.

At that moment the Green Ride turned abruptly towards the coastline, where the Martello Tower headland still made a natural harbour for incoming craft. There the smugglers had dismounted in the moonlight and led their horses down the steep incline, to find the boat that lay moored and lightless in the inlet below. Mick left the Green Ride on his right and kept straight on, his step quickening a little for the last lap. Home lay down in the hollow off the Green Ride. They had between them made their own track joining the top of the garden path to the Ride. It had been worn and beaten into quite a wide path by the home-coming hooves of Punch and Dinah and Bellman.

Caroline caught up with Mick, and they ran along side by side. The sound of the tide now sang in their ears and their noses sniffed up the new saltiness in the air. The little track swerved round and ran along the edge of a low basin made by the hills. Below them the waving bracken sloped away in shelves almost to the shore line. They trotted round a fold of the hills, and then round another. Sunlight bathed the whole hollow in a warm glow. A rabbit lolloped across the track ahead of the children. A blackbird piped busily in the rowans below in their own garden. They rounded a last corner and pulled up dead before a small green gate set in the fencing. Together they stood and looked down at the square white house, low built and serene, cupped in the hollow of the green hills with the sea singing and murmuring before its windows. Each child gave a sigh of profound relief at the sight of the familiar house after the night's voyaging through unwelcome adventure.

'D'you know, Mick,' Caroline said, 'I believe my inside's come all right again. I believe I could do with bacon and eggs after all.' She put out a grimy hand and unlatched the little gate. 'But we'd better go straight to the stable before we do anything else, hadn't we?'

Chapter 6

Disaster

'There's no need to go on tiptoe. It's our own house and
we aren't burglars,' said Mick reasonably, as they crept
furtively out of the stables, doubled up like a pair of pantomime villains.

Caroline laughed and straightened herself. 'I feel as
though all the windows were staring at us,' she said light-
heartedly. In the familiar environment of home and garden
the pallid Caroline of the Pol les Roches road had been
replaced by her more normal sprightly self. In the bright
daylight the house looked most reassuringly undisturbed,
just as though Thomas might come running out at any
moment or Daddy lean out of the dining-room window and
summon them to breakfast. You couldn't possibly go on
feeling frightened when you were back at the Point with
everything looking as it had done every day of the summer
holidays.

The visit to the stables had proved eminently satisfactory. Dinah and Punch had arrived back safely, obviously none the worse for the fancy-dress dissipations and
the ride home through the rain. They had greeted their
respective owners with every sign of approbation. Even
Bellman who usually rudely refused to acknowledge the
presence of any member of the family had condescended to
twitch his ears in their direction. The Beaumarchais'
groom had evidently put in some time in the Templetons'
stable for the whole place was neat as a new pin. The
saddlery was properly arranged on its hooks, the lids of the
bins were tightly shut, and each stall was filled with clean,
sweet-smelling straw. Manfully controlling their own pangs
of hunger, Mick and Caroline set to and fed and watered

and groomed – the last a little hastily – before closing the stable door behind them.

'We shall look jolly silly if the whole place is locked,' Caroline said apprehensively as they approached the back door. But the latch gave to the first pressure of Mick's fingers, and they walked into the silent kitchen with mud on their feet sufficient to have caused the scouring spirit of Jeanne to lie down and die.

How still it was! Except for the clock ticking in the kitchen there was no sound at all in the whole house. The children went softly from room to room. Daddy and the servants had evidently left in a great hurry. In the study a half-empty glass of lime-juice stood beside the phone where Daddy had hurriedly put it when the call from London had come. In the dining-room Thomas's unfinished tea lay on the mahogany table, a biscuit broken on his plate. In the little room where Jeanne and Marie clattered and sang like small humming-birds magazines and pieces of fine embroidery lay flung on the floor, where they had been thrown in the haste to escape the invaders.

The children opened and shut door after door almost stealthily. 'It's like the Sleeping Beauty's Palace,' thought Caroline as she put her head round the door of Mother's room. At any moment in this still house you might come upon Daddy and Thomas and Marie and Jeanne and Petit-Jean, all sunk in the enchanted slumber of that fabulous household with the dust already lying lightly upon them. She shivered slightly. With her voice echoing down into the empty hall she said aloud, 'Mick, if we're going over to the Beaumarchais' we'd better get on with it and have breakfast. Let's push back to the kitchen.'

Mick, upon whom the same vague unease had drifted down, concurred and they crept back to the kitchen by the back-stairs. Caroline strong-mindedly closed the door to shut out the rest of the house and proceeded to make as much to-do with the shining pans in the scullery as though she were exorcizing evil spirits.

There was bacon in plenty in the larder and tomatoes and eggs. There were a couple of sausages on a plate at which Caroline prudently sniffed, while Mick watched in a passion of anxiety lest they should be high. But everything went into the pan together and soon was merrily sizzling away upon the stove, while Caroline turned it over with the slice as it crisped and browned in a splutter of fat.

As the alluring smell of good mixed grill pervaded the kitchen the Templeton spirits again soared. Mick flung the yellow-checked cloth on to the table with a fine abandon and bore the blue-and-white breakfast crockery about the kitchen on one nonchalant hand, while Caroline prodded and pricked away at the stove. He even offered to take over with the slice if Caroline's inside should suddenly jib before such a prodigality of food. At length, down to the last curl of bacon, the last bursting sausage deliciously oozing browned globules of meat, breakfast was ready. Caroline set the pot of frothing coffee down on the sunny yellow table, and the meal began in a silence no longer born of disquiet but of frank rapture.

'Well now,' said Mick some ten minutes later, 'we've got to decide on our plan of action.' He wiped his mouth complacently with the back of his hand and tilted his chair perilously on its hind legs. Really life was not so bad. The whole show had been tough but they were coming through it quite nicely. Caroline was a good sort and had pulled herself together jolly well, and his own interior was now warmed and lined with the right kind of hot food. Taking all in all Mick felt, like Caroline some hours earlier, that he'd managed everything rather well. 'We've got a good deal to decide,' he repeated, leisurely balancing to and fro on his chair.

'Yes, well, we can talk things over just as well while we wash up.' Caroline ruthlessly manoeuvred her brother into the scullery and handed him a dish-cloth. She had had experience of the unwashed crockery from meals rising in alarming piles before someone was firm enough to deal with it. She put a kettle on to boil, collected the breakfast things on to a tray, unearthed from the cupboard Marie and Jeanne's chintz aprons and tied one on Mick and one on herself. 'Good job nobody can see us,' she commented, not for the first time since yesterday, 'we do look a couple of comics.' Caroline had earlier insisted that they put on their winter dressing-gowns and bedroom slippers while their clothes went into the airing-cupboard.

'Speak for yourself,' retorted Mick, pirouetting round the kitchen with Marie's apron daintily held out between finger and thumb like a ballet skirt. He looked wickedly at Caroline. 'What price Elaine the Lily Maid?' he inquired.

Caroline turned scarlet. Then she and Mick collapsed in shrieks of laughter.

'Oh, oh, oh, you did look funny with that sun-hat!' crowed Mick, staggering helplessly about the room.

'If you could have *seen* yourself in that frightful parade!' cackled Caroline, reeling up against the wall.

At last their sobs of mirth died exhaustedly and, still clutching their middles, they returned to comparative sobriety. 'We must get on.' Mick seized a plate and plunged it into the washing-up bowl.

'Here, I'm doing the washing.' Caroline, reconvulsed with giggles, rolled forward twirling the mop. 'And the silver goes in before the plates, thank you.' She took full possession of the sink and Mick leaned up against the table, waiting to fulfil his function as Dryer-up-in-Chief with the dish-cloth.

For a few minutes there was no sound but the clitter-clatter of the knives and forks in the washing-up bowl. Then Mick suddenly burst forth. 'You know,' he said, frowning intently at the marmalade spoon, 'I've been thinking a lot about this business of asking the Beaumarchais to take us in and –'

'O Mick,' said Caroline, 'so've I been thinking –'

'You mean – ?'

'What you mean –'

'That it'd be much better if we could stick on our own. Peter's father's such a fusspot. He'll boss us all over the place.'

'I don't really like him a bit,' said Caroline. 'Besides,' she added, feeling very noble, 'it isn't frightfully fair to go

and plant ourselves at La Falaise. The Nazis might find out
and shoot the Beaumarchais –'

'I believe they're pretty funny that way,' put in Mick, to
whom this aspect of the situation had not occurred. 'No,
Caroline, we're managing very nicely, and I think we'd
better stay on our own.'

'But however can we?' said Caroline wonderingly.

'I look at it this way,' answered Mick in a considering
manner. He propped himself against the sink, twiddling
his dressing-gown cord. 'I honestly don't see that Daddy
can do anything about us. It'll be a million to one against
there being any communications between England and
Clerinel. He'll probably go rushing round a lot of government departments and get tangled up in oodles of red tape,
and we shall just sit here in the meantime. Seems to me,
if we want to get away we've got to do it ourselves. We obviously
can't do it without a certain amount of help from other
people, and whoever helps us stands a chance of getting
copped. I think we shall have to ask the Beaumarchais –'

'Oh, *no*,' wailed Caroline, reflecting at the same time
how much easier it was to face nasty facts when you were
warm and full.

'Wait a shake. I've not finished.' Mick put up an ad-
monitory hand. 'There's an alternative, but I don't know
if you'll like it.' He cocked a dubious eye at his sister who
was absentmindedly swilling the soapy water round and
round the bowl while she listened to him. 'We could stay
here at a pinch. I mean, nobody knows we're here, and
there seems to be plenty of tinned stuff in the larder. We
shall have to ask M. Beaumarchais to help us get off the
island, but we needn't involve them in any trouble by
actually parking ourselves in their house until we can get
away. It lessens the risk for them almost to nothing, and
it'll be much nicer for us to manage our own affairs. What
do you think?'

He need not have worried about the reception of his idea.
Caroline was a most undomesticated person – she hated
sewing, her room was like a jumble-sale, she loathed the
sight of broom and duster – but there are very few people

who can resist the delight of running a house for somebody else. She spun round from the sink, her eyes shining. 'Oh, lovely, lovely,' she cried. 'O Mick, it's a wizard idea. We could manage here perfectly with me doing the house-keeping. Oh, you do have absolutely marvellous ideas, Mick. You are jolly clever. I never think of things like that. Of course it's the very thing. No one would ever come here and discover us –'

'That's O.K.' Mick cut off handedly across the babbling torrent. 'It'll solve the problem, too, for the moment of who's going to look after the ponies. I was getting a bit worried about that.' He strolled over to the side-window with his hands in his dressing-gown pockets, his face smug with self-satisfaction while Caroline pranced after him, smacking him in a congratulatory way on the back.

'That's all right then. We'd better see if our things are dried and go over to La Falaise and tell them what's happened. We ought to warn old Beaumarchais about your blue-feather friend. If he really did gate-crash the party yesterday it may mean the Nazis have got something on the Beaumarchais. Anyway, we must warn him whatever we do.' He rocked to and fro on his heels, surveying the corner of the front lawn and the sweep of the drive much as though he had created them. Caroline was rushing about stacking the china.

All at once Mick jumped. 'Golly,' he said excitedly, 'here's a bit of luck. Here's old Beaumarchais himself.'

'*What?*' Caroline put the last cup in the cupboard and hurled herself across the scullery to the window. Sure enough, slowly proceeding up the drive was a familiar blue Morris Ten. 'Goodness gracious, so it is. I thought for an awful moment it was somebody had seen us come in and had followed us. Mick, what a terrific bit of luck! I suppose he's come to see if the house is all right. I expect Daddy gave him the key before we left. He *will* get a shock, won't he?'

She switched round to find she was talking to thin air. Mick was already making for the front door. Caroline turned back and put out a hand to open the window. The car was moving more slowly on a lower gear. When it reached the bend at the corner she would lean out and wave her own greeting while Mick was dancing outside on the doormat. Gone were all the unkind thoughts she had ever cherished about Peter's father. He seemed now an archangel of deliverance. As the blue saloon swung cautiously round the bend in the drive she could see M. Beaumarchais sitting bolt upright at the wheel, a trim little figure in the yachting cap beloved of the Frenchman. Then she wrinkled her brow. Surely – that was funny! In the back of the car lolling against the upholstered corners were two passengers – the one a rather stout elderly somebody with a bald head, the other – Caroline's heart turned over.

'Mick!'

Caroline's whisper reached Mick just as he was turning the knob of the front door.

'Mick, whatever you do DON'T OPEN THAT DOOR. Come here QUICK.'

There was something in his sister's voice that sent Mick back into the scullery at a speed that surprised even him. Caroline met him at the door. She gave him barely time for one hurried glance through the window before propelling him across to the back door.

'They'll come into the house by the front door. Wait until they're out of sight of the back of the house, then make for the stable loft.' Caroline's urgent hiss showed that she had the situation in hand. They waited in breathless silence. Caroline darted noiselessly about removing all traces of their occupation. There was a long pause, broken only by the ticking of the kitchen clock. Then from the hall came the faint click for which they had been waiting, the fumbling fitting of Yale key to lock.

'Now!'

The children streaked quietly across the yard and in at the stable door.

Upon this occasion Dinah might quite justifiably have expressed both resentment and surprise, for the mild inquiring gaze she bent upon the flying form of her mistress as she shot past her stall and up the loft ladder met with no affectionate come-back whatever.

We Couldn't Leave Dinah

The long, low-rafted chamber that ran the whole length of the stable was dusty and hung with cobwebs. An indifferent light filtered through the grimy skylight in the slant of the roof. Nowadays it was used chiefly as a storage room for Petit-Jean's sacks of oats and bales of straw which lay stacked in great mounds round the walls. When Mick and Caroline had been of nursery rather than schoolroom age the loft was a heaven-sent escape from the minor tyrannies of the various nursery authorities. The game had been to rush headlong up the ladder, bang the trap-door down at the top and sit on it so that no entry could be obtained by persons other than yourself. It was to this procedure, long discarded except by Thomas, that the children now instinctively reverted. Mick waited until Caroline had leapt over the last rung of the ladder. Then he carefully closed the trap-door, and they both sat down heavily upon it.

'They can't get up here even if they want to,' Mick panted. 'If they do try they'll only think the place has been locked. I say, you're not going to be sick again, are you?'

Caroline was sitting cross-legged on the door and shaking like a small blancmange.

'N-n-no,' she chattered. 'I'm truly all right. I'm getting used inside to things happening, but I c-can't help shaking outside. It's n-not m-m-me shaking, 'f you understand. Mick, *what on earth is M. Beaumarchais doing with Blue Feather in the car?*'

'I don't know – any more than you.' Mick's face was troubled.

'I don't see how we shall ever be able to get him alone. We shall just have to wait until they've gone, and then go to La Falaise and see him there. I told you Blue Feather would turn up everywhere. And that other fat creature! Did you see he was in uniform too? Oh, poor little M. Beaumarchais! I'm sure those beasts have got hold of him and are making him take them on some sort of official tour of the island. They're probably pointing revolvers at him the whole time. Mick, you don't think they'll torture him, do you?' Her eyes widened in horrified recollection of the treatment the Nazis had been known to mete out to those under their protection.

Mick was looking more worried than ever. His short hair was standing wildly on end where he had run his hands through it and his mouth was set unhappily. He was scarcely listening to Caroline's running commentary.

'I don't like it,' he kept on saying. 'I don't like it. You see –' he hesitated and then spoke very fast. 'Caroline, we don't know that he doesn't *like* being with them. I mean, it's an awful thing to say, but we've no proof that he isn't one of them himself, have we? You know what Mr Lawrence said last night about treachery on the island itself. And Peter's father's not English. He's French, and a good many of the French really have Nazi sympathies –'

Caroline had turned rather white. Not Peter's father! It couldn't be true! It was a hateful idea! She thought feverishly back over the past few weeks in an attempt to find some vindication for M. Beaumarchais. But her effort had a dire result.

'Oh,' she exclaimed, and her hand shot up to her mouth, 'how awful! I've just thought of something so awful that I daren't say it.'

'Go on, only don't talk too loud,' said Mick wearily. The strain of the last twenty-four hours was beginning to tell on him later than on his more excitable sister. This last twist in the whole string of events was different from the other excitements. Those, much as you might regret them, were adventures of a kind – they were all situations that made demands upon you. They all had to be matched by your inventiveness and your courage. But this was just foul and degrading. Mick felt tired and heartsick and baffled by doubts.

'Mick' – Caroline sounded quite frantic – 'say you don't think it was the Beaumarchais who invited Blue Feather and those men with him to gate-crash the party in fancy-dress so that they would be on the island ready to signal the landing-parties into the harbour?'

'But that wouldn't account for their wanting to come to our party.' Mick's head was aching in the close air of the loft but now in his turn he was trying to exonerate Peter's father. 'If they couldn't land on the island in uniform they wouldn't be able ever to land in fancy-dress with the whole island smothered in island Guard.'

'But in Holland and Belgium the Nazis parachuted down dressed as peasants and nuns and things,' persisted Caroline.

'Well, then, supposing they were parachuted down at night why didn't they dress up like the Pol les Roches people and make their way straight down to the quay and hang about with the crowd until the planes arrived and everybody cleared off? Why come to our party at the other end of the island, miles away from where the Nazis were going to land, in comic fancy dresses? It doesn't make sense.'

Before Caroline could counter this potent argument they heard the scullery door open and a murmur of voices, followed by the tread of feet crossing the yard.

'The stables.' M. Beaumarchais' voice floated somewhat muffled up through the trap-door. Caroline raised an eyebrow at Mick. In all their controversy over M. Beaumarchais they had entirely forgotten to ask themselves what he was doing with two Nazi officers at the Point House. Mick silently shrugged his shoulders, and slithered quietly from a sitting to a lying position on the trap-door with his ear to the crack where the flap fitted into the uneven flooring.

'Ach so!' There was a pause and then the voices rose through the crack more clearly. The party had entered the stable.

'My Nannerl will be pleased.' The fat guttural voice, as though the speaker had swallowed an orange, must certainly belong to old Baldhead. 'She has to ride long wished.'

Up in the loft Caroline's ears twitched suspiciously. Who was Nannerl and why ever should she be pleased because there were horses in the stable? She wasn't going to ride Dinah, was she?

'They are nice liddle horses, *nicht wahr*, Karl?' That was Baldhead again. Nice liddle horses indeed! Patronizing old horror! Karl – so that was Blue Feather's name – made a harsh comment that neither child could quite catch. There was a rumbling laugh from Baldhead and a titter from M. Beaumarchais.

'The Templeton children were most enthusiastic horsemen. They rode with my son a great deal.' M. Beaumarchais was talking very quickly with more French accent than usual. His voice sounded rather squeaky as though he were not entirely at his ease. 'This beautiful bright-brown horse the boy, Michael, rode. I do not remember his name –'

'Punch, you fool, Punch,' muttered Punch's owner on the trap-door, shuddering at this description of the chestnut. Caroline smothered a hysterical splutter at the sight of Mick's outraged face.

'This one – Dinah – the girl rode. She was not so good as her brother. A leetle excitable, I fancy.' The remark ascended with devastating clarity to the loft, and it was Mick's turn to smirk at Caroline's flaming countenance.

'The little pony – Bellman,' intoned M. Beaumarchais – but the two Nazis had evidently had enough of the ponies for the children heard Karl Blue Feather cut across these introductions with scant politeness.

'This, then, is all the house?'

'Except for the loft which is empty. You have seen all. You are satisfied, monsieur?' There was a new, anxious note in M. Beaumarchais' high voice. 'You will be comfortable here?'

Mick and Caroline looked at each other, stricken into complete immobility with the horror of the moment. They might have guessed. It was just what Daddy had prophesied, and they had neither of them given it a moment's thought. Of course the Point House was just the place for a Nazi officer's residence, and especially an officer so high in rank as Caroline from her brief glimpse of Baldhead had surmised him to be.

'But yes' – Baldhead was speaking in condescending tones – 'you have not done too badly, M. Beaumarchais. The Reich will not forget your service in this great day of her history.'

'I want no reward – only – onlee –' M. Beaumarchais'

agitation was patent to the listeners above. Caroline yearned to stuff her fingers in her ears. It was terribly embarrassing to hear the father of your best friend grovelling like this.

'Zat will be attended to.' Was the peremptory voice of Karl also a shade contemptuous? Caroline writhed with shame for M. Beaumarchais, as she lay with her ear glued to the trap-door.

'Germany does not forget her servants.' Karl Blue Feather pompously repeated Baldhead's words. 'It would not have been easy for us to land our men, if we had not been enabled by you to take first your Tower that does the whole island command.'

The last clue! Unconsciously the tense attitude of the children relaxed. Daddy had always said the Tower could hold out for weeks. By getting the unsuspecting island Guard to allow him to lay his paper trail within the outer defences and then arranging for Karl and his men to gallop in with the Pony Club, Peter's father had successfully accomplished an immediate surrender of Clerinel's stronghold.

Caroline in a flash remembered how she had noticed, as the riders streamed past her on the shore just before she met Thomas, that Blue Feather was not to be seen either then or later on the lawn of La Falaise. Then during all that time she was urging Thomas to go home Blue Feather's detachment was overpowering the island Guard and capturing the Tower a couple of hundred yards in the rear. How frightfully simple it all was! And so that was the reason for the carnival, and the reason why Peter had been a bit offhand over the whole thing. Caroline felt at that moment that she would give anything in the world to see Mother come walking up the ladder, and those awful men go up in cinders. Mummy belonged to the clean ordinary world where things like this just didn't happen. She stole a glance at Mick. His head was resting on his arm, turned towards her. He looked as sick as a dog.

'We could come here at once, yes?' Baldhead was talking again. 'Nannerl, she is in Pol les Roches. I sent her from Germany two weeks ago to stay with friends until I should come. But now she can arrive here tomorrow. Our two servants from Berlin are also with her.' He gave a throaty little chuckle. 'We had some difficulty over the passports, but we managed. We managed. Today I will send out two of my men from our new headquarters in the town. They will the place prepare.'

'But of course. You must stay tonight at La Falaise, my humble residence. The servants here are gone. But the stable boy is still here to look after the horses until your own servant arrives. And Monsieur Karl will be welcome too.' M. Beaumarchais' obsequious tones were fading gradually out of the stable.

Almost at once the children heard the click of the latch on the stable-door and the sound of three pairs of boots leisurely walking across the stable yard. Mick got to his feet and stood on tiptoe to look through the dust-grimed window in the rafters. With Caroline peering over his shoulder he just caught sight of the big blue car starting up and rolling silently down the drive away from the house.

Mick turned away. Nobody spoke. Caroline planted herself on a sack of oats by the wall. Mick slowly paced up and down the loft. Caroline waited patiently with her chin on her cupped hands for her brother's pronouncement upon this new development. The whole thing was so frightful beyond believing that she felt temporarily bereft of speech.

At last Mick spoke. 'That,' he said, 'has just about cooked our goose, hasn't it? The Point House commandeered by the Nazis and our one hope, the Beaumarchais family, Fifth Column.' He gave a short little laugh to cover his longing to put his head down on his arms and burst into tears.

Caroline nodded speechlessly. There just didn't seem to be anything very much you could say. She got to her feet to go and pace up and down beside Mick because he looked so small and lonely in the middle of the room by himself. She opened her mouth to say that although their goose appeared not merely cooked but absolutely roasted black, she was sure something would happen. And at that instant something did happen, something that froze her against the sack of oats where she stood.

Somebody was coming up the ladder.

Chapter 7

Peter's Plan

The heavy trap-door lid was pushed back inch by inch until it stood squarely on its hinges, perpendicular to the floor. For a second it hid from the occupants of the loft the figure that was climbing so surefootedly out of the abyss. All they could see was the back of a dark slim head and a pair of narrow shoulders in a brown pullover. Then, in one movement, the door was lowered and the figure turned to face them. It was a tall thin-faced boy who was standing in the half-light at the far end of the loft. He was dressed in old worn riding-breeches with leather strappings and he carried a riding stick in one hand. He regarded Mick and Caroline unsmilingly.

Caroline broke the silence.

'Peter Beaumarchais!' she said, and sat down again with such a thump upon the sack of oats that the dust rose in clouds around her. The whole situation had taken so fantastic a turn that she did not feel at all surprised. It merely left her completely feeble-witted. She sat there gaping, with her mind entirely emptied of any possible comment or contribution.

What Peter might have answered in reply to this enthusiastic greeting never transpired, for at that moment a diversion from another quarter occurred. The strain and shock of the last half-hour had defeated Mick's endurance. Almost as the words left Caroline's lips there came a bellow from the far corner, and a small stocky figure shot, like pea from peashooter, out on to the middle of the floor, where it confronted the intruder with squared fists, wild hair, and a face white with fury.

'Get out, you beastly Nazi! Get out, get out! This is our

house. Get out, or I'll half kill you!' The floor-boards creaked ominously as he danced up and down with rage.

Peter merely bent a considering gaze upon this pugnacious apparition clad in a camel-hair dressing-gown, and shifted his weight from one foot to the other.

'D'you want a hiding?' Mick dropped into traditional schoolboy idiom, squaring up to the still figure with a great show of fist and rolled-up sleeves. Caroline continued to sit like an image upon her sack of oats.

'No, I do not. Don't be an ass, Mick.' The Pony Club President's words dropped like little cold pebbles into the middle of Mick's tempestuous challenge. But his eyes anxiously searched the faces of his former friends. 'I only came to see what I could do to help.'

At the sound of Peter's voice, with its very slight foreign intonation, Caroline's frozen brain began to thaw.

'So that you could run off and tell your Fifth Column father and his fat friend, I suppose? All right. You've seen us now. Run along and say your piece.'

'Mick.' Caroline spoke from her sack of oats. Mick's onslaught and Peter's quiet withholding had given her the time she needed to recover herself. As her brother hurled his taunts a curious peace of mind was settling down upon her. For the moment it didn't seem to matter to Caroline whether Peter came as ally or enemy. She had watched his unmoved face while Mick was storming at him and had seen the flicker of pain in his eyes. She had known a moment that quite startled her of compassion for somebody who was being badly hurt. She knew what she had to do, and she spoke with authority.

'Mick, shut up,' she said. 'Peter, what were you going to say?'

'Say my foot!' Before the assurance of Peter and Caroline Mick sounded less certain of himself. The atmosphere seemed somehow to have changed. He sensed an unspoken alliance between the two of them from which he was shut out. It made him feel bewildered and defiant, and he became even more truculent than before. 'What's there to say anyway? We're being hoofed out of our house by his Nazi friends, aren't we? I don't see that there can be anything more to say.'

Peter and Caroline took no more notice of him than of a bellicose starling.

'Go ahead,' Caroline invited. It was to her that Peter spoke.

'I saw you,' he said, 'this morning. I was out with Pepper, and I saw you in the distance running down the Green Ride. I daren't shout and I couldn't get to you through the bracken. I was in the car, too, with those officers, General Schleicher and his nephew. But I told Father I wanted to walk home over the cliffs. He put me down at your gate, and I came round at the back and waited until they'd cleared off. What are you going to do now?' he finished abruptly.

'D'you think we're going to tell you that?' said Mick rudely but in somewhat more subdued tones. Caroline itched to kick his ankle to recall him to some manners. But it was again to her that Peter had addressed himself.

'Haven't the foggiest idea,' Caroline answered him across the room. Her mind was beginning to run along other tracks. In a queer way she felt now that she was in control of this tense situation, although it was upon Peter that their fate obviously depended and upon Mick's acceptance or rejection of Peter's terms. It was she, she knew, who must set about healing this breach between Mick, suspicious and un-understanding, and Peter, hurt and desperately dignified. It was all very odd, she thought. There had been quarrels before – plenty – but they had always been quick flare-ups about, oh, Pony Club plans and so on. This was different. She fumbled after a new idea. This was the kind of misunderstanding that made people hate one another for ever. Caroline felt for a moment that the sorrow of the world was upon her shoulders. Then she realized that Peter was speaking again, and pulled herself together to listen.

'Of course you must be taken off the island.' Peter seemed now to have definitely taken them in tow. He hadn't even inquired, Caroline realized, how they had come to be left behind in this ignominious fashion. 'There are plenty on Clerinel who will not tolerate a German occupation,' he went on, 'and they will leave – somehow. Escapes have been made from other occupied countries and they will be made again from here. I expect that was what you had in mind, why you came back to the Point?'

He paused. Caroline nodded. She was not going to tell him that they had meant to enlist his father's assistance in this project. Peter continued, walking up and down as he spoke.

'It can be arranged. Of that I am quite, quite certain. But it may take time. We shall not be able to smuggle you away today, nor yet tomorrow. There are certain pre-liminaries – one has to feel one's way very carefully to discover who is planning a secret escape. Nobody will wish to shout it from his doorstep. But it can be done, particu-larly if one jingles money. It is the meantime that is the problem. Where to eat and live and sleep – and be hidden from the Nazis. You can't possibly stay here because Schleicher's men will be over from their headquarters by lunch-time. You – can't come to La Falaise,' he reddened slightly, and Caroline looked tactfully at the ceiling. 'I rather wondered how you'd like to go along to our own Headquarters, Pony Club I mean, until we can get you away.' The climax came abruptly on top of this summary of the situation.

Staggering, stupendous, brilliant idea! And propounded rather humbly by Peter as a mere suggestion! Had the relations between them been more normal the Templetons at this point would have leaped on Peter with congratu-latory hoots and smacks.

As things were Mick merely looked suspicious and Caro-line eyed him gravely. She had no real doubts about the feasibility of the plan. As Peter had diffidently suggested the scheme her heart had soared at the prospect of a release from the mousetrap in which they were caught. The quarrel with Peter, coming straight on top of the departure of the Nazis, had almost driven out of her mind the really appalling straits into which she and Mick had been plunged. The Cave would indeed be the one solution!

'It sounds just the goods to me,' she said. 'What do you think, Mick?'

Alas, it was at once lamentably apparent that Mick had entered upon that unfortunate aftermath of bad temper, the purely obstructive mood that comes when we fear that we have made fools of ourselves. Both Caroline and Peter waited for his answer. It came after an appreciable pause in distant tones. 'I really don't know at all, I'm afraid' – gazing remotely into space.

Usually Caroline was reduced to nervous prostration beneath the hydrangea bushes when this mood overtook her brother. Today she was mildly surprised to discover in herself only a strong impulse to slap his face. 'All right,' she snapped, 'then I do. It's a splendid idea, Peter. I think we'd better start right away.'

'Yes,' said Peter. He hesitated, and then, without so much as a glance at Mick, 'You needn't worry, you know, about me splitting on you. I shan't say anything. But you'll have to trust me until I can explain about the whole thing.'

'We aren't worrying,' answered Caroline comfortably, her mind already on the future as she dragged up the trap-door lid. 'You can tell us the whole story when we get to the Cave. For goodness' sake, let's get on. I'm petrified of those awful men coming back.'

They clambered singly down the ladder and ran back across the yard into the house. Peter who was as much at home in the Point House as in La Falaise made straight for the larder with Caroline at his heels.

'You'll need food,' he said. 'Tinned things. Enough for, say, five days. Can you get them from the back, do you think, so that the Nazis won't see anything missing? They've got eyes at the backs of their heads.'

Caroline shot past him and started recklessly to plunder Marie's neat store cupboard. Pork and beans, glazed tongue, tomato and spaghetti, tinned sausages, green pea, mushroom, celery and mulligatawny soups – they stood, tin to tin, in orderly rows. She handed them down one by one to Peter and spaced the remaining tins out over the gaps to cover her pilferings.

'Salt.' Caroline rushed to the Cerebos tin nailed against the wall.

'Frying-pan.' She unhooked the omelet pan and a large aluminium saucepan, hanging the lids of the other saucepans over the marks they left on the wall.

'Bread.' There was enough in the bin for four days.

'Bacon.' Caroline seized the last four rashers remaining from the early morning maraudings.

'Butter and lard.' She sliced the greaseproof packets in half and Peter wrapped them in fresh paper.

'Jam. Would it be an awful luxury, Peter?' Four days of bread and butter did make one's heart sink, even in wartime.

'Tea and cocoa.' Tea for breakfast, but lovely thick syrupy cocoa for tired campers recumbent around the glowing camp-fire. Really it was all going to be a super picnic. Caroline's imagination excitedly envisaged herself pouring out the perfectly brewed mugfuls for Mick as he lazily recuperated from the ardours of the day.

'Crocks, cutlery, and washing-up things are all there,' Peter ruthlessly cut across her dream. 'That ought to be enough to feed a regiment, Caroline.'

Caroline looked with dismay at the array on the larder floor. It seemed enough to stock a grocer's shop twice over.

'It's O.K.' Peter answered her unspoken thought as he turned to go back into the kitchen. 'I've got an idea about transport. Now – sleeping things –'

'TIN-OPENER!' shrieked Caroline and darted back into the scullery.

At last they had all the miscellaneous assortment collected together in the kitchen. Mick had condescended unasked to be responsible for bedding, and had staggered down buried like a Christmas-tree beneath a pile of rugs and sleeping-bags. Caroline at the last moment remembered toothbrushes, combs, flannels, and bath-towels and rushed upstairs to rummage furiously in various drawers and cupboards, while Peter yelled after her up the stairs to for goodness' sake leave everything tidy. She hung over Mick's shirt-drawer but decided that their peasant get-ups, uncomfortable as they were, were too good disguises to be abandoned, and called in at the airing-cupboard on her way down to collect them, nicely aired and warm.

Mick in the kitchen was meanwhile surveying the growing mound with jaundiced eye. Not for worlds in his present mood would he have asked precisely how Peter intended it should be transported to the Cave. It was plainly impossible for it to be man-hauled. As Caroline bounced back waving a bouquet of toothbrushes and combs Peter answered his question by dividing the pile into two.

'I thought we would take one of the ponies,' he said casually. 'It's a good job we've got the little cave fitted up.'

Caroline's face was blazing with delight.

'Punch, not Dinah,' Peter added warningly. Caroline's mouth turned down. 'He's sturdier than Dinah and more reliable. We must have a weight-carrier,' said Peter with sympathy. He knew how Caroline felt about Dinah. Privately he thought her a bit silly in her refusal to recognize the merits of any pony other than the beloved Dinah. Peter considered Punch in his own way every whit as good as Dinah. 'Besides,' he went on, 'Dinah would be missed. Punch is in a dark corner of the stable and I don't suppose the General looked very carefully at him. Richard left his chestnut with us after the carnival last night, and I can easily ride him over and smuggle him in in Punch's place.' He threw the last words over his shoulder as he crossed the yard.

Caroline stood still at the scullery-door with her hands clenched and her mouth mutinous. 'It's not fair,' she muttered fiercely. 'S'not fair. I want Dinah. I won't leave Dinah behind. Dinah's quite capable of carrying all that stuff.'

She started across the yard after Peter to tell him that she really did want Dinah very badly, and that it couldn't make all that difference which pony went to the Cave. Then, suddenly, she pulled up so short that Mick, watching sulkily through the kitchen window, wondered what she'd forgotten. She turned and walked soberly back into the scullery, hoping Peter had not heard her footstep on the cobbles. It really would be rather dreadful to make a scene so soon after Mick's performance. Peter would think them a pretty feeble pair of babies. Besides – Caroline became very quiet – this wasn't all just for fun. It wasn't really just a marvellous picnic. People all over Europe were being made miserable by the Nazis, and were being turned out of their homes in a far more terrible way and with far less chance of escape. And there was she, Caroline Templeton, whining because she couldn't take her pony along with her. 'I'm a pig,' she said furiously. 'I'm a plain pig.'

There was a little sound behind her in the kitchen. She turned and saw through the open door Mick checking over the stuff and making an inventory. His face still looked unhappy and irresolute, and when he saw his sister looking he pretended to be searching for something in the mounds. With a flash of intuition Caroline divined that poor Mick felt perfectly frightful but was not yet able to bring himself to any state of grace.

'Perhaps it's as well it is Punch that's going,' she thought as she tactfully went out into the yard and stood in the sunlight.

With Peter absorbed in the stable and Mick quietly occupying himself indoors it seemed to Caroline, alone in the warm sunshine, queerer than ever that life should have changed so much for her and Mick within a night and a day, and yet everything round about them should remain so completely unaltered. If they'd come back to the house to find that it had turned scarlet and was hanging upside down in mid-air Caroline felt that she would have understood that the general upheaval had affected the house too. But it was really quite amazing to crawl back as hunted refugees and discover it still dreaming in the hollow of the hills, untroubled of change and horror. It was rather pleasant. It warmed you. It reassured and comforted you, reflected Caroline, leaning up against the sunlit wall and letting her head loll drowsily forward.

She was brought to by the familiar clippety-clop of Punch's hooves. He emerged, led by Peter, out of the stable with his head tossing up and down with pleasure in the sunlight and the prospect of a ride. It was obvious that he was yet in ignorance of the travail he was to undertake. Peter had cleverly fastened two large gardening baskets on either side of him with a strap of webbing and a pad of horse-rug.

'Load up as quick as you can,' Peter called as he adjusted the balance of the baskets. 'The General will have telephoned to Headquarters from our place, and those men will be well on the road by now. He's in charge of the Army of Occupation, and he knows how to get a move on. We'll go by the Green Ride to avoid running into them, but we ought to get going.'

Five minutes later a curious little procession could have been seen trailing up the path between the hydrangea bushes. The casual onlooker would have been hard put to place it. Except for the dark boy at the head the children and the pack-horse might have belonged to some travelling tinkers. The chestnut pony did not, however, seem at all accustomed to the load he was reluctantly carrying. He proceeded gingerly up the hillside with ears pricking nervously to the clish-clash of aluminium that resounded from the one basket.

'You needn't worry,' Peter said to Caroline as she strove to pad the offending frying-pan. 'Nobody's about up here to hear us.'

Peter was right. The children could see in the valley below farms and fields quite deserted where the men were usually working in the midday sun. There were no figures about on the opposite hillside nor on the white ribbon below them that was the road into Pol les Roches. There were no little ships chugging their way along the coast-line, and there were no distant squads of island Guards outlined with their rifles against the skyline as they stood on defence duty. The Nazi invasion, if it had apparently changed nothing outwardly, had stifled all the busy workaday life of the island.

Up in the hills it was hot and sleepy. The scent of bracken and foxglove was overpowering. Peter made them walk in single file and very quickly, and, despite what he had said about nobody being about, he made them talk in lowered tones. They turned off down the La Falaise fork at a junction of the tracks. It wound downhill back towards the coast and then branched again, the one track going direct to Peter's house. The narrower path which the procession took led down to the cliff edge and the Cave.

At one point Peter stopped dead and pointed silently down to the distant road. There, going in the direction of the Point House, crawled a minute speck like a grey dusty beetle. 'We weren't too soon,' commented Peter grimly. 'That's the lorry with the General's men.'

'You *are* quite sure we shall be hidden in the Cave?' Caroline questioned anxiously. Somehow out here on an open hillside you felt as though a thousand enemies might be watching you from the all-hiding bracken.

'You'll be perfectly safe,' Peter turned his head over Punch's withers to reassure her. 'There's only one thing you have to be careful about. Your bit of foreshore can be seen from the Tower headland. You'll have to set up some sort of mark half-way down between the Cave and the water's edge and not go beyond it. Actually if you don't go down farther than the jutting-out bit of cliff that's at the end of the next cove you'll be all right. But the Tower itself is in Nazi hands. What's more, it's under the command of Karl Muller, General Schleicher's nephew. I believe the General pulled some sort of string to get him appointed. He's a nasty piece of work. He was with old Schleicher this morning.'

'I saw him yesterday at the carnival,' began Caroline, and then stopped. The slow flush spreading down the back of Peter's neck was not entirely due to the sun. 'I won't believe it, I won't, I won't,' she raged to herself. Mick in the rear said nothing. He had not spoken since they had left the Point.

'Peter, who's Nannerl?' Caroline hastily covered up her blunder as skilfully as she could.

'Nannerl?' Peter guided Punch down the narrowing steep little track. The stones kicked up by the pony's hooves almost drowned his words. 'Nannerl? I suppose she's the

General's wife. I heard him speaking about a Nannerl in the car.'

'She's coming tonight,' announced Caroline gloomily. 'And she's going to learn to ride. It's a bit late in life, isn't it? Especially as we've taken the only weight-carrier out of the stable. She's sure to be fat and flaxen. The German women always are,' she ended dogmatically.

'Oh, I don't know,' Peter murmured diplomatically, knowing perfectly well that Caroline was picturing an enormous blonde frau bucketing round Clerinel on Dinah. Really, reflected Peter, it's no good Caroline going on about Dinah. The animal's got to be exercised and somebody's got to ride her before the Nazis are turfed out of Clerinel.

But before he could insinuate his point of view the path took a last twist, a cold little wind blew up into their faces from the sea which disclosed itself almost beneath their feet, and the track sloped down over the cliff-edge. They had reached sanctuary at last!

There it was – the Cave! Just as it had been on that memorable morning only about a forntight ago when the Pony Club had formally possessed itself of its new Headquarters.

'Goodness, how odd!' Caroline murmured, as with Peter and Mick she stood looking at the now deserted Headquarters. Both boys nodded. Everybody understood quite well that what Caroline meant was that it was jolly odd to be coming back to the Cave not as Pony Club members, but as fugitives.

Peter led Punch into the smaller cave and unloaded him and hung his bridle on the hook near the entrance. Punch appeared quite at home in the new stable and cast an approving eye at the oat-bin, and the shelf for brushes that Nick Lindsay had fixed up with rawl-plugs. He cast a slightly less favourable glance upon the barrier that the boys had erected to swing across the doorway. But whether he really liked it or whether he thought it was a poor sort of show the point was that the first Pony Club pony was now stabled in the new Headquarters. Even with the Pony Club disbanded under particularly mournful circumstances it was quite a solemn moment!

In the Cave itself everything was standing ready for the midnight picnic that never came off. The three survivors stood silently on the threshold and looked round at the neat shelves of white new wood, stored with the Club's blue and white china, the table with the green cover on which reposed the famous Beatrice stove that had nearly burnt out the Lawrences' shed when Kit had overturned it, the nine stools set at equal intervals round the table, the pictures balanced precariously on the protrusions of rock around the walls, the stocky little kettle waiting for somebody to boil it, the painted mugs ready for the sugary cocoa, the cheerful rugs on the bumpy floor. How homely and friendly it all looked! Caroline experienced a prickly sensation at the back of her nose. Poor little Cave, waiting so expectantly for the children who never came!

'I'll just help you unpack and then I must be off.' Caroline came to with a jump. Peter was standing rather uncertainly in the mouth of the cave, his eyes on the ground. It was a rather awkward moment. Mick made no comment.

Oh – Caroline thought feverishly – Peter couldn't possibly be allowed to go off feeling all hurt and with this frightful breach between them unhealed. The notion was unthinkable. Caroline took a deep breath.

'I'm terribly hungry,' she said untruthfully. 'Peter, you simply must stay to lunch.' Oh dear, now she sounded just like one of those awful gushing society hostesses. What could she do! She looked despairingly at Mick who had his back to her and was unpacking one of the baskets. Peter was also looking at Mick. Caroline realized that Peter would only stay if Mick seconded the invitation. The issue lay now between the two boys. She had done her best. There was a dead silence in the Cave. Then – 'Lunch would be nice,' said Mick in a gruff voice.

Hurrah, hurrah, the tension relaxed with catapult speed. Mick was going to come round, Peter was going to be mollified, everything was going to be quite all right. Caroline, garrulous with relief, hurled herself upon the tin-opener.

'Come on,' she chattered, 'I'll cope with the food. Mick, you nip up to the spring and get the water. Peter, you fish out the knives and forks and lay the table. We'll all three have lunch *straightaway*.'

Chapter 8

Peter Explains

'Now then, fire ahead, Peter,' commanded Caroline as she propped herself comfortably up against the outside wall of the Cave. Her houseproud eye roved over the symmetrically-stacked crockery drying against the rock-face, the cutlery all neatly wrapped in an old piece of green baize on the table, the little larder so dexterously contrived in the recesses of the Cave, and the two replete figures sprawling in abandoned attitudes outside on the ledge. Nobody, thought Caroline proudly, could ever say that she didn't know how to feed people, even if she couldn't keep her bedroom quite tidy or darn her stockings properly.

Like most meals eaten under a bright clear sky and beside a strip of sparkling blue sea lunch had been almost surpassingly delectable. Pork and beans fairly dripping with rich oily tomato sauce, hunks of bread, farmhouse butter, and raspberry jam, washed down by piping soup – really, as Caroline had observed at the time, it was a meal fit for the Royal Family at Buckingham Palace, let alone homeless outcasts. She privately wondered if Peter could possibly narrate a coherent story after the amount he had eaten, and if she and Mick could possibly keep awake along enough to listen to it.

'Do carry on,' she urged Peter's prostrate form as she shifted herself to where a natural hollow in the cliff-face made a comfortable place for her back. At the same time she sent up a fervent prayer that whatever explanation Peter was going to offer them would not widen that strange rift that had opened but would close it for ever and aye.

'There's nothing much to tell.' Peter sat up, looking momentarily overcome at all the attention about to be focused upon his private affairs. Mick rolled over sleepily and lay facing Peter, shading his eyes with his hand from the glare off the water.

Caroline had a sudden brainwave. 'Hold on a shake,' she ordered and scrambling to her feet dashed into the Cave. She reappeared waving an unpleasant little paper bag of aged aspect. 'Fruitdrops. I found them in my handkerchief drawer,' she explained as she passed the bag to Mick.

Lunch had limbered Mick up enormously, thought Caroline. He had got quite chatty over the beans, while Peter had thawed steadily throughout. Goodness knows what miraculous effects the fruitdrops might have, Caroline reflected hopefully as she hunted for a red one.

'Off you go,' she said. Peter waited to see if there were to be any further interruptions. Then –

'We're not Nazis.' The abrupt statement shot out in the middle of an afternoon siesta almost winded Caroline, the idea was so uppermost in her mind. Having got his audience thoroughly awake Peter rattled the fruitdrop round his mouth and continued:

'I know it must look as though we were. But – what do you know of Nazi Germany?'

He shot the query so unexpectedly at Mick that that young man jerked into a sitting posture as though galvanized. Caroline cast frantically about. What did she know about the Third Reich? Heaven knows everybody was always talking about it.

'Jews,' said Mick weakly.

'Concentration camps,' Caroline backed him up in an effort to sustain the family's reputation for intelligence. Really, Miss Biddle seemed to talk about nothing but Hitler's Germany in the Current Topics class at St Dorothy's. Caroline racked her brain but nothing more illuminating emerged. Peter was smiling at the contorted expressions on his friends' countenances.

'You are like everybody else,' he said, 'nobody knew anything about Germany. Not France nor England nor America nor the Great League of Nations. If they had known – thought a little harder, watched a little closer – there would have been no war.'

Mick and Caroline said nothing. They could not compete with Peter in a discussion on world-affairs. It was upon these occasions that both children dimly realized how much more Peter had knocked about the world than they in their short lives. Caroline found herself suddenly speculating what she would have been like if, instead of passing her days either at school or on Clerinel, she had been carted from hotel to hotel on the Continent. I'd much rather be me with school and ponies and the family, she said firmly to herself. Then she looked at Peter. 'Why do you want to know what we think about Germany?' she asked curiously. 'What's it got to do with us now?'

From the expression on Mick's face, where one cheek bulged fatly with his boiled sweet, it was obvious that he was dying to ask the same question.

Peter answered Caroline's inquiry without hesitation. 'I only really wondered how much you did know about Germany,' he said. 'You see – I lived there until I was ten. I really am half German. My mother was a German. She was born in Mittenwald, and she lived there till she married my father.'

Caroline had given a gasp, and choked over her fruitdrop. Mick never moved a muscle. He merely leant over and thumped his spluttering sister gravely on the back. Peter smiled, a small, frosty smile.

'Ye-es,' he said, 'I thought that would surprise you. I lived in Nuremberg with my grandmother and my aunts. It was not suitable for a small child to go out to that part of South America where my father worked, and after my mother died I was sent to Germany. I was very happy there. We lived in a tall old grey stone house, like the ones in your Hans Andersen, Caroline. It stood near the river, and it had geraniums and hanging purple flowers growing in its window-boxes. Grandmother and Tante Anna and Tante Frieda were very good to me. I went to the kindergarten nearby and then to the school for older boys. My friends were all German boys.'

'But did you like it?' Caroline sounded quite staggered at the idea that anybody could possibly have been happy living in Germany.

'Yes. I tell you I was happy. And when the Nazis came into power I was still happy. Nobody noticed changes at first. Gradually the little German boys were brought into the Nazi Youth Movements and there seemed to be less time for play. But that was all. Grandmother and the Aunts believed in the Party. They were great admirers of Hitler. I used to hear them talking of the wonderful things he was doing for Germany. And then' – Peter's voice hardened – 'Father left his job in America. He came to fetch me. He had heard things in America, and he knew Germany was now no place for a French child to live. I didn't want to go with him. We went to France first and lived in hotels in Paris and Rouen, and in other cities. Then we heard of Clerinel, and we came to see it. Father wanted to settle somewhere, and many years ago his ancestors had lived on this island. Father bought La Falaise and sent me to school in England.'

He stopped. Caroline writhed with impatience on the warm rock. What had all this got to do with the betrayal of the Tower? If anything it weakened Peter's case to admit that he was a German on his mother's side.

Peter glanced at her. 'You're wondering what all this has got to do with yesterday's business, aren't you? Well, here you are then. When I left Germany I went because Father foresaw that one day there might be trouble between Germany and France, and I was primarily a French citizen. You would think, wouldn't you, that it would concern nobody that one small unimportant French boy should leave a vast country like Germany? That the Nazi Party would not interest themselves in what happened to a ten-year-old child? No. I wrote home each week to Grandmother and the Aunts. They answered me each week. Father thinks now that the letters were opened. For five whole years Germany kept track of us as we moved from town to town. And then quite suddenly she pounced. Two months ago some naturalized Germans' – Peter's voice was stinging with contempt –

'called on Father at La Falaise. They told us a great deal of news about our relatives in Nuremberg, how well they were, how good, how kind they were, what good citizens they were. We were so pleased to meet friends who knew our relations. And they knew my friends too, and brought me messages from them. It seemed such a pleasant meeting. And then just as they were going they told us why they had come. It wasn't to bring us loving greetings and news of our friends. It was to tell us that if we did not do as the Government wished our relatives in Nuremberg, good Nazis though they are, would be arrested and put into a concentration camp.'

The silence was broken only by the stamping noises Punch was making in his new home.

'What could we do?' Peter emphasized his words by pounding with his fist on the ground. 'I ask you, what *could* we do? We could not appeal to the French Government because it is German-controlled. They did not want much, they said. The Führer wished to take Clerinel without bloodshed. The Tower was a vital point. It could hold out against everything except air bombardment. This the Führer did not want to employ. Would we kindly arrange for some strategy by which the vital point could be delivered intact into his hands.'

Caroline nodded slowly, her eyes wide with sorrow and horror. There was no need for Peter to say any more. She understood the whole pitiful tragedy now.

'You don't think I wanted the beastly carnival, do you?' Peter said savagely. 'I'm French, but I've not been to an English school for three years without knowing how you English hate making fools of yourselves. But it was the only way. There was no other means of taking the Tower except by a bluff. I hoped up to the last that it wouldn't have to happen. That morning, Caroline, you asked me on this very spot whether I thought the Nazis were coming; I did not believe, indeed I did not, that they were. But I was wrong. Some days before the carnival Karl Muller and his men were parachuted down in darkness. All that time they went about the island unrecognized. We had their fancy-dresses waiting for them at La Falaise. We dared not let them join the carnival from the beginning in case any of you wanted to know who they were in spite of the masks in which we purposely asked you all to come. But – you do see, don't you, how they forced Father's hand, how we could do nothing else?'

It was obvious that Peter cared tremendously that he and his father, to whom he was devoted, should be vindicated in the accusing eyes of the Templetons. If they shrugged their shoulders at his story he would still carry out his promise to help them and see them safely off the island, but never again could there be any real friendship between them. His relations with Caroline and Michael Templeton would just have to be written off as another of those good things spoilt by the Nazis.

'It was not like betraying a country,' he insisted vehemently. 'That Father would never do. The Tower would quite soon have been bound to fall.' He threw a defiant look at Mick, but Mick's face was inscrutable as he sat crosslegged, rocking meditatively to and fro.

Caroline's mind was in a flat spin. She felt dreadfully confused. It was a ghastly story, a terrible position to be put into by those unspeakable Nazis. You couldn't leave your own family to be tortured, and yet – and yet – she frowned and pushed her two pigtails back over her ears in her endeavour to think clearly. Somehow she couldn't picture Daddy doing what M. Beaumarchais had done, not even if she and Mick and Mummy and Thomas were all involved like Peter's people in Nuremberg. But supposing the Beaumarchais had gone all heroic and refused to help the Nazis, what good would it have been? Wouldn't they have bribed someone else and wouldn't the Nuremberg grandmother and aunts in the grey fairy-tale house have been tortured for nothing?

Caroline's thoughts spun round and round trying to find a satisfactory solution. She looked up exhaustedly. Peter was sitting on the rock at the end of the ledge where he had moved while he was telling his tale. He was staring out to sea. His narrow shoulders were drooping dejectedly and his hands hung limply over his bony knees. He did not look a scrap like a defiant intriguer, but only like a rather tired boy of Mick's age who was far too proud to beg the English children to go on being friends with him in spite of everything.

Suddenly Caroline knew that the only thing that mattered was that they should all go on being friends simply because they all liked each other. They could go on arguing the rights and wrongs of the story till the Judgement Day, and M. Beaumarchais could betray every Tower in Europe, but what really mattered was that she and Mick and Peter should go on doing things together.

On the impulse she cried out, 'O Peter, *dear* Peter, it's quite all right. Truly it is, isn't it, Mick? And we're terrifically sorry for you, aren't we, Mick? It's a beastly business. Don't worry, Peter, please don't worry, because we truly do understand and we don't mind two hoots, do we, Mick?' She longed to rush over and hug Peter, but realizing how little he would welcome such a demonstration of affection contented herself with glaring truculently at Mick in an attempt to jolt him into joining her assurance to Peter that everything would be quite all right.

For the second time that day the whole affair swivelled upon Mick. Caroline knew that Peter would want an independent verdict from her brother, that he wouldn't want him to back her up half-heartedly or out of mere politeness.

Mick said nothing for nearly a full minute. He merely extracted the yellow fruitdrop from his mouth and inspected its progress. Then he put it back and mumbled through a drastic suck, 'Lousy swine,' and hurled a pebble very fiercely at an old tin can on the beach.

Caroline breathed again. This ambiguous pronouncement could be safely interpreted as referring to the Nazis and not to the Beaumarchais. Mercifully Peter elected to accept it as such. 'We'd better all have tea.' She cut recklessly across this embarrassing reconciliation scene, regardless that the crockery was scarcely yet dry from the last meal. She seized the kettle and rushed off to the spring. Both boys leaped simultaneously upon the larder. The crisis was over.

We Couldn't Leave Dinah

'I really shall have to be getting back,' Peter said, half an hour later, laying down his empty cup reluctantly. 'The General's with us for another night, and I don't want him poking his nose into what I've been up to.'

Tea had been a most voluble meal with everyone talking at once in their relief at having reached an understanding. Despite the quantity of food consumed so short a while before none of them seemed to be noticeably suffering from lack of appetite.

'Are you sure you'll be all right?' Caroline was more alive than ever now to the precarious position of the Beaumarchais during the Nazi occupation. Peter reassured her by promising that he would pretend he had been into Pol les Roches.

'I shan't say anything about you having got left behind to Father,' he added. 'It might lead to trouble for him if the authorities ever did find out about you after you'd gone.' Caroline noticed that he didn't mention anything about getting into trouble himself. 'I'll start snooping round tomorrow for some means of getting you away. I'll have to keep in very close touch with you. But don't get worried if nothing happens immediately. I can't go making too many inquiries or I shall rouse suspicion. You've got plenty of food, and there's heaps for Punch because I laid in enough for two ponies. And as long as you don't go down beyond that jutting-out bit of cliff you can't be seen from the Tower. Nobody's likely to find their way here so you needn't worry about being discovered.'

He had risen to his feet while speaking and stood looking down at Mick and Caroline.

'I say,' said Mick suddenly. He had been brooding for several minutes while Peter was talking. 'How are you proposing to keep in touch with us exactly? It's not going to be safe for you to come down here much.'

Peter smote his head. 'That's true,' he said. 'I never thought of that.'

'Couldn't we have some kind of signalling system?' interrupted Caroline breathlessly. Her imagination, fired by Peter's story, was now kindled to all the usual apparatus of the adventure books on her bookshelf. Both boys looked at her.

'Go on,' commanded Mick.

'Well – er' – this wasn't so easy – 'couldn't Peter wave something or semaphore from the cliff over there?' Caroline pointed vaguely to the far cliffs that enclosed the whole bay of which their small cove was only a minute part.

Peter shook his head regretfully. 'If I start waving flags about up there the men at the Tower will see it as easily as you.'

'I've got it,' cried Mick jubilantly. Caroline and Peter turned to him.

'Your dinghy's all right, isn't it?' Mick addressed Peter who looked surprised.

'Yes,' he answered, raising his eyebrows inquiringly. 'It came back from Pol last week. Why?'

'Well, look here, then. You're known round the island as a keen fisherman. Could you possibly come out for an hour's fishing every morning between, say, half-past nine and half-past ten in the bay just opposite here?'

'I don't see why not,' answered Peter in puzzled tones. 'I quite often do fish off this cove anyway. That's how I first noticed the Cave.'

'Right,' said Mick triumphantly. 'Now you listen to me. Your Uncle Michael's a great man. Our key will be the number of rods with which you fish. See?'

'No,' chorused Caroline and Peter together.

'Poops. If you sit fishing with *one* rod we'll know you've got nothing to report. If you put out *two* rods we'll know there's something in the wind. It'll be a kind of "Alert" signal. But if you put out *three* rods it'll mean you've got definite news for us, and we'll come and meet you so that you aren't seen making your way here.'

'Jolly good,' breathed Caroline, awestruck before this scintillating display of intelligence.

'It *is* good.' Peter spoke more cautiously. 'It's an awfully good idea, Mick.' Mick looked pleased. 'One rod for no news, two for "Be ready", three for definite news. We can manage that perfectly. You'd better give me some sort of return signal to show you've picked me up. It doesn't much matter what you do, provided you do it from inside the mouth of the Cave.'

'We'll wave something white. Dishcloth probably. Then it'll be seen against a dark background,' said Caroline excitedly. 'Don't you think we ought to have a danger signal too? Just in case something goes wrong and you have to warn us?'

'Yes,' said Peter thoughtfully, 'we most certainly ought.'

'Four rods –' began Caroline.

'Haven't got 'em,' said Peter, disposing of the nightmare idea of a code of cumulative fishing rods. 'No, I tell you what. If there's danger I won't use any –'

'But you can't just sit and *rock*,' cried Caroline. 'People will think you're mad.'

'Wait a moment. I'm not going to do anything so silly. I was going to say I wouldn't use any *rods* but I'll put out a spinner and trail for mackerel with my outboard engine going. If you see me careering across the bay with my line trailing you'll know it's danger.'

Caroline by this time was dancing round and round in ecstasy at this elaborate scheme, and even Mick's imperturbable face was quite pink with excitement. They examined the code from every angle. It appeared both watertight and foolproof.

'And we'd better arrange to meet at the Ruined Cottage – it's under cover most of the way and nobody ever goes there – say, three hours after you see me go home when I've signalled I've something to report,' said Peter finally. 'I shall have to go on fishing for some time after signalling to keep up appearances. And three hours after I land will give me time to get leisurely out of the house so that nobody will think I'm in a peculiar hurry. Now then, I really must go.'

The three of them parted in high spirits. Mick and Caroline stood just inside the danger mark and waved good-bye to Peter as he climbed up the sandy track. They saw him reach the top and snake over it just in case anybody should be watching. He turned and glanced down at them before disappearing, but he did not wave – just in case...

*

It was not until late that night that Peter's story was mentioned.

They had washed up the supper crocks behind the black-out curtain by the yellow oily glow of the Beatrice. They had said good night to Punch. They had tidied the Cave, and, lastly, had unrolled the sleeping-bags and climbed and slithered into them. The black-out curtain had been rolled back so that they could see the white line of the foam upon the shore and the constellations wheeling across the night sky. It was very quiet.

'Mick.' Caroline poked her head out of the mound of rugs.

'Uh-huh?'

'I say. If you had to choose between having your relations tortured and betraying a bit of your country, what would you do? Would you do what Peter's father did?'

She heard Mick thump round like a dog in a basket.

'Depends.' The sleepy whisper sounded muffled by the darkness. 'I might if it was Daddy or Mummy or Thomas or you the Nazis were going to torture.'

'Thanks very much,' murmured his sister with drowsy sarcasm.

'On the other hand,' went on Mick, yawning heavily, 'if it were Aunt Marcia or Hubert and Penelope the Nazis could do what they jolly well pleased. G'night.'

Chapter 9

Caroline Makes a Discovery

The next morning promised to be as fine and warm as its predecessor. The weather was just what it had been three weeks before, when they had first discussed the possibilities of an invasion.

It seemed to Caroline, as she stood barefooted and tousle-headed on the ledge in her pyjamas, that summer simply couldn't bear to relinquish Clerinel completely to autumn and the Nazis. She had woken up well before Mick, and had crawled on hands and knees across his cocoon-like form to emerge blinking upon the pearly dawn landscape. Sea, sky, and sands seemed to merge in varying tones of grey, with only a faint creamy line to show where the sea infringed upon the shore. The wind had dropped and the sea lay calm and unwrinkled beneath a tranquil sky. Caroline felt that she was a very small and lonely figure standing at the edge of the world.

She yawned widely and wished it was safe to run down to the water's edge and paddle in the sweeping shallows. Surely the soldiers in the Tower would still be peacefully rolled up like Mick in their rugs. Perhaps, though, an invading army never slept? Perhaps the men were even now crouched with rifles at the ready round the Tower watching for enemies?

She rubbed her eyes and stretched out her arms in a long sleepy movement. How frightfully queer it was that she and Mick and Punch should be sleeping in a cave while the rest of the family had sailed away and left them! How queer it was that they could no longer live in their own home! How queer that the Beaumarchais should be all tied up with the Nazis! How queer – how very, very queer – that the Nazis should consider it their business to be on Clerinel at all! . . . Caroline turned back into the Cave, caught her foot, and fell over on top of Mick.

By the time Mick, looking smaller and squarer than ever in his blue-striped pyjamas, had pronounced himself awake, Caroline had the kettle blithely singing on the Beatrice, and was reminding him that they mustn't take too long over breakfast because Peter might be fishing before half-past nine and it would be too awful if they weren't ready.

Mick was more concerned over the problem of exercising Punch. He had run before he was dressed into the little stable to see if Punch appeared to have passed a satisfactory night, and he was prepared to gobble his breakfast down at a great rate so that he could get his pony groomed before Peter arrived on the scene. 'I shall have to risk exercising him on the cliffs towards dusk,' he announced to Caroline, as she followed him into the stable after breakfast. 'After all, if anybody did see us they wouldn't think a boy riding a pony was anything particularly out of the ordinary. I can always speak to them in French and pretend I've come over to one of the farms from Pol les Roches.' He started to curry Punch's bright satiny coat.

Caroline hung about a trifle wistfully at the entrance. It was nice for Mick to have his pony with him, of course. But she still couldn't help wishing in her heart that it were Dinah. It wasn't the same helping with Punch, even if Mick needed any help. It would have been marvellous if it had been Dinah who had to be exercised at nightfall. It was hateful wondering if fat Frau Schleicher was already falling off Dinah's back at the Point. Caroline did not pause to consider that Frau Schleicher had barely as yet arrived at the Point. She handed Mick the soft cloth from the shelf and went back to the washing up. When she next looked out of the Cave Mick had led Punch out of the stable and was solemnly walking him up and down the sand well within the danger mark. Was it fancy that Punch looked a shade bored with this restricted form of exercise?

As half-past nine drew near the children's excitement rose. Every five minutes from nine o'clock onward Caroline kept rushing out on to the ledge to see if Peter could conceivably have appeared in the bay yet. 'Not,' Mick reasoned, 'that he's likely to have anything of importance to say and, even if he has, he's got to stay put there for at least an hour, so we shouldn't be likely to miss him.' However, in spite of this pose of detachment when Caroline's wristwatch showed nine-thirty to the minute he was sitting by Caroline with his feet dangling over the edge and his eyes glued as firmly as hers to the far point.

Five minutes passed.

'He's not coming. He's been found out. Blue Feather's got him. He's probably been put into a concentration camp.' Caroline was as usual prey to a whole panorama of dreadful contingencies.

But at last the distant chug-chug of a small auxiliary engine was heard round the point. Caroline let out a squeak of excitement and grabbed at Mick's jersey as a low, rather clumsily-built red dinghy nosed a passage into the bay. They could distinguish in the stern a small crouching figure with one arm resting on the tiller.

'Peter,' breathed Caroline unnecessarily.

The little boat slowly plodded its way across the bay. The children never took their eyes off its progress. They heard the altered note of the engine as the boat slackened speed. Then they heard the engine die away altogether with a protesting splutter. Presently the boat rocked itself to a standstill. The small figure could be seen to heave out an anchor, and then busy itself in the bows.

'He's not hurrying himself, is he?' murmured Caroline, her eyes watering with the strain of keeping them fixed so long upon one spot.

At last the little figure straightened itself, and they could see the sun flashing on the bait-can it put on the seat. The figure rose to its feet. It held something long and slim in its right hand. Both children stiffened like a pair of setters, and Mick leaned forward and shaded his eyes. The figure raised its arm in a swift arc and brought it down again.

'First rod,' muttered Mick.

They waited anxiously for another cast – or would the

figure make the first rod fast before proceeding? But the figure merely sat down again. The little boat rocked placidly on the calm sea – and there to all intents and purposes rocked, too, a fisherman with his rod enjoying the pleasant sunny morning.

'One rod – nothing to report,' said Caroline disappointedly as she got up to fetch the answering signal from the Cave.

There had been a slight contretemps earlier about the employment of the one dishcloth as a signal, Mick contending that after Caroline's washing up the cloth was no longer so much white as dirty grey. As a result Caroline had in some dudgeon agreed to the usage of the only other white article, namely her vest, upon the broom-handle. Ostentatiously shivering with cold she waved it backwards and forwards, backwards and forwards.

'I told you there'd be nothing to report.' Mick also felt quite unreasonably disappointed as he watched Caroline sending out the reception signal. Then he nudged Caroline and drew her farther back into the Cave.

'Look,' he said, and pointed in the direction of the Tower peninsula.

On the rocks at the very farthest tip a well-built form was standing, silhouetted against the skyline. It held a pair of binoculars in its right hand focused upon the little red boat and the fisherman.

'Cousin Karl.' Caroline would have known the stalwart outlines of that figure if she'd seen it in Brazil. 'Thank goodness we're too small for him to see here,' she added with a shiver.

Cousin Karl remained a few more minutes with binoculars raised, and then the two watchers saw him turn away as though satisfied that no enemy to the Reich lurked within the dinghy.

'I'm not at all sure I don't prefer Cousin Karl when he is in full view. You do at any rate know he's not up to any mischief,' Mick commented as the stout figure clambered its way cautiously out of sight over the rocks.

'My word,' said Caroline as she struggled into her vest,

'Peter was right. You can't be too careful with the Nazis. They seem to see *everything*.'

The rest of that day passed uneventfully, and, truth to tell, a little boringly. Camping in a Cave-de-luxe with your own pony to hand and the glorious blue sea just in front of you sounds perfect. But when you cannot leave the Cave except just to sit about outside, and when you cannot ride your pony or bathe in the sea, the fun begins to wear a bit thin after a time. In any case the main event of the day, Peter's appearance, was over so early that anything else would have been an anti-climax.

In the afternoon Mick and Caroline sat outside on the ledge re-reading all the old Pony Club literature. It was quite amusing at first going through the loose-leaf minute book, and recalling all the incidents noted down by the successive secretaries. There was the account of Mick's famous gymkhana when Richard had sprained his ankle in the Thread-the-Needle and the Club had rushed out with first-aid kit. There was the whole story in Pam's sloping backhand of the discovery of the Green Ride. There was the occasion when the Club had found a starving pony fallen down the cliffs, and the police had come with ropes and Peter and the other boys had helped in the rescue. There were accounts of all the meetings they had had, the disputes, the momentous decisions, the motions and amendments and financial statements.

'You know,' Mick said, producing a pencil, 'we ought to add to this an account of how we have found sanctuary in Headquarters. After all, it is a Pony Club episode in a sense, isn't it? And it's quite the most exciting thing that's happened to any of us yet.'

So the early part of the afternoon was whiled away by writing the narration of the fugitives' flight to the Cave and the stabling of Punch in the Headquarter stables.

'We can't fasten it into the book,' said Mick, 'in case anybody finds it after we've gone and it gives the show away.'

They decided to roll it into a screw and put it in a crevice of the Cave wall and cover it with chips of sandstone.

'That must be one of the first things we do when we come back after the war,' said Caroline, putting the last chip into place. 'We must come and unearth it and put it into the minute book.'

But even this episode did not sufficiently fill up the remainder of the day. By supper-time it was quite plain that an enemy at least as potent as the Nazis was Boredom. Even Mick's short and uneventful ride on Punch did not greatly cheer either him or the envious Caroline. Altogether it was a somewhat disgruntled pair that rolled into the sleeping-bags that night.

The next morning dawned in precisely the same way as the morning before. This time Caroline did not eagerly arise to greet the dawn. She considered privately that the day would be quite long enough without lengthening it at the beginning. Exactly the same episodes occurred at breakfast – same old difficulties with the tin-opener, same old food, same old washing and tidying up. Caroline became more and more silent, while by nine o'clock Mick was positively morose with boredom. At last Caroline could bear it no longer.

'I shall go mental if Peter's done nothing by now,' she moaned as she tied the shoulder-straps of her vest round the broom-stick in a clumsy granny.

'I don't suppose he has yet,' returned Mick dispiritedly. 'That knot'll never hold, Caroline.'

'I don't care if it doesn't,' said Caroline in a cross voice. 'Do you think Daddy's discovered we weren't on board the *Queen of Clerinel* by now? I should think he's tearing his hair out.' She was feeling thoroughly homesick for Daddy and Thomas. It wasn't, she said to herself, that she didn't like camping. But this was such a sickening kind of camping.

'I should think Aunt Marcia's rung up half the Embassies in Europe by now,' said Mick sardonically.

This led to a fruitful discussion as to what Hubert and Penelope would have done under similar circumstances. They had just reached the conclusion that Hubert and Penelope would at the outset have gone and wept on the Nazis' shoulders when the sound of Peter's engine was heard.

We Couldn't Leave Dinah

The same elaborate show of dropping the anchor and preparing the bait was staged. Mick and Caroline watched without undue optimism. The performance staled with repetition, and when Peter again put out only one line Mick groaned aloud, less at there being no news than at the prospect of another day hanging about with nothing to do.

'My holy aunt, how sickening! Get the vest, Caroline. At any rate we'd better let him know we're still alive. Pity we didn't arrange some signal to show when we became raving lunatics,' he said drearily.

Caroline lethargically picked up the broom-handle. 'Oh, look,' she said without enthusiasm. 'I believe he's gone and caught something. How killing!' If we could only go and catch dabs it'd be something, she told herself. She waved the broom-stick to and fro like a Morse flag.

'Oh *gosh*,' she said in a sudden burst of temper, 'why doesn't something happen?'

And such was Caroline's luck that at that very moment something actually did happen!

As the words left her lips she accompanied them with an extra vigorous sweep of the broom-stick as though she were banging Hitler and all his Nazis over the head. The granny came undone, the shoulder-straps flew apart, and the little vest twirled up into the air and sailed down on to the beach.

'Golly!' said Caroline.

'Coo!' said Mick. 'That's your vest gone.' He stared entranced at the spectacle.

'Gone nothing!' retorted his sister with spirit. 'How d'you think I'm going to get along without my vest? You wouldn't like to go about without your pants!'

'I don't know what you think you're going to do about it. It's in the next cove by now.

Caroline's vest
Has gone West,'

jeered Mick, dancing up and down with pleasure in this trifling incident that was breaking up the day's monotony.

Sure enough, the little vest was bowling merrily along the shore. Even as the children looked the breeze suddenly lifted it up in the air again and deposited it in the cleft of a rock just beyond the cluster of piled-up rocks that marked the limit of the cove.

'I'm going after it. So there!' Caroline was thoroughly roused at the sight of the defiant little garment now coyly waving its hem at her from between two rocks. She bent down and wrenched off her shoes and hurled them into the Cave behind her. Then she took a flying leap down the path on to the beach.

'Here, hi, whoa!' Mick was more than alarmed. 'You can't do that. Caroline, come back. I say, Caroline, you'll be seen from the Tower.' Had the girl gone off her head?

'Rot,' Caroline pranced backwards below the ledge and cocked a snook at her agitated brother. 'I'm sick of the old Cave. And nobody's going to see me. They're all busy goose-stepping. Watch me.' As she spoke she dropped flat on her tummy and wriggled a passage between the rocks where her quick eyes had spied a narrow gully.

Mick watched her apprehensively as she disappeared from view. It would be too sickening if Caroline went and spoilt everything at this juncture, even if she was tired of the way they were living. Then he realized that she was actually as safe in the next little cove as in the one they were in, because both were really part of one big cove and the same barrier of rock protected both from the Tower headland. However, one never knew what Caroline might do next in one of these turns. He wondered whether he ought to go after her and try and stop her behaving like a skittish colt. Then he remembered Punch. He mentally washed his hands for the time being of the exasperating Caroline and went off into the stable.

Out in the bay the patient fisherman was still dutifully pulling in dabs in ignorance of the uproar ashore.

Mick stood for some time patting Punch's gentle nose and stroking his neck with long-practised movements. He was in his undemonstrative manner devoted to his pony and not at all sorry to be left in peace with him for a few moments. Punch was settling down in his new quarters far better than the more restless Dinah would have done. He turned his head and nuzzled quietly at Mick's shoulder as the boy talked to him in a low murmur. Mick tugged gently at Punch's ears and ran his fingers through the short mane. So engrossed was he with Punch that he completely forgot all about Caroline, until about five minutes later he was suddenly recalled by a conspiratorial voice from the other side of the rocks.

'Could you come here a minute, Mick, please?'

The voice sounded so unnaturally meek that Mick hastened to wriggle through the gully in some terror lest Caroline should have further complicated matters by going and spraining her ankle. Nothing so disastrous had apparently occurred. There was Caroline in the cove behind the rocks kneeling almost doubled up over a tiny rock-pool. In one hand she was grasping the errant vest, none the worse for its adventures.

'Look at this.' Caroline did not turn her head as Mick swarmed through the rocks and joined her by the pool. 'Somebody does come here,' she said in stricken tones, and pointed with her free hand.

Mick leaned forward over her shoulder. It was a small but particularly exquisite specimen of a sea-water pool. A steep piece of rock rose sheer above it and a fringe of seaweed swept its surface like a cascade. It sparkled far down in its depths with a translucent green light, and was starred with limpets and sea-anemones. Mick looked at it more closely. Caroline was indeed right. Floating serenely in the middle was a smallish square lump of cork. Trails of seaweed from the overhanging rock festooned its grained, worn surface, and it bobbed up and down in a jaunty manner upon the miniature wavelets caused by Mick's hand as he plunged it into the water.

'Whoever's put his catch into a pool above the high watermark will be coming back for it pretty soon,' remarked Mick, drawing the cork towards him. It came more lightly than he expected through the water. Evidently the basket to which it must be attached was not a heavy one. He rolled up his jersey sleeve and submerging his arm to the elbow felt for the thin rope that would be joining basket to cork.

To his surprise it coiled easily into his hand as though the object at the other end was of no weight at all.

'Whatever is it?' Caroline spoke in a fearful whisper.

Mick hauled up the last few inches of dripping rope, and carefully detached the shiny wet object that was lashed to a small stone around which the rope was passed. It lay on the palm of his hand – a little folded oiled-silk wallet. In dead silence the children bent over it, and Mick untied the soaking tape and unrolled the minute bundle. Inside was a flat square of oiled silk made like an ordinary envelope.

'All very watertight,' murmured Mick as he slid his fingers inside the silk envelope to extract a tiny slip of paper. The oiled silk had done its work well. The paper was as dry as when it was first put into the wallet, and the writing stood out as clearly as though the writer's pen had only just touched the paper.

Mick gave one glance at the jumble of letters. 'It's in code,' he said disgustedly. He spread it out on the rockface and held it in place with a couple of pebbles. Then he bent over it again, and brooded absorbedly upon the array of Gothic characters in which the message, if that was what it was, was written.

A sudden suspicious sound from behind his right shoulder made him look up hastily. Caroline was still kneeling beside him. She was staring at the paper, her face frightened and her eyes tearful. 'I don't like it. Somebody does come here,' she repeated with another gulp. 'We aren't a bit safe after all. It – it might be anybody.' She looked huntedly round the quiet cove, up at the cliffs, at the rocks, at the sea itself. The sea still danced and gleamed in the sunlight, the white sands were still as inviting, but the whole atmosphere seemed to have changed. The silence of the little cove was no longer that of profound peace. The cliffs towered over them no longer protectively but in hostility. The rocks were no longer the barrier to keep their foes away. They were themselves the hiding-place of the enemy. There was an indefinably eerie quality in the quietness of the cove since Caroline's discovery.

Mick looked down at the message again. What a beastly

thing to have happened just when they were beginning to feel a bit more secure.

'I don't like it,' Caroline was saying in a queer high-pitched voice.

'Here, take a pull, old girl,' said Mick alarmed, thumping his sister hard on the back. But it was too late. With a sniff and a swallow Caroline was in floods of tears and dabbing madly at her eyes with the crumpled vest.

'Put it back, oh do put it back,' she sobbed, completely unnerved. 'Let's go right away from here – anywhere, I don't care where. We can't stay here with these awful things happening every moment of the day. Oh, whatever are you doing?'

She had looked up to see Mick calmly copying the message off the strip of paper into the notebook which always reposed in the pocket of whatever suit he was wearing.

'What are you doing that for?' hiccuped Caroline between sobs.

'Because,' Mick answered with more patience than tact, 'I'd like to try my hand at solving the code, and whoever that message is meant for is going to come and collect it some time.' He eyed Caroline apprehensively, anticipating a fresh collapse at this prophetic utterance. But the astonishing girl only blew her nose with a trumpeting sound and got out 'Orright. But you'd better [gulp] lemme tie wallet up again or [gulp and sniff] they'll guess you've been at it.'

Mick silently handed over wallet, paper, stone, rope, and cork. Rent at intervals with devastating sobs Caroline managed with shaking fingers to tie the whole contraption up so neatly that nobody could possibly have detected the work of alien hands. She lowered it back into the pool with scarcely a splash. Then with a final gulp she turned to Mick and said, 'For goodness' sake, let's get back into the Cave. I feel quite worn out. Such a lot seems to happen.'

Chapter 10

The Code

'Why on earth,' Caroline reasoned, 'the Nazis should want to leave messages tied to corks for other Nazis to find when they own the whole island and can tell each other what they want to say beats me.'

'That is precisely what we want to find out,' retorted Mick as, with a patience that was almost exasperating, he turned to a clean page of his notebook and made another start.

It was now late afternoon, and ever since they had crawled back, damp and dishevelled, through the rocks they had sat on the ledge working on the code. A dozen times had Caroline raised her head despairingly to say, 'Oh, for goodness' sake, Mick, let's stop. After all we're only doing it for fun.' A dozen times Mick had maddeningly answered, 'We can't give it up and just be beaten by it. We'll get it soon.'

Mick had no intention of relinquishing the attempt to solve the code until the whole secret message lay deciphered before his eyes. While Caroline's quick erratic brain produced every few minutes some brilliant and quite unworkable hypothesis he quietly and methodically worked through theory after theory, crossing out and rejecting until page after page of his notebook was covered with his neat handwriting.

Once when Caroline had protested at the waste of time, saying that obviously, even if they did solve the code, they could do nothing to put a spoke in the Nazi wheels, Mick had firmly registered his own protest. He had raised his head, and told Caroline in no measured tones to stop being a beastly nuisance and a hindrance. Even if they could do nothing at the moment, he added, he supposed that some day before the war ended they would be in England again, and then they could hand the messages in to the authorities. They'd look pretty silly, wouldn't they, if they couldn't hand in some sort of solution at the same time. He snorted with disgust at what he considered Caroline's casual attitude towards so serious a matter.

The afternoon gave place to evening. The rocks turned to a dark purple in the sunset. The sea ebbed to an even deeper calm, with blue shadows streaking across towards the horizon. At intervals Caroline leaped to her feet, and strode up and down the ledge in a frenzy of pent-up energy. Long before supper-time she retired inside the Cave, and could be heard working off her boredom in a furious attack of spring-cleaning, banging and swishing round with broom and mop and duster. Once she came to the entrance, her pigtails tied up like a busy housewife's in a duster, to observe that she did hope their German would be up to understanding the gist of the message, when Mick did manage to decode it.

Mick merely grunted at this. His pencil flicked over another page. He, too, felt a bit rocky where the German language was concerned. The two older Templeton children had had a German governess during the holidays a good many years ago, and both had learned to chatter away quite adequately. But how far their knowledge would stand up to stuff like this Mick was not prepared to say. However, time enough for that bit of trouble when the code was solved. Actually, Mick, at the moment of Caroline's dishevelled appearance at the doorway, was pondering another bit of bother. He'd just had a pretty uncomfortable idea.

A few minutes later when Caroline came again out of the Cave with the bucket to fill at the spring she found Mick sitting with a brooding look upon his face that she knew all too well. She put the bucket down on the ground with a bang, stuck her hands on her hips, and surveyed the hunched figure in the blue jersey with a grim look.

'Go on. Cough it up,' she said shortly. To one who had lived with Mick since babyhood it was more than obvious that something was weighing quite heavily upon his mind.

'Eh? What?' – innocently – 'S'nothing to cough up, is there?'

'Aw, can it, buddy.' Gangster Templeton assumed a threatening attitude. 'Go on, Mick. You'd better tell me what it is because you know I always find out in the end.'

Mick capitulated. He did indeed know Caroline's capacity for prising out one's most cherished secrets.

'Well,' he began guardedly, keeping a wary eye on his sister's face, 'I was only just thinking, you know, about what we said about somebody coming to fetch that message. Looks rather as though they don't particularly care for parading about the beach in daylight, any more than we do. So' – he nervously hurried on beneath Caroline's ominous eye – 'it did strike me, but I may be absolutely wrong, so don't take me for gospel or anything –'

'Oh, come off it,' said Caroline wearily. 'I suppose what you want to say and daren't is that you think they'll come at night. So do I think so. I thought it ages ago, too.'

'Oh.' There was no very obvious reply to this. Mick appeared slightly stunned at the vagaries of a girl who could weep like a fountain at the mere discovery of a code message in an oiled silk wallet, and contemplate with equanimity the prospect of the arrival of a posse of enemy Secret Service agents under cover of darkness to recover the message.

'I suppose what you want to do is to set a watch tonight.' Caroline voiced Mick's thoughts in dour tones. She was standing over him with arms akimbo, the very picture of Amazon inflexibility steeled to desperate adventure.

'As a matter of fact, I do think perhaps we ought to,' said Mick on a slight note of apology. 'Not that there's very much point in it because we can't do a thing if anybody does come. But if we go to bed knowing that there's the chance of someone coming we shan't get a wink of sleep, and we shall be as jumpy as a pair of kittens. There's another thing, too.' He hesitated. 'I said there wasn't much point in it. There's this much point. We clearly can't stymie their plans but we can collect every bit of possible data. It might be awfully useful to the Secret Service at home.'

The path of duty did indeed lie plain before Caroline's

unwilling eyes. It would, she consoled herself with Mick's first argument, be impossible to sleep anyway. She couldn't help saying though, as she picked up the bucket again, 'It will be fun if they discover us in the Cave, won't it?' She knew if she didn't voice her secret fear it would haunt her with increasing intensity through the evening's ordeal. She flung it over her shoulder as she walked off to the spring.

Mick looked after the disappearing figure of his sister. He did not vouchsafe any answer. Absently he slipped his note-book back in his pocket. It was getting too dark, anyway, to go on. Caroline had, of course, hit on the snag in the whole scheme. Supposing the mysterious agent, or agents, used the Cave as *their* headquarters, supposing they already knew of the presence of intruders in the Cave! There was no comforting reassurance he could offer Caroline on this point. He shrugged his shoulders and went off with sombre face to bridle Punch for his exercise. Supposing – supposing –. It was the one big danger – the fly in the otherwise rather exciting ointment.

But as things turned out Mick need not have worried unduly. The whole affair was in the end curiously undra-matic – in fact it was very nearly tame. 'Perhaps we're getting hardened to adventures,' Caroline hazarded after-wards in an attempt to explain their blasé attitude towards what to most people would have been a highly unpleasant episode.

Darkness fell quite early. The children ate their supper in the twilight out on the ledge. It was still warm enough to be able to sit out of doors until the stars were well in the sky. Mick hung up the black-out curtain while Caroline cleared away the remains of the meal, and then they both ensconced themselves behind the curtain ready to peep out at the first stealthy footfall. Mick had put the broom-stick ready to hand as the nearest approach to a lethal weapon, while Caroline fully intended to swing the bucket down on the enemy's head as he crouched at the entrance. Actually the black-out curtain, erected by Richard and Peter for the Anniversary Night celebrations, gave them both a far greater feeling of security than they had expected. Mick privately hoped that if the night-jay should find entry to their stronghold he would fall into its thick folds *en route* and he and Caroline could then busy themselves with bucket and broom-stick before he recovered.

They did not have long to wait, not long enough for nerves to become over-taut or tired brains to spin with sleepiness. Almost as soon as night had completely descended upon the little cove and the only noise was the rhythmic falling of the waves at the tide-line, Caroline nudged Mick. Her quick ears had caught an unfamiliar sound. It was an unexpected sound too. Neither child had thought about the enemy coming by any way than on his two feet. The approaching dip-and-plunge of muffled oars from over the water took both by surprise. They lay on their propped elbows, with heads peeping round either side of the heavy curtain, staring into the night. The next sound was the slight bump of a boat upon the sand. It sounded, Mick judged, like a very light dinghy indeed. Followed the flash of a carefully-shaded torch as someone took bearings. Both Mick and Caroline deduced independently that only one man was concerned in these operations. It was evidently somebody who had been before for there was no fumbling approach to the little pool. The listeners heard the faint swish and drip of the rope as the cork was cautiously drawn through the water. Then there was a long, long silence. Evidently the stranger was decoding the message by torch-light. Perhaps he was even answering it. Caroline writhed at the thought of the key to the code being so close at hand, and yet she was not able to move hand or foot to reach it.

Whoever the stranger was he was no novice in the art of secret and stealthy movement. The next sound was not that of footfalls returning across the sand but the creak of row-locks and the pad-pad of the oars dying away again over the water. Mick and Caroline simultaneously leaned out beyond the black-out curtain, vainly striving to distinguish the outlines of the small craft that had come and gone so mysteriously in the night. But darkness, like a black-out curtain itself, hung before their eyes. They could see nothing, and almost at once the dip of the oars died in the distance.

We Couldn't Leave Dinah

The only sound left was once more the falling of the sluggish waves upon the beach. The children drew back into the Cave, feeling rather flat. The show was over, and very little seemed to have happened.

*

Caroline was wakened next morning from heavy slumber, not only by that peculiar certainty of having grossly overslept but also by a crude bellow in her right ear.

'I say, do wake up. I believe I've got it.'

'Go' wha'?'

Caroline heard an unintelligible noise proceeding from her own throat and opened one eyelid with an effort. Even in this semi-comatose state the hazily perceived rapture upon her brother's usually phlegmatic countenance silenced upon her lips the righteous fury of the thus rudely awakened. With a terrific effort she heaved herself to a sitting posture in her sleeping sack. Outside the Cave she could see by the brightness of the sun that she was far later in waking than upon the two last mornings. Still dazed with sleep she reached feebly for the two slips of paper that Mick was holding.

'Have you got another message?' she inquired.

Mick nodded. It was plain that he was almost beside himself with pride. Caroline suddenly was overwhelmed with affection for him. He stood there waiting for her verdict looking so small and square and pleased. Darling Mick! How obsessed he was with his old code! She could dimly remember now half waking in the night to perceive him, with his little torch glowing under the cover of his sleeping bag, bent over his notebook, quite unable to tear himself away from it even for sleep.

'I went and collected the new one,' he was saying, 'while you were still asleep. We were right, Caroline. Whoever came last night did leave an answer in the pool.'

She looked down at the one slip of paper. Under one of the longer jumbles of letters Mick had printed in block capitals the one word:

SCHLEICHER.

'Old Schleicher, you see!' burst out Mick, unable to

contain himself any longer. 'That gives us a start all right, doesn't it? We ought to be able to work out the rest from that easily enough.'

'However did you do it?' Caroline played up nobly to Mick's pleasure.

'Oh, easy,' said Mick with a casual air. Then more truthfully, 'Well, no, it wasn't really what you'd call easy. I put the new message down by the side of the first, and then I noticed a whole word that had a kind of *sameness* as the old jumble I'd got so stale over. It seemed to give my mind a kind of jolt, and I jiggered the thing about a bit and then quite suddenly I hit on old Baldhead's name and it came out. I've been trying to work out the key ever since. Look.' He took his notebook out of his pocket. It was doubled back at a page upon which was neatly tabulated a cryptic and quite meaningless collection of letters.

Caroline gave one look, more of respect than comprehension, and handed the book back to Mick with the comment, 'It's no good. My mind just doesn't work that way. But if this war goes on I should think the Secret Service will absolutely go on their knees to you to do their codes for them.' She crawled out of her bag as she spoke. 'I'm going to get dressed and get breakfast. You go and sit quietly out on the ledge and get ahead with the key.' She realized that it was quite hopeless to expect Mick to discharge any domestic duties satisfactorily while his mind was set on his precious code.

An hour later Mick was still working out his key before starting to decode the two messages. Caroline had cleared breakfast away, put the cave to rights, and was busy tying the vest on to the broom-handle to flag Peter when he had done his piece for the day.

The party this morning was infected with a far more perceptible spirit of gaiety than on the preceding day. Both Mick and Caroline were relieved at having something definite to do, especially something that really was going to be a grand success like the code. Secretly, too, both of them were thankful that the night, with its grim watching, was over. In the bright light of day the actual significance of the code seemed to be unimportant, and the sinister network of espionage that it represented not so terrifying. Caroline had caught something of her brother's pleasurable anticipation, as the messages really began to look as though they might not remain for ever just a maddening teasing word puzzle. Her washing up was receiving very sketchy attention this morning. It was impossible, she found, to concentrate in two directions at once. When she had laid the broom-stick up against the cave entrance until Peter should arrive, she spent the intervening time dashing between her bowl of suds and her brother perched on the ledge outside. 'I shouldn't expect too much,' Mick kept on saying. 'Don't forget even when I do get it out it's going to be in a language we've both rather forgotten.'

'That's what I told you yesterday,' Caroline returned as she rushed back to slap her pots and pans with renewed vigour.

Just before half-past nine when Peter was due Mick quietly laid his pencil down. He raised his head and looked round for Caroline to tell her that the key was at last completed, and that they could now decode the messages straight away. He felt curiously tired with all the effort he had put into the work since yesterday morning, and yet now that the solution lay to hand, very exhilarated. Caroline was in the Cave. He could hear her singing away to herself. Mick did not call her. He simply sat still in the warm sunlight with his hands dangling over his knees. He wanted to put off the moment when he would apply the key to the code messages. It seemed like a miracle to have reached the ending of all his labours like this. It had been worth, more than worth, all the toil and the tiredness and the recurring defeats and disappointments to feel that the solution, like the tiny kernel of a hazelnut, lay at last beneath your fingers. He felt like a king crowned. He sat peacefully there in deep contentment for another minute, savouring the experience. Then slowly he reached for the two slips of paper which he had stood under a stone to keep them from blowing away. He put his notebook on his knees open at the key, and picked up his pencil again.

Some ten minutes later he was dimly conscious that Caroline was standing beside him with one hand shading her eyes and the other grasping the broom-stick.

'Peter's dead on time, isn't he?' he heard her say. Mick gave one quick glance as from a dream at the little red boat now pushing its way across the bay. But even the morning appearance of his friend, bringing with him the possibility of release from this Crusoe life, failed to excite him. He bent over his notebook again, frowning at something that was puzzling him very deeply.

'Caroline,' he heard himself say, 'Caroline, come and look at this.'

'Whatever's he doing?' was the only response from the figure beside him.

'Caroline.' Mick looked up to see Caroline standing tensely, leaning forward on the broom-handle.

'What's he doing?' she repeated sharply.

'Caroline, I say, Caroline. This is jolly odd.'

'What say?' She gave him only half her attention.

'Caroline – these messages aren't in German at all. They're in English – *English*.'

But Caroline was paying no attention to him.

'Gosh,' she was whispering. 'Gosh, Mick, look at Peter.'

And at that Mick did look across the shining waters of the bay to the little red boat so quietly rocking up and down, where Peter sat fishing with three rods.

Chapter 11

Three Meet

The excitements after two days of solitary confinement came so quickly upon one another that Mick and Caroline were completely dazed.

Caroline flopped down exhaustedly on the ledge beside Mick after she had finished her war-dance of celebration, remarking that it was a mercy they'd arranged to let three hours elapse before meeting Peter at the cottage as she would be in no condition sooner to make intelligent plans. 'I do wonder what he's arranged,' she kept on repeating happily as she fanned herself with her signalling vest. It was marvellous to think that there really and truly was a chance of seeing Daddy and Thomas again. Even the prospect of a prolonged visit to Hubert and Penelope seemed more bearable now.

Mick was also wondering how Peter proposed to get them off the island. He gave a little imperceptible sigh as he made the appropriate replies to Caroline's running comments. It would be super to escape from Clerinel. Of course it would. It would be grand to feel safe again, and know that there was no chance of a sudden pounce from Cousin Karl, but . . .

Luckily Caroline was far too excited to notice Mick's lack of enthusiasm. He picked up his notebook and fingered over its pages. It was a bit difficult to appear terrifically pleased and thrilled when all the time you were secretly longing to know what was going to be the outcome of the mystery upon which you had so unexpectedly stumbled. Mick knew that it was none of his business and that there was nothing he could do to help the writers of those messages, but after all he had spent a long time racking his brains over the code and in the end he had been successful. It was a bit hard to think that some doorkeeper at the Admiralty, or wherever you did hand in those kind of things, would just take it from him and he would walk away back to Eaton Square and never hear any more about the matter. Poor Mick heaved a sigh so gusty that Caroline stopped talking and looked hard at him.

'What's up?' she inquired.

'Nothing,' replied Mick shortly.

Caroline's eyes fell on the notebook. She gave a little squeal. 'Goodness,' she cried, horrified at her apparent lack of interest, 'I'd entirely forgotten about the code in all the excitement. What did you say about them? I wasn't listening properly.'

'I said they'd come out in English,' said Mick patiently. It was quite plain that Caroline was only pretending to be interested. Her whole mind was entirely given over to the latest development in the situation, and the pursuits of yesterday were to her already a thing of the past. Mick handed her over the notebook open at the now decoded messages. On the left-hand page he had written out the first message that Caroline had discovered in the pool. It ran:

SCHLEICHER HAS INFORMATION SUSPECTED DATE-CHANGE. ACCESS IMPOSSIBLE.

The second message left in answer to the first was terse:
IMPERATIVE OBTAIN DATE.

'But why are they in English?' Caroline raised puzzled eyes. 'Nazis don't write in English – unless it's to make it all more difficult to detect.'

'Which it wouldn't be. One of *their* enemies reading that would understand English better than German – like us. No. I believe those messages were written by Englishmen.'

'But – golly, you mean they're not Nazis at all. They're our side.' Caroline's interest was rapidly quickening.

'Looks like it,' said Mick. 'It did look fishy all along that the Germans should be sending messages in this way when they hold the whole island. I never thought of it being our Secret Service. I should think the one man is an agent actually on the island, and the man who came last night by boat was landed from a destroyer or a seaplane or something.'

Caroline bent over the two messages again. 'Wonder what

they're about anyway,' she said. 'Looks as though the Nazis had got some plan and we found out the date and then they changed it, doesn't it?'

'And as though old Baldhead knows the new date,' supplemented Mick. 'We apparently can't prise it out of him. I should imagine that's what that "ACCESS IMPOSSIBLE" means.'

'It's evidently jolly important that whoever wrote that has got to get the information somehow,' Caroline observed. 'The date seems to be the king-pin of the whole show.'

'It's probably locked up in the office safe at Headquarters,' said Mick, taking his notebook back and putting it in his pocket. 'Place'll be stiff with military. Poor devil won't stand an earthly of getting near it.'

'It might be at the Point, too, among the General's papers,' said Caroline. She looked at her watch. Her interest was waning as the time of their appointment with Peter drew nearer. 'Pity our man can't dress up as Frau Nannerl's maid or Baldhead's batman and snoop round the house that way.'

Mick grunted. It was no joking matter in his opinion.

'Anyway,' Caroline went on cheerfully, 'it's nothing to do with us. We can't get at the date, and in any case we're off almost at once – or I suppose we are.'

Mick grunted again and got to his feet. He strolled in to see Punch who was always an antidote against depression. He felt in his heart that it was all wrong that he should feel so downcast when the news was so good. But he wanted so much to know more about the two lonely Englishmen who had leagued themselves against the whole Nazi occupation on Clerinel.

Caroline, on the other hand, was hard put to it not to shriek and scream with joy at the prospect of leaving the island. But she was a kind-hearted girl and realized dimly that Mick was feeling a little low about this code affair. Inwardly she thought, 'Thank goodness it *is* nothing to do with us. I hope I never have anything to do with oilskin wallets again as long as I live.' Aloud she only said, 'Well, anyway, it was fun while it lasted.'

There was no reply from the stable until some twenty minutes later Mick reappeared and said, 'I'm ready, Caroline, if you are.'

Caroline had meanwhile been bustling round to make the Cave look as much like the Clerinel Pony Club Headquarters and as little like the Templeton family's private residence as possible. It was unlikely, she argued, that Cousin Karl or his fellow Nazis would come poking round in their absence, but it was as well to be on the safe side. Sleeping bags and washing apparatus were cunningly hidden away and the nine stools set round the table as though the Club Committee were due to sit at any moment.

When the children set out up the cliff path Caroline was hopping and bouncing with relief at being released from the narrow confines of the cove, and even Mick's gloom had lightened. The weather was not so fine as could have been wished for this first excursion into the haunts of civilization. The sun which had shone brightly enough for breakfast had withdrawn into a pale grey sky and turned into a sulky-looking orange ball. Almost as Caroline announced that she could smell fog in the air Mick pointed to the first beginnings of a sea mist creeping over the horizon.

'It's a good job,' he said, 'that we're not going to be much longer in the Cave if the weather's breaking up – and it's a very good job if there's going to be a fog for us to escape in. It'll make it much easier for a boat to get away from the island unseen.'

'We haven't yet thought what we're going to do about Punch,' Caroline reminded him as they cautiously skirted the hollow in which La Falaise lay and turned across the sweep of hills to descend to the cottage.

'I hadn't forgotten,' said Mick. 'I was hoping Peter might take him. He can't go back to the Point if Richard's Robin is there. I'm sure Peter could put up some sort of story to his father and Punch would never be discovered at La Falaise.'

'I wish Dinah could go to La Falaise with Punch,' sighed Caroline. 'She'll be absolutely miserable with that awful fat Frau Nannerl. Besides, we don't know at all who Baldhead's found to look after the stables. I say' – she gave a little skip – 'we shall have something to tell Peter as well as him us. He'll be green with envy when he hears about those messages.'

Mick stopped dead in his tracks. 'My hat,' he said, 'I'm jolly glad you mentioned it. I meant to say earlier that whatever we do we musn't mention the codes to Peter. After all' – he felt for his words hesitantly – 'we're sure Peter's all right, but M. Beaumarchais – well, he's *all right,* but there's always a chance that the Nazis might force it out of him somehow. Don't you think so?'

Caroline nodded disappointedly. Then – 'Ooh, look,' she cried, 'there's Peter.' She broke into a run with Mick behind her. They were coming down the hillside opposite the ruined cottage, and her sharp eyes had espied a figure sitting waiting on the distant doorstep.

With an elaborate caution born of three days of fugitive living the children waited for a moment in the deep bracken while they looked round to make sure the landscape was empty before crossing the clearing to the cottage. Then they stepped out into the open and marched across to the ruin. Peter rose from the doorstep and gravely saluted the expedition with his butterfly net like Neptune with his trident.

It was almost a historic moment. Caroline felt quite solemn and uplifted as Peter advanced. It was, she decided, like the meeting in darkest Africa between Stanley and Livingstone. There was a brief pause. Then everybody grinned sheepishly and talk burst forth like a long dammed torrent.

'Signals worked all right, didn't they?' Peter said. 'I saw you flying yours terrifically clearly.'

'Did you see my vest fly into the next cove?' began Caroline eagerly.

'Oughtn't we to go into the cottage in case anybody's about?' Mick cut hurriedly across the coming indiscretion of his sister. Caroline turned scarlet, Peter looked from one to the other and said nothing. Mick led the way inside the cottage.

It was a most romantic spot for a secret meeting. Little

more than a shell, the ruined cottage had defied Channel winds and rains for half a century since its last occupants had gone off with bag and baggage to the more friendly town. The rafters were black and almost eaten away with age, moss and baby fungi had pushed their way up between the floorboards, and the rustling in the old chimney suggested the domicile of birds. Cobwebs swinging from lintels and ceiling brushed the tops of the children's heads as they trooped into the silent hall. A delicious eerie shiver crawled down Caroline's spine. What better place for the disclosure of Peter's plot?

'I can't stay long,' Peter said as they sat down on the rickety staircase. 'The Nazis are swarming everywhere. They've let La Falaise alone only because the General has us taped.'

'How are things going on the island?' Mick inquired. He felt as though he had been out of the world, like Rip Van Winkle, for countless years.

Peter shrugged his shoulders. His face was clouded. 'There've been no "incidents" if that's what you mean,' he said shortly. 'I don't suppose there will be until the Gestapo arrive. The military have received instructions to treat the civil population decently, and only arrest if strictly necessary. But nobody dare open his mouth. The men are standing idly about on the quayside without speaking, the women scarcely dare say "B'jour" to each other in the market place. Everywhere the Nazis take what goods they want from the shops practically without payment. Oh, on the face of it things are quiet and apparently all right but ...' Peter's eyes were bleak as he shook his head, and stared moodily out through the open doorway. Then he went on in lighter tones, 'But I've managed to make arrangements for you to clear out.'

The sober expressions of his audience brightened. Peter rose to his feet and strolled to the entrance. He cast a casual glance round the clearing before returning to his seat on the stairs. Then he leaned forward. The three heads almost touched in conclave. Peter spoke low and rapidly.

'The two le Mesurier brothers, the ones you fish with,

Mick, are sailing on the tide at midnight tonight. I spoke to Meurice. He will take you both if you are at his cottage at eleven-thirty. The old boy's apparently known for his anti-Nazi talk and has been persuaded to go before the Gestapo arrive. It's a risky job for them taking passengers, but I rather hinted that your father would make it worth their while. That all right?' He paused and looked inquiringly at the Templetons.

'Gracious yes,' said Caroline trustingly, 'Daddy'll pay anything to have us back.'

'Good. That is arranged then. Eleven-thirty tonight. You will be able to find your way into Pol in the dark, won't you? I warn you –' Peter hesitated and then went on gravely, 'You do realize, don't you, that it is all a pretty tricky business? There is always more than a chance of being caught. The Nazis are hot on this form of escape.'

'We know.' Mick answered briefly for both of them. 'But there's no other way, is there?'

'Absolutely none,' agreed Peter sombrely. 'Every channel of communication with England seems to have been broken off. Other boats will escape of course – but it may not be for some time. By the way, I didn't tell Meurice who it was who was going with him. I simply said two friends of mine. It seemed wiser to mention no names. I told him you would be in ordinary island dress, and would tap lightly on his door three times and say, "Can you give us a bed for tonight?"'

'Gosh,' marvelled Caroline, 'it's just like a book.'

'He's got to identify you somehow. If anybody should overhear you you would only appear to be two islanders from an outlying village who had got stranded.' Peter appeared to the naïve eyes of Mick and Caroline to be moving through this chequered pattern of intrigue with the nonchalance of an accredited Secret Service agent.

'Now about Punch.' Peter turned to Mick. He seemed to have forgotten nothing, thought Caroline admiringly. 'I thought I'd come over to the Cave tomorrow morning and ride him back to La Falaise and keep him there. You can stable him all right for one night alone, can't you?'

Mick looked as though the last weight had been removed from his shoulders. 'I'd like that,' he said, 'I'd like Punch to be at La Falaise until – until we all come back.' There was a short silence, broken by Caroline.

'I suppose you haven't heard how the ponies are being looked after at the Point, have you?' she asked. It was almost more than she could bear to hear all these plans being made for Punch and to know that darling Dinah was going to be left to Frau Nannerl's mercies.

But Peter understood very well. 'I can't do anything about Dinah, I'm afraid,' he said gently. 'But I'm sure she'll be all right. Until they can find a proper stable-hand the General's batman is looking after the stable. They seem to think that your Petit-Jean is still on the island and may be persuaded to go back there. But don't you worry, Caroline. I'll keep an eye on Dinah.'

'Peter.' Before Caroline could express her gratitude Mick, who had been very quiet, broke abruptly into the conversation. 'Couldn't you come with us? Couldn't the le Mesuriers take the three of us? You oughtn't to stay here with all this going on.'

'O Peter, do, do,' Caroline besought him. 'We can't possibly leave you here and not see you again till the war's over. Daddy'd be thrilled if we brought you with us. Oh, do come too.'

'I can't. Of course I can't.' Peter spoke decisively. He looked slightly surprised at the suggestion. 'It might get Father into frightful trouble if I disappeared. Of course I must stay.' Somehow his prompt disposal of Mick's suggestion made both Templetons feel a little small.

'I do feel a miserable skunk leaving you behind,' said Caroline mournfully.

'Rot,' said Peter. 'I'll be all right. Besides, we shall probably have whacked them before long. I shall go along to Headquarters occasionally and dust it. And you'll have to keep the Pony Club going in England, you know.' Caroline felt as though she were a small child being comforted by a kindly grown-up.

'That's what Mr Lawrence suggested,' said Mick

thoughtfully. 'I wonder if we could. There won't be very many of us, though.'

But Peter was pulling a bit of paper out of his pocket. 'Lend me a pencil,' he said. He spread the paper out on the staircase and wrote busily for a moment. He then handed the result over to Mick.

'I hereby appoint,' Mick read out loud, 'Michael and Caroline Templeton to be joint temporary Presidents of the London Branch of the Clerinel Pony Club during its residence abroad, and I give them full powers to enrol members and carry on the business of the Club according to their and their committee's discretion. Signed: Peter Beaumarchais, President.'

'There,' said Peter, feeling rewarded at the sight of Caroline's delighted face, 'that ought to keep you busy for the duration. And then when you come back to Clerinel you can elect one of your new members to carry on the London branch.'

Mick slowly pocketed the paper. 'It's a fine idea,' he said, 'a fine idea. We'll jolly well do it.'

'We've settled everything, I think,' said Peter in business-like tones, getting to his feet to cut short Mick's thanks. 'I must be off. You won't forget tonight's proceeding, will you? If there should be any change of plan I'll signal you from the boat and we shall just have to meet again. With any luck there'll be a bit of a fog tonight, and you'll get clear of Clerinel under cover of it.'

The trio walked across the clearing and stood on the fringes of the bracken jungle. 'Well,' said Peter very seriously, 'good-bye and good luck.'

Caroline was blinking rapidly in a frantic effort not to disgrace herself by dissolving into tears before the two boys. Saying good-bye was always among the most distressing incidents of her thirteen years. Even Mick was looking a bit blue, and had set his mouth in a tighter line than usual. Peter shook hands gravely with both of them.

But for once the misery of parting was not unduly prolonged. Caroline had barely mastered her incipient tears, Mick had barely wrung Peter's hand and muttered 'G'bye and g'luck,' before all at once they saw Peter's face change. Simultaneously Mick and Caroline swung round and stood open-mouthed, gazing at a distant spot in the bracken.

'EE-YAH-OW. EE-YAH-OW. EE-YAH-AH-AH-OW.'

For the love of Mike! It sounded like all the black men of Africa.

'EE-YAH-OW. EE-YAH-OW.'

The peculiar trumpeting came nearer and nearer. The trio remained paralysed at the edge of the clearing. In the distance Caroline could see the bracken tops agitatedly waving as though some terrific jungle animal were tearing a passage through the undergrowth towards them.

'AY-YAI-YAI.'

Peter dropped flat and slid like an eel among the tall bracken stalks. He evidently expected the others to follow him. But Mick and Caroline stood transfixed by the sound, which as it came nearer and nearer took on, to a brother and sister with a younger brother in the nursery, an uncanny familiarity. Caroline could scarcely believe her ears. The peculiar sound ringing across the welkin resembled nothing so much in the world as good honest nursery howling, of the kind usually dealt with by Nanny's hand applied hard. Before Caroline could communicate this to Mick the noise doubled like the trumpeting of a herd of elephants, the bracken was thrust ruthlessly aside, and out into the clearing, with stamping feet and purple enraged countenance, charged a small fat girl slightly older than Thomas. Thump! She cannoned headlong into Mick.

'Ee-yah-yah-ow.' The fat little legs thumped up and down on the spot as their owner, convulsed with rage, took no notice whatever of the obstruction. Mick recovered his balance and started to shake with laughter. It was left to Caroline to rise to the demands of this situation. She looked wildly round. The bracken stalks concealing Peter were also beginning to shake. Controlling herself with an effort she took a step forward, aimed a kick at Mick's shins, and seized the bawling child by the shoulders.

'Be quiet,' she ordered, 'or I'll turn you over and spank you.' She did not want any stray Nazis attracted by the din. 'Be quiet,' she repeated in a firm tone. The reiteration of the order had an instant effect. The howls died to sobs, and the sobs to noisy and unrestrained hiccups.

'Where's your hankie?' said Caroline crossly.

'Urgly-gig-gug-hic,' said the infant choking. She looked up at the obstruction that had impeded her raging progress.

'*Wer ists?*' she demanded.

There was a dismayed silence. It had occurred to nobody that the infant might be an invader's offspring.

'*Wer ists?*' the child demanded again, hiccuping nastily.

Quick as thought Caroline rose once more to the occasion. Very well. If the child wanted to know who they were she jolly well should. With a grin and an elaborate wave of the hand she indicated her gaping brother. 'Petit-Jean,' she said. Then, keeping a wary eye upon the tear-blotched face, she beat her own breast dramatically, 'Gabrielle.'

The child appeared totally unmoved by these introductions and Caroline breathed again. She was just looking round to summon Peter to complete the party when the tear-stained object proceeded to drop its own bombshell. Drawing itself away from Caroline's restraining hand and clicking its heels together it made a funny little bow of self-introduction. 'Nannerl,' announced a squeaky complacent voice.

Mick and Caroline stood rooted to the spot. There was a slight commotion in the bracken like a rabbit as Peter beat a hasty and strategic retreat.

Chapter 12

Nannerl Upsets the Applecart

Nannerl laboriously straightened her portly little figure from the stooping position she had assumed to peer short-sightedly after the non-existent rabbit. She was not, thought Caroline, looking dispassionately at her, a prepossessing child. Short, stumpy figure clad in a blue-checked pinafore with waist squeezed into a black leather belt, long flaxen pigtails tightly braided and raked off the forehead, cheeks like shiny little penny buns with blue boot-button eyes, Nannerl Schleicher looked like a picture out of Thomas's *Struwwelpeter*, Caroline decided. But the squeaky voice, rather like the voice that proceeded from the interior of Thomas's old plush duck, was speaking again. Caroline jumped. It was addressing her.

'We will spik English,' the plush duck's voice was saying. 'You do not spik German, no?'

'N-no,' answered Caroline uncertainly. 'We spik – er, speak – English and French,' she supplemented a little lamely, and glared at Mick to induce him to take his share in this laboured dialogue. But Mick had lapsed into a watchful silence and was evading her stern eye. Of Peter there was by this time no sign. Caroline prepared to shoulder the burden of the conversation alone since Nannerl showed no sign of imminent departure. Aloud she said to the apparition at her elbow, 'Where did you learn English?' She spoke with a slight French accent to sustain the illusion that she and Mick were simple island peasants.

The question was evidently a lucky one. The penny bun cheeks creased into a wide smile, all tears forgotten, and the currant eyes snapped. Nannerl prepared to tell her newly-found audience her life's history. 'I learn the English at our

house in Berlin,' she began importantly. 'I do not yet spik it so good as my grandfater. He learn the English and the French for many years so zat one day we may to zis island come. I have the English governess *zu Hause*. She is in Berlin – in in-tern-ment,' she finished carefully.

Caroline paled and Mick shuffled his feet uncomfortably. Could one ever escape these awful people? Caroline racked her brains for a change of subject. But Nannerl was wound up like a clockwork mouse.

'We like zis place. We shall here for ever stay,' she announced improbably, looking from one to the other as though she would brook no difference of opinion about the outcome of the war. Mick concealed a grin and Nannerl eyed him suspiciously.

'Why were you crying?' Caroline burst in with more speed than politeness. This was awful. The little comic showed no signs of departure and Mick was being entirely unhelpful.

The General's granddaughter drew herself up with a show of dignity like a dowager duchess. She looked, Caroline thought, exactly like the picture she had had in her mind of the original blonde Frau Schleicher. 'I was crying,' she stated with no traces of embarrassment, 'because I have from – nein, because I have fallen from the horse.'

'What horse have you been riding?' inquired Caroline quickly. Mick gave another grin at the question. Caroline glared at him. Luckily Nannerl was too preoccupied with her recital to notice this family by-play.

'I do not know its name,' she was saying, 'but I call it Gretchen. It was in colour a very dark brown –'

'Bay,' interrupted Mick to the accompaniment of a faint moan from his sister.

'Grandfater wished me to ride ze leetle horse. But I wish to ride Gretchen. My Cousin Karl – I do not like him – say he come mit me to teach. We wa-a-lk – so – on to the hill and Gretchen stop to eat grass. Karl say "Kick her". I say if I kick I fall. He say No. But I know Yes. So I vip –'

'You what?' chorused her audience. Nannerl made a terrific effort with the elusive 'w'.

'I say I we-eep 'er mit stick. What does Gretchen do?' cried Nannerl, warming dramatically to her story. 'She throw up her behind and I am over. Look.' She switched round, and in the middle of her blue-checked person was a large green stain. 'So I run away,' she continued with a telling gesture. 'I cry and cry. And Karl leads Gretchen home again.' She looked from Caroline to Mick, and then with narrowed eyes more closely at Mick. 'You – Petit-Johann' – a stumpy forefinger shot commandingly out – 'Grandfater is looking for somebody called Petit-Johann. He say, "Find zat boy, pay heem his money, and he shall look after my horses and teach Nannerl to ride." I shall tell Grandfater I have found you. Ven you coming?'

'Gosh,' said Mick helplessly. He looked at Caroline for support in this new development.

'You shall come,' Nannerl's voice started to rise, and Caroline looked nervously round the clearing.

'You *shall* come and teach me to ride Gretchen. I ride Gretchen with you, hein?'

'What? O my hat, yes, I suppose so,' said Mick in a desperate sort of manner.

'*Yes.*' Nannerl and Mick stared at Caroline, quite startled at her thunder of affirmation.

Caroline had again taken matters into her own hands. She was beginning for the first time in her life to appreciate her hitherto concealed gift for impersonation, as she described it to Mick later. 'Yes,' she asserted, drawing herself up to her full height, 'Petit-Jean shall come. He shall come tomorrow. He is – er, staying with his sister. He did not know that he was wanted or he would have come before.' In her turn Caroline evaded Mick's appalled eye as she gave voice to this very misleading declamation. It was, she knew, the only way out.

'*Ja, ja.*' Nannerl was bouncing clumsily up and down with pleasure. It was as though a miracle had suddenly happened. The little old-woman face beamed, the button eyes sparkled and softened. For a brief moment the General's small granddaughter looked quite pretty. 'I vill tell my grandfater you vill come tomorrow. You ride with me, yes?' She seized Mick's arm and swung on to it. Caroline was conscious of a rush of pity for the lonely child.

'Yes.' Mick, unused to such demonstrations of affection, answered awkwardly.

'Now we must go,' Caroline interrupted this scene quickly. 'Petit-Jean needs his dinner,' she improvised.

'I go too,' nodded Nannerl happily. 'I go to my dinner too.' She was still jumping about the clearing with excitement and anticipation.

'Well, good-bye,' said Caroline firmly, determined Nannerl should be sped well on her path before she and Mick departed themselves.

'*Wiedersehen*, Gabrielle. *Wiedersehen*, Petit-Jean.' Nannerl's trusting politeness made Caroline feel oddly shamefaced about the whole deception. She flinched away from the picture that rose in her mind of a disappointed child watching for the new friend who would never put in an appearance. But before she could bid a further more enthusiastic farewell to Nannerl, to her intense surprise Nannerl's short legs clicked to attention and an arm shot out in salute. 'Heil Hitler!' The stentorian squeak quite startled a sparrow that had just dug up a worm close by.

'Heil Hitler!' Caroline gravely raised her arm and looked pointedly at Mick. 'Heil Hitler!' said Mick sheepishly.

The representative of the Herrenvolk nodded to each like a benign Sunday-school teacher. Then without another word she trotted away through the bracken in the direction from which she had burst upon the startled Templetons only a quarter of an hour before.

'Give her ten minutes to get out of sight,' whispered Mick as Caroline made a move herself.

They waited, tracing Nannerl's progress by the waving bracken-tops, until the pinafored figure emerged at the top of the hill, beyond which lay the drop down to the Point House. On the skyline Nannerl took a stance for a moment, surveying the landscape with the air of a conqueror. Then she disappeared over the summit.

'Phew!' said Mick, mopping his brow elaborately. 'My heavenly aunt, she's a holy terror, isn't she?'

'Poor little brute.' Caroline was inclined to be tolerant of Nannerl Schleicher. 'It must be awfully dull for her with no one but that foul Blue Feather Karl to mess round with. I rather gathered there were no parents, didn't you?' They had started slowly on their return journey to the Cave, and were climbing the hill that led to the boundaries of the La Falaise grounds. Peter had presumably long since arrived and was probably sitting over his *déjeuner* by now. Caroline suddenly started to laugh. 'Peter was a bit out in thinking Nannerl was Baldhead's wife, wasn't he?' she gurgled.

'He only said he thought she was his wife,' corrected Mick, sniffing the damp air with some distaste. 'I wish we'd got coats,' he went on uneasily. 'This mist is settling down jolly thoroughly.'

'Never say I can't act.' Caroline took no notice of Mick's interruption. 'I got us out of a nasty hole with that child just now, I'd have you know. I say, I hope to goodness she's not going to be allowed to ride Dinah. Gretchen! I nearly *fainted* when she spoke about whipping her. I don't want Dinah got into bad habits. I cured her of bucking, you know. It's a pity you can't really go as stable-boy, Mick. You could persuade her to stick to Bellman and leave Dinah alone. You know she rather cottoned on to you, I thought. She'll be frightfully disappointed when you don't turn up tomorrow. Funny to think we shall be miles and miles and miles away from Nannerl and Baldhead and Cousin Karl and everyone by then. It was rather funny her mistaking you for the real Petit-Jean, wasn't it? I say, you didn't think it awful of me to make up all that rigmarole, did you?'

Caroline rattled on without a break, neither seeking nor expecting an answer. Inside she was so excited about the prospect of escape from Clerinel that she couldn't stop talking about anything and everything that came into her head, while her heart was singing its own song of rejoicing. She felt she could afford to snap her fingers at such minor complications as Nannerl Schleicher.

As far as Caroline, at any rate, was concerned their

escape was already accomplished. Already they were on board the fishing smack, hidden under piles of net and tarpaulin, slipping across the inky waters of the Channel, the merciful sea-mist concealing their passage from the enemy. Already, crouched in the bows, she and Mick, stiff with cold, were gazing upon the approaching white cliffs of England. Already, stumbling with fatigue and exposure, they were walking into the hall in Eaton Square with Daddy and Thomas dashing out to greet them and Hubert and Penelope in regrettable hysterics of envy on the stairs. Caroline hopped and jumped as energetically as Nannerl in front of Mick, humming a tune.

If she had not been so absorbed in the enthralling pictures her imagination was weaving from the coming adventure, she might have noticed a change flicker across Mick's face when she commented lightly upon Nannerl's mistaking him for their late stable-boy, Petit-Jean, now safely established in England. It was as though some idea so startling, so stupendous had come to Mick that it altered for a brief second his entire face.

'We shall have to make an early start tonight.' Caroline's busy brain was racing ahead so fast that she did not notice Mick's absorbed silence. 'Mick, we shall have to feed and water Punch before we start, shan't we?' She turned round and walked backwards before her brother with light-hearted little dancing steps – and it was only at this moment that she realized that something was wrong.

Mick was moving along like an automaton, his feet dragging heavily over the springy turf. His head was dropped down on his chest and his shoulders hunched as though he were solving some problem of far greater moment than that of the code which had so preoccupied him earlier. As Caroline spun round he raised his head and surveyed her. It was as though he were bringing home his thoughts from some very distant place. It was funny but Caroline had a fleeting impression that Mick was terribly sorry for her about something.

'Caroline.' Mick, incapable of tactical strategy, plunged

straight to his point. 'Caroline, I can't go.' He looked straight ahead down the green track.

Pause. 'Can't go? Can't go where?'

'I can't leave the island possibly. Don't you see it's a chance in a thousand?'

'Whatever do you mean?'

Caroline was standing deathly still, blocking his passage down the track. Her eyes had lost their happy, eager light and her mouth was set in a straight line.

Mick took a deep breath. 'The information those English agents want Schleicher's got,' he said quietly. 'It may be in the Point House or it may not. They can't get access to the house but I can. I can go as their rotten stable-boy tomorrow morning. It was your saying that to the kid gave me the idea. Now do you see?'

'You're nuts.' Caroline spoke coldly and without any expression in her voice. She was suddenly chilled to the bone with fear. 'It's none of your business. It's nothing to do with you. You said so this morning.'

'It's my business now because I can help in it. It was only when I couldn't do anything that it wasn't,' said Mick stubbornly.

'They won't want –' Caroline paused for a cruel enough phrase. 'They won't want little boys interfering.'

'They will if they can help,' countered Mick unmoved. Brother and sister stood very still facing each other. The sea-mist crept round them, wreathed itself over their garments, clung to them persistently with long damp fingers.

'It's wrong of you.' Caroline spoke after another pause in an icy tone of fury. 'It's wicked of you. Daddy –' Caroline was almost beside herself with fear. In her heart she knew that she was fighting a losing battle.

'Oh, shut up.' Mick was goaded at last beyond endurance. 'You don't think I want to stay on the beastly island, do you? And you go gadding off to England? But you'd feel pretty skunkish if you made me come with you now. You're not a baby like Nannerl Schleicher. Why can't you be sensible? I'm only asking you to get yourself off the island before me. I'm not proposing to stay for the duration.'

'We're only children.' Caroline's defence was rapidly weakening but she was still fighting desperately. 'Nobody expects us to help like that, like what you want to. We only have to collect money and knit and – and collect scrap-iron and things.'

'Tripe.' Mick's temper was shortening in yards. 'Bunk. And you know it. You do know it. You know I'm right, don't you?' He took a step nearer Caroline and glowered furiously at her. 'What's age got to do with it?' he demanded. 'It doesn't matter what age we are if something turns up that isn't knitting or collecting scrap. It's our war, isn't it, as much as *theirs*?'

Caroline backed literally before Mick's onslaught. She gazed fascinated at this spectacle of her phlegmatic brother with his face scarlet with anger advancing upon her.

'You know I'm right, don't you? Don't you?' Mick's jaw was thrust bellicosely forward. He was determined to force Caroline to an admission.

The fog was creeping in relentlessly from the sea. Drops of moisture were hanging on their clothes and dripping from Caroline's pigtails. It seemed very much colder. Caroline shivered. She felt suddenly very tired. In her heart she did know that Mick was right. 'Yes,' she answered, 'yes.' You couldn't go on struggling against your real convictions. 'All right, Mick. I'm sorry. It was sickening of me. But – *if you think I'm going without you you're terribly mistaken . . .*'

*

Down on the shore the fog had obliterated all the familiar landmarks. It closed gently down over rocks and cliffs and sea. Its white spirals rose to greet the children as they groped their way down the cliff-path. With it came a profound silence. The gulls could be heard squawking as they flew along the shore-line. The waves could be heard falling lazily upon the beach. But all other small sounds of outdoor life were stilled. Even the children themselves fell silent.

Mick and Caroline found the Cave filled with the damp, clammy mist as though with smoke. Quickly and methodically they made preparations against a long evening of fog-bound waiting. Caroline pushed the table aside and set the Beatrice in the middle of the floor while Mick unhooked the black-out curtain. The oily fuggy heat of the stove started to warm the Cave almost as soon as Caroline had set match to the wick. She piled the rugs and sleeping-bags round the circle of light. In the twilight she and Mick huddled over the stove, cosily swathed in a mound of rugs, planning, planning. There was so much to plan. So little time to plan was left.

In the stable Punch with the old horse-blanket over him stamped with boredom. Outside, the wall of fog pressed up against the entrance so that Mick, lifting the curtain to peep out, gazed blindly into whiteness. But the interior of the Cave itself began to take on a soft, sleepy warmth. The children talked in whispers, almost unconsciously.

'How shall you know what it is you want to discover at the Schleichers'?' Caroline murmured.

Mick had been thinking about this important point all the way home, when they had decided to leave all discussion until they had coped with the fog and reached the Cave. He had his answer ready. 'I shall put a note in the oilskin wallet myself,' he said in low tones. 'The man who put in the first message – the one who says that access to the information is impossible – is sure to come tonight. He'll find a message from me saying that I can help them, and telling him I'm in the Cave. He'll probably come up here then and talk things over.'

'Just supposing,' whispered Caroline, 'that they really are Nazis all the time and the English they wrote in is only a blind.'

'We shall have to risk that,' admitted Mick. 'But it's unlikely.' He took out his notebook as he spoke and tore a blank page out of the middle. Then he wrote his message in large capitals and signed it 'English refugee'. Caroline watched him. 'I'll go and put it in the wallet straight-away,' he said. 'It'll be one thing settled.' He got to his feet and slithered past the black-out curtain, carefully letting as little fog as possible into the Cave as he made his exit. A few minutes later he was back in his place, rubbing his clammy hands over the stove to restore them to warmth.

'There are two more things,' he said. 'First, I'm awfully afraid one of us will have to go over to Pol tonight and tell Meurice le Mesurier we aren't coming. He's such a kind old man that he's more than likely to miss the tide thinking we're late and waiting for us. And, Caroline, I'm sorry but it'll have to be you. I shall have to stay here for that man if he comes tonight.'

'All right,' said Caroline. 'I don't mind going a scrap. I shall go on Punch.' She felt quite eager to set out on such a mission. It meant that she really was cooperating with Mick in a practical manner instead of being simply a drag on the whole procedure, and she badly wanted to show Mick she meant to help and not hinder after that unpromising beginning upon the cliffs.

'The other thing,' went on Mick, 'is what we're going to do with you while I'm at the Point.'

This consideration had also occurred to Caroline, but she was so anxious to be helpful and unselfish that she had determined not to mention the matter until it came up for discussion in the course of events. 'I can stay here,' she said, trying to simulate some sort of enthusiasm. It was not a very alluring prospect – an indefinite sojourn in the Cave with the weather breaking and no companionship.

'I think you'd better talk it over with Peter,' Mick said. 'It's not very good your staying here. And Peter's bound to know what's happened. He'll be over in the morning for Punch and he'll find you here at any rate. I suppose I ought to be at the Point by breakfast-time. You could go over to Petit-Jean's grandmother on the other side of the island. She'll hide you. She ought to be jolly grateful to Daddy for taking her grandson off the island. But you'd better not decide until you've talked to Peter.'

'Ought we to tell Peter?' said Caroline doubtfully. 'It doesn't seem any fairer now than it did before to drag him into it.'

'Tell him,' replied Mick. 'He's bound to find out we've not gone.' Actually there was no real need for Peter to know they were still on Clerinel. But Mick secretly wanted Peter to help Caroline while he was away and to be responsible for getting her off to England if anything should happen to him. He felt thoroughly uneasy at leaving his sister to fend so much for herself. But he could this time see no help for it.

'Talk the whole matter out with Peter in the morning,' he insisted. 'Whatever you settle it'll only be, I expect, for a few days. If that change of date really is true – then, if I don't discover it, I shan't have anything further to do at the Point once whatever the Nazis' plan is has come off.'

'Mmmm.' Caroline saw the argument. Perhaps the outlook was not quite so black as she had earlier imagined. Perhaps Mick would soon be able to stop being Petit-Jean and come and find her and make his escape properly with her. Caroline yawned and slid into a full-length position in the radius of the warmth from the stove. The Cave was now deliciously fuggy. She stretched her arms out to their full length and rolled over and put her face down on them. She felt like a sleepy, purring little cat. Tonight, with its ride to Pol les Roches through the fog, seemed a long, long way off. Caroline relaxed every muscle in drowsy contentment. Dimly she heard Mick get up and draw the black-out curtain aside. 'What is it?' she murmured as a breath of cold air drifted across the warmth. But Mick had let the curtain fall again and had come back to his place.

'I only thought for a moment I heard an engine out in the bay,' he said. 'But there's nothing there. Isn't it beastly? But I think it'll lift before you have to go. Anyway, nothing very much can have happened since we saw Peter.'

'You're sure it wasn't Peter you heard?' Caroline sat up anxiously.

Mick shook his head. He looked at his watch. 'Five o'clock,' he said. 'If you leave about half-past eight you ought to do it nicely. No, there's nobody out in the bay. One always imagines one hears things in a fog.'

Five o'clock. The green hands of Mick's Luminex watch gleamed in the dark Cave. The children drew their rugs closer and settled down like Esquimaux in an igloo to wait for dark.

Out in the bay, with the fog muffling every sound, Peter chugged his engine backwards and forwards across the strip of ice-grey water, hoping against hope that its noise would penetrate the blanket of mist and convey his message to the children on the shore: '*Danger. Danger.*'

Chapter 13

Caroline Rides to Town

'I feel just as though I were riding in some queer fairy tale,' said Caroline to herself as Punch moved forward again.

'Two and a half kilometres to Pol les Roches.' The old milestone, half hidden in the tangle of the hedgerow, was already swallowed up behind them in the fog. 'Two and a half kilometres,' Caroline whispered into Punch's patient ears as she swung herself once more on to his back. It was a mercy nobody had seen them stop by that milestone and flash the torch across its ancient face. Caroline was inwardly quite proud that she had managed to ride all across the cliffs as far as the road without using the torch at all. 'It's just like a fairy-tale ride through an enchanted country,' she repeated.

Plid-plod. Plid-plod. Punch's hooves echoed eerily through the still night. Mick had insisted on tying them up in the dishcloth and the tablecloth, cut into pieces, because he thought it would lessen the sound.

'Trot, Punch,' whispered Caroline, pressing his damp flanks with her heels. Punch broke into a gentle trot on the wet grass by the roadside. Clever little Punch! He seemed to understand the need for silence as well as she did herself. He trotted gallantly along much, thought Caroline, as she or Mick might run on tiptoe.

It was getting on for two hours since they had left Mick crouching over the Beatrice in the Cave. Almost at the last minute he had balked at the idea of her setting out alone like this. 'I don't know what to do,' he kept on saying irresolutely. 'I don't a bit like your going all that way by yourself.' He had seemed so miserable and undecided that at last Caroline had taken matters entirely into her own hands and said stoutly, 'Well, I *am* going and I shall be quite all right. I'm not a baby and I don't mind a bit.' It was not strictly true for when the moment came for setting out into the fog she discovered that she did mind a good deal, and would have given a lot either for Mick's company or to be staying in the security of the Cave herself.

The fog had lifted slightly by the time she left, but not enough to make the Pony Club's old landmarks distinguishable. The journey across the cliffs had been one long dreary series of dismountings to search blindly for cross-paths and turnings. Caroline's back fairly ached from the number of times she had ungracefully hauled herself in her long hampering skirt up on to Punch's broad back. Still, they had only lost their way once.

The fog had accomplished one good result, too: there was absolutely no traffic on the roads. Mick had warned her that the Nazis might put a certain amount of mechanized transport out between Pol and the outlying villages. But no lorry or car or motor-bike would venture out in fog like this. The road stretched emptily before her with the hills closed round it.

Punch deftly picked his way over a couple of drainage ditches and Caroline leaned forward and patted his bristly neck. 'It's a good job,' she reflected, 'that we had Punch with us. I should simply have hated coming all this way at night by myself.' Punch's sturdy self-confidence was very inspiring. When a gigantic bough had flapped its leaves in their very faces Punch's contemptuous shake of the head had preserved Caroline from emitting a piercing shriek of terror. And when something white and ghastly had whirled from the darkness under his hooves Caroline's panic stricken gasp had ended in a giggle at the withering manner in which Punch had planted his dish-clothed hoof on the elderly paper-bag.

But it was cold – my word, it was cold. Caroline, blowing on her fingers, remembered yearningly her camel-hair dressing-gown hanging on its hook behind her bedroom door at the Point. She wondered what Nannerl would do with all the clothes lying in the chest of drawers and in the white-painted cupboard. Would some frugal governess cut them down to fit Nannerl's solid little frame? She rather wished she'd told Nannerl to borrow Thomas's breeches instead of attempting to ride in that pinafore thing. Poor little wretch! She was obviously keen to ride. It was a shame Cousin Karl had given her such a bad start. Perhaps Mick would really be able to teach her something and then when they left Peter might be persuaded to carry on the good work. Bellman was an excellent pony to learn on and both boys were good, patient teachers.

Caroline's heart warmed with charity towards Nannerl, until she all at once recollected that she hated the very idea of any one whatsoever riding Dinah, and that Nannerl shouldn't be encouraged to borrow breeks and have riding lessons because she would almost certainly want to ride Dinah and not the amiable Bellman. Caroline's lips tightened at the offensive notion. She tried to feel angry at the bare idea of any one riding Dinah. But somehow it was not so easy as usual to feel angry, because suddenly there just didn't seem to be any reason at all why Nannerl shouldn't ride Dinah. In fact it seemed pretty dog-in-the-mangerish not to expect her to. Caroline thrust the thought quickly out of her mind, and at that minute Punch stopped dead, with his ears pricked forward.

'Goodness, what's he seen?' muttered Caroline apprehensively. She leaned forward to gaze into the fog. But it was only the big cross-roads above Pol les Roches. Punch had not quite liked the sight of the traffic light, twinkling a lonely rotation through the green, yellow, and red.

Just beyond the cross-roads she could perceive the horrid little stucco bungalows lining the road. Caroline knew that it was time to turn off the main road again. At any moment someone might lean over one of those green-painted gates and inquire what she and Punch were doing out on such a night. She touched Punch again, and they turned off to the left, where the dim outlines of the little bungalows soon gave way to tall narrow hedges as Punch skirted the town.

There was not a soul about, and not a light to be seen as Caroline stood in the stirrups to look over the hedge and down upon Pol les Roches. The little fishing town lay in profound darkness under the ruthless hand of the German invaders. It was queer to think that Pol les Roches was no longer blacked out against the coming of the Nazi bombers but against the R.A.F.

Quarter of a mile along the road Caroline drew rein. Punch stopped, blowing the fog away from his nostrils in great gusty snorts. Somewhere – ah, here it was! Caroline turned the chestnut down a narrow alleyway that ran down-hill between two high old brick walls. When she and Mick raced their bikes into Pol they generally took this short cut which led straight down to the harbour at the back of the modern residential quarter. It marked the spot where you could start safely to freewheel and continue freewheeling, whizzing rapturously all the way down the sharp incline until you sailed out in triumph on to the open quayside. It was the same alley up which she and Mick had crawled exhaustedly only a few mornings ago after that dreadful night in Pol les Roches.

Punch moved quietly along between the high walls just as though he realized the increased danger of discovery now that he and his rider had reached the precincts of the town. Punch, Caroline admitted to herself, really was behaving extraordinarily well – considerably better, she suspected, than her own beloved Dinah would have behaved under similar circumstances. Punch made you feel as though every-thing must come out all right in the end, Caroline pondered gratefully, realizing that Punch was largely responsible for her own calmness of mind during this night-ride. Perhaps I really am getting used to adventures, she thought. Or – she experienced a sudden burst of illumination – perhaps it's because we're coping properly with things that happen that we no longer mind them so much. The whole sequence of the events of the last four days rose before her – the carnival, the mad dash to the boat, the dreadful night on the quayside, the return home and the arrival of Baldhead and Cousin Karl, the Cave – above all, the Cave. That was an adventure indeed. 'Goodness,' she whispered to Punch, 'what a lot's happened to Mick and me!' She urged him to a slightly faster walk as the alley temporarily flattened to the level.

As it turned and twisted in its descent to the quayside the narrow passage seemed to fill with fog as though the sea were pouring its wet clinging mist down the neck of a bottle. Caroline would never have believed that fog could have made such a difference to a journey that she had made so many times since they had first come to Clerinel. She put a tentative hand out into the darkness. Yes, the old rough bricks of the wall were still there. Her destination was not quite reached.

A minute later the wall on Punch's offside receded into the night and gave place to a row of small cottages. Caroline could just discern the high pointed eaves. She heaved a sigh of relief which spent itself like a tiny wisp of smoke on the chilly air. That was all right. She was now on the last lap of her long cold pilgrimage. She had only to find the second alley on the right and the sixth cottage, and the whole journey would be finished. At that moment the bells of St Marie, the church by the market-place, rang out heavily in the half-hour. Half-past eleven. She was not really any too early. 'In another thirty minutes,' Caroline reckoned, 'the le Mesuriers' boat will be slipping quietly away from Clerinel on the tide, and if it hadn't been for me and my vest Mick and I would be on her.' She surprised herself by pondering upon this thought without any regrets. She merely hoped now that they would in due course manage to get themselves off the island somehow, and that Mick would be able to justify the whole change in their plans by finding something really worth while at the Point House without getting himself caught by Baldhead or Cousin Karl in the process.

Here was the alley at last – or had she miscounted? No. Because there was the little *estaminet* where she and Mick had often stopped for coffee on their excursions into Pol. The Coq D'Or stood at the corner, fronting directly on to both alleys with its sign creaking drearily overhead. Caroline guided Punch into the shadows and slid noiselessly off his back to lead him past the darkened *estaminet*. Not a chink of light escaped through the wooden shutters as she walked the pony past the door. But the faint murmur of voices within announced that the Coq D'Or was, as usual, full of customers for its good wines, even if those customers were of a different nationality from its habituals.

As Punch placidly followed her past the door the strains of an accordion floated out on to the night, played perhaps by some Austrian soldier sick for home. It was the first sound Caroline had heard since she had left Mick all those hours before. She stopped with one hand on the bridle to listen. It was as well that the clatter of the pony's hooves on the cobbles did cease, for at that moment the door suddenly opened and a bunch of soldiers stumbled out into the darkness. For an awful second Caroline thought they would turn in her direction and perceive Punch's stocky form standing in the shadows. But luckily they reeled off in the direction of the town with linked arms and singing lustily. She could hear the raucous sound of their song dying away in the distance. She gave them another minute, then tugged gently at Punch's bridle, and crept down the passage-way.

One, two – three, four – the cottages stood in pairs, with fenced gardens between them and the alley. At the back of each cottage a yard and a small slipway gave on to the river that ran into the harbour. Caroline's skirt dragged against the piles of blackened nets flung across the low railings to dry. A strong smell of stale fish and rotting seaweed pervaded the fishing quarter of Pol les Roches. Caroline was now in its most picturesque district. She and Mick were particularly fond of these rows of little old cottages with their shell-bordered gardens, dolphin-headed door-knockers, and tiny model ships nailed over the low doorways.

The outside of number six looked in the fog no different from its fellows, Caroline thought, as she carefully looped Punch's reins on the fencing that ran along the little passage between the alley and the river. Punch stood quite quietly on his four legs with his head drooping docilely over the railings into the michaelmas-daisy plants in the minute garden.

Caroline unlatched the gate as quietly as she could and stole up the path to the door. As she stepped into the gloomy little porch the bells of St Marie rang out the three-quarters, the echoes dying away like ghost-bells across the river. The whole cottage appeared completely blacked-out, and as silent as a tomb. Nobody would ever guess that at the slipway a boat was lying ready to cast off for safety.

Rap-rap-rap. Three knocks Peter had told her. A shiver of anticipation ran down her. She waited for the shuffle of footsteps behind the closed door that would inform her that the le Mesurier brothers had heard and accepted her signal. She rehearsed under her breath the password that Peter had taught her that morning so that there should be no delay once the door was opened. It would be dreadful to hold the le Mesuriers up and make them miss the tide.

The minutes ticked past, but nobody seemed to be answering her signal. There was no footfall inside the silent hall, no fumbling of an old gnarled hand at the bolts.

Caroline lifted the knocker again with numbed fingers and repeated her three knocks as loudly as she dared. *Rap-rap-rap.* They echoed, to her mind, with the hollow thud that betokens an empty house.

It was deathly cold in the doorway. The damp struck up wickedly through her thick clothes from the wet ground. The fog drifted round her head in grey curls. Caroline felt all at once chilled to the bone with terror in the porch of this empty cottage. For empty it undoubtedly was. She was positive there was no life behind those darkened windows. What, oh what could have happened? Where were the le Mesuriers? Was she late and had they already sailed, or – ?

'Mademoiselle.'

The sibilant whisper reached her like a breath of the fog itself. Caroline for a moment was not certain if her imagination had not betrayed her.

'Mademoiselle – come, if you please, to the fence.'

The whisper was coming from her left-hand side, from

the garden of the next little cottage, number five. Perhaps Meurice had gone next door for a last-minute farewell. Caroline slowly groped her way across a small earthy flower-bed. She remembered having heard that the le Mesuriers' cousin, Jacques Dupuy, lived there. She felt her way along the railing, and a movement in the darkness told her she was opposite the whisperer.

'Mademoiselle, my cousins were expecting you tonight?'

Caroline realized that the man she was talking to was as cautious and uncertain as she herself. The knowledge gave her confidence. 'I was told to say, "Can you give us a bed for the night?"' she murmured.

The figure on the other side of the fence appeared satisfied. 'I will come round,' it whispered, and its dark outlines disappeared into the fog. Caroline crept back across the flower-bed to the gate. The figure was already waiting for her.

'Jacques Dupuy.' Then it was the cousin himself and not one of the le Mesuriers. A shadow of uneasiness lay across Caroline's mind. 'Wha – what's happened?' she gasped faintly, unable to restrain her apprehensions any longer.

'I greatly regret, mademoiselle, that it will not be possible to accommodate you and your brother tonight' – the low, level tones broke a little – 'my cousin Meurice, mademoiselle, was this morning taken by the Nazis.'

Caroline looked speechlessly at the short, spare outline confronting her at the gate. 'He was not wise,' the quiet voice continued, 'he said foolish, angry words in the Coq D'Or and they were overheard. They arrested him and took him away immediately. My cousin Pierre was warned not to come in from his fishing. He took his boat round the coast and has gone to his sister in Bec de Querels before he could be arrested too.'

Caroline felt quite stunned. 'I'm so sorry,' she whispered, thinking how inadequate she sounded. In the darkness she saw the little old man bow to her with dignity.

'Mademoiselle is very kind. I am sorry for her disappointment. Pierre asked me when I met him at the quayside this morning to warn Monsieur Peter Beaumarchais and to give him his deep regrets. But Monsieur Peter has evidently not been able to pass the warning on.'

Unless that really was Peter's engine that Mick heard? The recollection chased across Caroline's brain. 'I'm terribly sorry,' she repeated helplessly. What else could you say before a tragedy like this?

'You must go now, mademoiselle,' said the old man gently after a moment's pause. 'They may come at any time to search the cottage. You are going back – where?'

'Towards South Point,' said Caroline, realizing that Jacques Dupuy had no idea who Peter's friends really were. 'I've got my pony here,' she stammered.

Jacques Dupuy made neither comment nor inquiry. It did not apparently disturb him that anyone should bring a pony with them when they were going to sail immediately away to England. He asked no questions. He was not interested in Caroline. He had delivered the message as he had been asked, and he was prepared to see mademoiselle off the premises before those accursed Germans arrived. He beckoned to her across the gate. 'Come with me, please,' he said.

Caroline, who had opened her mouth to tell him that she and Mick had decided not to go to England and that she had only come into Pol that night to explain the position to the le Mesuriers, shut it again. The old man had opened the gate for her and was now shuffling round to where Punch was still peacefully standing eating the heads off the michaelmas daisies.

'The Coq D'Or is coming out, and it is not safe for mademoiselle to return up the alley,' Jacques Dupuy said under his breath as he put the reins into Caroline's hands. 'If she will come along this way –' He walked slowly a yard or so ahead of Caroline and Punch down the alley towards the harbour. Just before they reached the end where the alley opened on to the quayside he branched off down a passageway on the left and plodded silently along for another twenty yards. Then he stood and waited for Caroline to come up to him. 'This will lead you up on to the big road at the back of the town,' he said. 'You will turn left at the top and you will come to the roundabout with the lights.' Caroline murmured her thanks. The old man patted Punch's neck and bowed to her. There seemed absolutely nothing further to say. Feeling more than ever that she was moving in some mysterious dream Caroline mounted on to Punch's back. It was quite comforting to feel his broad withers under her hand. They, at any rate, felt quite real. Punch moved forward.

'*Adieu*, mademoiselle,' said Jacques Dupuy. He was swallowed up instantly into the fog.

Punch walked quietly up the passage. Caroline realized that it must run parallel to the original alley down which she had ridden some twenty minutes or so before. She knew that the fishing quarter of Pol comprised a whole network of confusing alleyways that only a native of the district could possibly negotiate. She had been fortunate in finding a man who had been ready to set her on a homeward path that would not, with any luck, involve her with the enemy.

Punch carefully picked his way up the stony ascent that twisted and wound up on to the main road. Caroline sat him in a trance. She felt quite sick with sorrow and horror at the tragedy that had befallen the two old brothers who had always been so kind to her and Mick. It was as though some awful nightmare had overtaken the happy little island. 'O God,' she said passionately, 'for goodness' sake, help us beat the Nazis. The things they keep on doing are absolutely *frightful*.'

At that moment Punch stepped out of the alley on to the main road. It seemed chillier than ever up here above the town. The cold ate through Caroline's blouse and ran down her arms to her shivering finger-tips. She huddled herself together on the chestnut's back. Everything she had on seemed wet – her hair, her face, her clothes, her feet. The fog closed round her again. It would take at least two hours to get home, and already Punch was stumbling with fatigue.

'I can't do it,' Caroline said out loud. Her heart failed within her. 'I can't go another step.' She peered into the darkness. At the next bungalow she came to she would stop and ask whoever was in it to give her bed and shelter and warmth for the night. It didn't matter if it was a Nazi. She was finished.

Then – 'Caroline Templeton,' she said sternly, 'you're simply awful. All over England there are people sitting in air-raid shelters being bombed, and you're grumbling because you've got to ride home in a fog. Take a pull on yourself, my girl.' She had spoken out loud. Punch quickened his step into a trot at the sound. Caroline posted to his motion. There were the traffic lights. There was the South Point Road. Soon they would be on the cliffs. Soon they would be riding down to Mick and the Cave. Caroline and Punch trotted on into the darkness.

Chapter 14

Mick Keeps Watch

While Caroline and Punch were pursuing their way to Pol les Roches Mick was undergoing an equally unpleasing evening alone in the Cave. The only advantage the Cave had to offer him over the dripping Pol road was warmth and dryness. For the rest it seemed no less lonely and eerie than Caroline's fogbound progress.

As soon as the sounds of Punch's hooves had died away on the cliff path Mick secured the black-out curtain firmly and turned the Beatrice's rather sulky glow to a flaring orange light, careless of the black smoke protestingly emitted. Warmth at all cost, Mick vowed to himself, dashing the black smuts casually off his nose. He blew on his fingers, swung his arms, and stamped in and out of the inky corners of the Cave, before subsiding by the side of Beatrice and spreading his hands over her fierce little flame. He settled himself to wait in a perilously balanced tent constructed out of the pile of rugs and sleeping-bags.

'Hope to heaven whoever is coming to fetch that wallet does come tonight,' he worried. 'It'll be rotten if Caroline has to stay in the Cave tomorrow night and nab him.' Poor old Caroline! She did seem to be having a rough deal. She genuinely hated all these happenings, and just when everything promised well and they were on the point of escape – oh, well, it couldn't be helped and she'd stood up to it all right. Looking back Mick scarcely even felt guilty over his own decision. As far as he could see there was nothing he could do but offer to take his chance as stable-boy with the Schleichers. Precious idiot he'd look if he made a muck of it! Anyway, he comforted himself, even if he couldn't get hold of the information they wanted, at any rate he'd be able to see that the ponies were being properly treated and instil a bit of riding sense into that young Nannerl, poor little devil!

The minutes slipped by. Golly, it *was* cold! He recklessly turned Beatrice so high that she hissed angrily and cast black flickering shadows round the walls. Mick looked at his watch. Half-past ten. Caroline ought to be well on her road to the town by this time. He rather wished the man would turn up before she arrived back so that they could both get a good night's rest. It was awfully still outside. So still that it made him feel quite creepy. Waiting for a mysterious stranger in a fog-closed cave on a lonely beach in enemy country was not quite the pleasant, easy matter it had seemed earlier in the daylight!

Mick resolutely clambered out of his tent and fetched another rug. Perhaps the less he thought about the mysterious English stranger just for the moment the better. He wrapped the rug tightly round himself and a warm glow began immediately to creep down his back. He looked again at his watch. Caroline ought to be almost there now. He yawned. Pity he hadn't got one of his old bird books with him to keep him awake. The cosy oily warmth of Beatrice was really making him quite sleepy, he noticed, as his mouth involuntarily shaped itself into two more yawns in succession. Might as well lie down? In the silence outside he couldn't possibly miss the slightest scrunch of a footfall. He drew his little fuggy tent closely over his head and lay staring into Beatrice's yellow glowing heart. It was such a bright heart that he shut his eyes against it. His limbs felt long and lazy as the heat crept into their bones, his back lay padded comfortably by the woolly rug, his mind reposed pleasantly drowsy. All the disturbances of the day floated serenely out of sight. At the very moment when Caroline was knocking on the desolate cottage door far down in Pol les Roches Mick, on a slow wave of blissful content, drifted into slumber, peacefully cradled in the snug warmth of Beatrice and the dark, friendly, flickering shadows.

*

CRASH! SCREAM!

'Ow, Mick, Mick!'

'*Mon Dieu!*'

Dazed with sleep, eyelids glued together, hair on end, Mick plunged down the cliff-path in a semi-coma into the night. As he reached the sand he fell straight between two wrestling bodies, knocking them apart with the uncanny accuracy of a billiard ball. How long he had slept, what his sister was doing, who the dark struggling intruder was, were questions his slumber-sodden mind refused to answer. All he realized vaguely was that things were not going according to plan.

Before he could collect himself the two figures hurtled together again, fell over him and crashed, with him well underneath, on to the sand. Quick as lightning the tallest figure disentangled itself, made a grab at Mick's neck and hauled him to his feet. From over Mick's head the voice of Caroline screamed like a ship's siren, 'It's Cousin Karl! It's Cousin Karl!'

'Oh my gosh,' thought Mick, the cold air and shock combining to stir his paralysed wits, 'if it's Cousin Karl we're finished.' But was it Cousin Karl? Was it? Was it? Mick scuffed his heels in a sudden frantic effort to escape the hold on his neck. At the same moment the disengaged hand of his captor clicked a cigarette lighter and a small spurt of flame illuminated the children's faces – Mick's desperate and still crumpled with sleep, Caroline's white and agonized and spent.

'Michael. Caroline.' The stranger's voice held no surprise but – could it possibly be amusement?

Mick furiously racked his brain. He knew that voice. That voice was as familiar to him as Caroline's or Daddy's or Peter's or – got it! 'Monsieur Beaumarchais,' he said dully. His head spun dizzily. What in heaven's name was Peter's father doing here?

Before M. Beaumarchais could reply Caroline elected to cause a diversion by giving a small sob and burying her head in M. Beaumarchais' coat. 'I'm so tired,' she wept apologetically.

We Couldn't Leave Dinah

'*Pauvre petite*,' M. Beaumarchais' voice was gentle. 'You are living in the Pony Club Cave, are you not?' Mick noted the air of authority with which the little Frenchman addressed him. He nodded dumbly. 'Then let us,' said M. Beaumarchais calmly, 'retire there.'

A snuffling noise out of the darkness indicated that the suggestion was all to Punch's pleasure. Mick caught at his pony's bridle where Punch was patiently waiting until some one should take some notice of him in all this midnight confusion. Evidently, Mick realized, Caroline had come down into the next cove by mistake in the fog, had led Punch along the beach and had cannoned straight into M. Beaumarchais, who somehow or other had discovered they were in the Cave and had come himself to find them. Mick, as he led Punch up to the Cave with M. Beaumarchais half carrying Caroline in the rear, decided upon the utmost caution in answering any questions that M. Beaumarchais might think fit to put.

The small stove was burning merrily as M. Beaumarchais set Caroline down in a weary heap in the little circle of light. He covered her deftly with Mick's rug and pillowed her head on a sleeping-bag. While Mick stabled Punch he took off her shoes himself and dried her damp pigtails.

'I perceive the familiar Pony Club mugs and by their side an inviting tin of cocoa,' observed M. Beaumarchais meaningly as Mick stepped back into the Cave and stood watching his ministrations.

And so began one of the strangest picnics at which the children had ever assisted. Caroline lay exhaustedly by the stove, too worn out by her ride to take any interest, while Mick vigorously stirred the cocoa in the mugs and M. Beaumarchais hammered open the ideal milk with an imperturbable smile upon his wrinkled face. The cocoa frothed, brown and creamy, over the edges of the mugs. M. Beaumarchais closed Caroline's cold fingers round the handle and held her head while she drank. Then he settled her down snugly in the rug.

'She will sleep now,' he smiled with a friendly, conspiratorial air to Mick who had gravely seated himself on the opposite side of the stove. 'You must now excuse me one little minute,' he went on. 'I have just to read a note I have received, and then we will talk.' He offered no further explanation as he fumbled in his pocket.

Mick, wearily watching the little Frenchman, wondered desperately how he was ever going to get in touch with the English agent for whom he had waited so long now that M. Beaumarchais had blundered across his carefully laid plan. 'Should think the man's come and gone by now,' he reflected bitterly as Peter's father leaned forward to untie some object he held in his hand by the light of the stove.

All at once Mick's jaw dropped. In his turn he leaned forward. 'Why –' he stuttered, 'you – you – where – ?'

M. Beaumarchais looked up sharply. His eyes narrowed in the soft flickering light as he followed Mick's fascinated stare. 'Why, what do you know about this?' he asked swiftly. He held up a small oiled silk wallet. It reflected the red flame in miniature upon its satiny surface as he dangled it before Mick across the stove.

Mick swallowed hard, his brain whirling. Never in all his fourteen years had he felt so confused. How had M. Beaumarchais come to intercept the code messages? Was he working in very truth for the Germans? Was Peter's tale about his father being an *unwilling* tool of the Nazis just a fine pretentious excuse? Mick stared wretchedly round the Cave, at Caroline's slumbering form, back at M. Beaumarchais, still silently, watchfully waiting for his answer. Which was the best thing to say, the safest line to take?

And then – he remembered again Peter's story. He remembered how pitiful he had found it, and how certain he had been that Peter had been speaking the truth. When they had sat outside on the sunny ledge and Peter had spoken in his sorrowful voice he remembered how angry and ashamed he had been that he had ever doubted Peter, and how he had wished he could bring himself to apologize properly for his own behaviour. At any rate he need not make the same mistake with Peter's father. He cleared his throat. 'You've not opened it yet, have you, sir?' he said nervously. 'You'll find there's a message from me there along with the other.'

'From you?' M. Beaumarchais sounded surprised as he drew out the two bits of paper, Mick's message and the message left the night before.

While he slowly unfolded the messages and smoothed the crumpled papers out on his knee Mick told him briefly of the events that had led up to the writing of the message, from the original discovery of the wallet after Caroline's vest had pointed the way, up to the encounter with Nannerl that had prepared his entry to the Point House.

'I see.' M. Beaumarchais stroked his chin, his sallow face thoughtful. 'And to whom were you signalling with Caroline's vest?' he inquired.

It was the question Mick dreaded. He had no wish to bring M. Beaumarchais' son into this story. But before he could parry it Caroline, hearing her name, opened one sleepy eye and said in trusting tones: 'Peter, of course,' and dropped to sleep again.

M. Beaumarchais laughed outright at Mick's troubled expression. 'I had guessed,' he said reassuringly. 'I guessed Peter had some secret from his frequent expeditions, but I did not know indeed *you* were still on the island.'

'He didn't want you bothered with us,' put in Mick, determined Peter should not be blamed. 'And he didn't know anything about us finding the messages. He thinks we've left tonight as he arranged for us. He'd no idea I was waiting to meet the English agent to find out how I could help.'

'Well,' said M. Beaumarchais consideringly, 'you've met him now, and he'll tell you what you can do.'

'What do you mean?' Mick looked startled.

M. Beaumarchais grinned. 'I am sorry to startle you,' he said, 'especially when you have been picturing me as the poor weak Frenchman, the unhappy instrument of the cruel Nazis –' His face sobered. 'I know the tale Peter will have told you,' he continued. 'It is true. I am French, I have my wife's people under Nazi threats in Nuremberg, but there is such a thing as the double-cross. You have undoubtedly heard of the double-cross in the adventure stories you have read?'

He stopped suddenly, leaned back, and pulled the black-out curtain a little to one side. The murmur of the sea echoed louder, and a swirl of fog drifted into the Cave. There was nobody about. He let the curtain fall and turned to Mick again.

'You must trust me as I am going to trust you,' he said quietly. 'I am the agent to whom you have written this message. It is I who am unable to obtain access to the information we want. But I am also the clever Fifth Columnist who so skilfully hands over strategic points to the Nazis. You will have to make up your mind quickly whether you are prepared to trust me. If you are you can help us.'

He looked questioningly at Mick. Mick's eyes were wide with excitement. There was no doubt whatsoever written upon his square countenance.

M. Beaumarchais went on. 'I shall have to tell you all this very briefly. It is a long story. After the fall of France,' he said in low rapid tones, 'we knew that Berlin was planning to invade England. Slowly but ruthlessly Hitler's plans are now coming to fruition. While England speculates "he will land his troops here, he will land his troops there" the German High Command intends to land its troops all round the English coast. Each separate county will stand as a separate battleground.

'In the ports of France, in the harbours of Holland and Belgium and Norway the invasion barges are concentrated. Many have been sunk by the Royal Air Force, so many that Germany cannot afford to go on losing and replacing them. Consequently she cast last June her eye around for further bases. Where else can she hide her invading forces that they may land in those places that will most paralyse the life of England? She takes the Channel Isles. They are opposite the Dorset coast – one whole sector in itself. She takes Clerinel, but she pretends that it is for an *air-base* that she needs the island. She knows that the R.A.F. will fly over and bomb to bits any air base she uses on Clerinel.

Good, says Germany, *let them*. England is not to know that she is destroying only a dummy aerodrome, that the real menace to her is not in plane concentrations but in *barges* – barges concealed by cunning camouflage up the inlets for which the island is famous.

'Michael, I tell you that the plan is diabolically worked out to the last detail. Those barges are intended to land their men on the Devon coast, supported by dive-bombers, to blast a way across the county to cut the south-west peninsula off from the rest of England. There is to be a German line stretching from Plymouth across to Bristol, supplied in part from this island. Behind that line thousands of English civilians will be isolated. The Nazis argue that the morale of that section will be weakened. And similar actions will be taken in every sector. The plan, as a whole, is to attack the civilian morale in various sectors and break down resistance piece by piece. The Clerinel-Plymouth-Bristol line will be one of many.'

Mick's eyes were glued to M. Beaumarchais' face as he talked in a quiet, confident voice. By his side Caroline snored stertorously on her pile of rugs. Beatrice threw her shadows across the picnic party with wreathing wisps of escaping smoke.

Mick drew a long shivering breath. 'Where did you say the barges were?' he said, trying to steady his shaking hands. He felt oddly unnerved by M. Beaumarchais' story.

'The barges came over from France by night in convoy, and they are hidden in the most obvious place,' began Peter's father.

'Not the Tower inlet?' whispered Mick.

'Why do you think the Nazis were so anxious to obtain so unobtrusively the Martello Tower and the consequent command over that inlet?' M. Beaumarchais confirmed Mick's guess with a smile. 'They went to the trouble of a complicated piece of strategy in that carnival business to take it bloodlessly so that their occupation of that whole bit of coast should not cause particular comment. You try going into that area today, Mick. You are challenged at every yard –'

'But if you knew all about these barges in the inlet, and weren't taken in by the dummy aerodrome, why haven't you got a message across to England telling the R.A.F. so that they can come over and bomb the barges?' interrupted Mick.

M. Beaumarchais poured himself out another round of cocoa and refilled Mick's mug before replying. 'This,' he said slowly as he warmed his hands round his mug, 'appears to be where you come in. We are, frankly, in a jam, and I do believe, mad as your whole stable-boy scheme sounds, that you may be able to help. Michael, the date for the invasion of England had been secretly fixed by Germany for next Wednesday week, twelve days from now. Our agents in Berlin notified us of this discovery. On Wednesday at dawn the barges, loaded with troops and light artillery, will leave their secret base and cross to their sector on the English coast. Now, listen carefully, for this is the crux of the whole affair. There are still twelve days before the invasion date. If the R.A.F. bomb the inlet now they will have to return again and again to bomb the barges with which Germany will replace those that are destroyed. Also to bomb them at the last moment just before they leave is to destroy them loaded and to prevent fresh plans being made at a short notice. You will realize that a far more effective raid can be delivered at the last moment before they sail.'

'Tuesday night,' nodded Mick, who could not for the life of him see what M. Beaumarchais was getting at.

'Quite,' said Peter's father. 'Tuesday night would, as you so rightly suggest, be admirable. The only snag is that we now have reason to believe that our agents have deliberately been allowed to discover a false date. The Germans know we shall act on this information and raid on the Tuesday night. Either the invasion is planned for an earlier date, in which case there would be no raid for the barges would have landed their troops already in England, or else it is arranged for a later date, in which case the R.A.F. would be attacking empty barges and new dispositions could easily be made. That is the significance of the phrase in the message you found saying, "Suspect date changed."

We Couldn't Leave Dinah

'As you've gathered, the Secret Service is working on this show. I am operating in touch with Headquarters in London. The Nazis entertain no suspicions of me. I have even betrayed the Tower into their hands to keep them quiet. But it has been impossible on so small an island, where the whole place has been overrun, and at such short notice – the speedy occupation of the island took us very much by surprise – to arrange for me to meet the Headquarters' agent. The best we could manage for the moment was this cork-and-wallet business by which he landed from a destroyer by boat and left a message that I picked up when I could. I selected that particular pool deliberately as it is, so far, in one of the quietest spots along the coast, and can be found easily in the dark by taking a bearing from the Cave. I knew all about the Cave because it is your Pony Club Headquarters. It is not quite coincidence that you and I have picked upon the same place.

'However, to continue. In this last message that you found Headquarters insists that the change of date must be discovered, despite my assertions that it is impossible to obtain access to Schleicher's documents. The new date is imperative. We – must – have – that – date.' M. Beaumarchais banged his left fist on the palm of his right hand to emphasize each word. 'This is where you come in.'

Mick jumped as the Frenchman suddenly leaned towards him. He was staring wide-eyed at this strange new M. Beaumarchais who had replaced the tiresome fussy little man who had always annoyed him and Caroline in the dear departed days at the Point.

'How much German do you know?' demanded Peter's father peremptorily.

'A fair amount – or at least I used to. I understand it now better than I speak it.' Mick shook his head regretfully.

'Never mind. They must not know that you understand their language. The main necessity is that there should be somebody in the Schleicher household who can keep his ears and eyes open for a date – just a date. Just the chance word. Any date you may see written. Any date at all. Mind you, Michael, I do not like you doing this. I would much prefer to take you two children and hide you in La Falaise until we could get you away. But I am prepared to risk your chances of escape to obtain this date. And even then' – he sighed – 'I do not in my heart think that there is much hope of your finding this date at the Point. At the Town Hall, yes, among the military documents. At the General's home, no. Not unless he is a less careful man than I believe. And yet again there is always the chance. The risk is not too great for *you*, actually. You look like an island boy – I noticed that myself when you rode in at the La Falaise gates in your blue jersey on the afternoon of the carnival. And until the Gestapo arrive, which will not be until the invasion has been launched, nobody will inquire too closely into the credentials of your Petit-Jean. You will not meet with anyone whom you know out at the Point. No, the whole idea, the meeting with the Schleicher child, might have been the beneficence of Providence. If Providence will only grant us one further kindness –' M. Beaumarchais paused and shrugged his shoulders with a typically French gesture.

There was a long silence, broken by Caroline's snores. M. Beaumarchais drew aside the rug and looked down at her sleeping face.

'I was going to send her to the real Petit-Jean's grandmother until I could leave,' said Mick in parental tones.

'She had better come to La Falaise,' said M. Beaumarchais. 'She will be well hidden there, and a few days in bed after all this exposure won't do her any harm. The Nazis are bound sooner or later to ferret out this place. The sooner you both leave the better.'

Mick gave a short unconscious sigh of relief. There was a great deal to be said for grown-ups who took the really weighty responsibilities off your shoulders.

M. Beaumarchais looked at his watch and rose to his feet. 'I ought to be going,' he said. 'Mick, one last word – if you discover anything, however unimportant it may appear to you, make your way somehow to La Falaise. It is the only safe way of communicating with me. You will be given a certain amount of freedom, and your comings and goings will not be under suspicion. I will send Peter over to fetch Caroline and Punch in the morning – oh, he was coming anyway, was he? Perhaps this will teach him not to try and keep his poor old father out of all his goings on.'

He moved round the stove and stood with one hand on the curtain, looking down at Mick. 'I'm not going to worry you with advice,' he said gravely. 'You Pony Club people always seem able to manage your own affairs very well. There is one thing you would do well to bear in mind, though. You are going to play a part, are you not? To pretend – like a nursery game of charades?'

Mick assented wonderingly. What was M. Beaumarchais getting at now?

'Then,' said M. Beaumarchais, 'do not allow yourself to start by thinking "I am going to pretend to be a stable-boy." *Be* a stable-boy. Live yourself into your role from the moment I leave you here tonight. Forget that Michael Templeton ever existed. *Be* Petit-Jean. Think like Petit-Jean – even when you are alone. It is the best, the safest advice – really, the only advice – I can give you.'

He smiled at the boy. Then a shadow crossed his face. 'It seems quite fantastic to allow a child like you to go into a household of Nazis,' he said slowly. 'I don't like it. I feel I ought to give you many more instructions. I ought to show you how to protect yourself against discovery more adequately. I ought to –' He threw out his hands in despair. 'But what can I do? The whole thing is so nebulous. We are not sending you to discover some secret paper hidden behind a panel in the wall, like a story-book. Only to listen – to make your mind like a wax gramophone record – to absorb anything you may hear or see.'

He looked worriedly at Mick, who said nothing. Then he gave another quick smile. 'Oh, well,' he said, 'we shall see, we shall see.' He raised his hand in mock salute. 'Good luck, whatever happens,' he said.

He drew back the black-out curtain and slipped out.

Mick sat back on his heels, very still. There was not a

sound, not a footfall, not a stone displaced. The Cave seemed to be sunk in absolute silence. Caroline lay peacefully sleeping, lulled in the security of warmth and comfort.

Mick continued to sit gazing into the hot gleaming core of flame. Round him shadows danced and played. He no longer felt lonely on that beach so far away from human dwelling-place. His mind ran absorbedly along its own track. Like Caroline on the Pol road, a panorama of the past days ran before his eyes. 'Jolly queer that we should have fallen on all this,' he brooded.

In his mind's eye he saw again the small dapper figure of Peter's father standing in the dim light. 'He's the bravest man I've ever met,' thought Mick dreamily, pondering the appalling dangers that the little Frenchman was incurring every moment of his double life upon Clerinel.

He passed to tomorrow. The dear picture of his home rose before him – the quiet square house, the stables, the ponies. It would be good to see it all again, whatever the outcome. He curled up beside Caroline in the circle of golden light.

Be – do not pretend. What did he know about Petit-Jean, he asked himself.

Petit-Jean had lived all his life on Clerinel. All he had known was a cottage full of older brothers and sisters, clattering and shouting in and out of the few tiny rooms, school with the little satchel strapped to his blue-jerseyed back, fishing with big brothers in the family boat, splendid shining visits to the town where a small Petit-Jean in his shabby clothes and wooden shoes pressed a button nose against the toy-shop windows. Church on Sunday in best blacks and long trousers, school again on Monday – fishing, town, school, church . . . that was what it was like to be Petit-Jean.

And Michael Templeton? Where was he? Why, Michael went off to England to his aunt and cousins when the English left Clerinel. He nearly missed the boat but he went, oh yes, he went. There were no Templeton children left now on Clerinel . . .

We Couldn't Leave Dinah

In the drowsy heat and glow of the tiny stove Petit-Jean, the Schleicher's new stable-boy, turned like a hound in his blanket and drifted into sleep.

Chapter 15

Bellman Takes a Hand

'Rise up and down, mam'zelle. Rise up and down, mam-'zelle.'

The General, his grey fieldcoat hugged round him, smiled broadly as the words floated in a rhythmic singsong across the fuchsia hedge. He stepped heavily across a flower-bed, and supporting himself with difficulty against a young larch peeped through the mesh of twiglets into the paddock.

'*One*-two. *One*-two. Rise up and down.' The new stable-boy's voice with its slight island accent was quite breathless as its owner ran alongside the fat little pony upon which the General's granddaughter bounced and bounded.

'That was vairy good, mam'zelle.' The stable-boy leaned panting against the little pony, one brown hand still clinging to the bridle. A nice-looking lad, thought the General, as he took a stride backwards on to the grass and strolled across the lawn to the paddock gate. One day that boy would make a good batman for a general – that was, when he had lived a shade longer in a good German household, and when he had perhaps received some slight Party discipline in the new Youth movements that the Reich would before long institute in its protectorates.

The General fumbled with the iron catch and swung the five-barred gate back on its hinges. He sauntered across the muddy field, the early morning autumn sun cosily warming his bald pate. His sentimental heart was delightedly embracing the so-charming picture of his Nannerl upon her first pony, with the square, funny little stable-boy standing quietly at the pony's head. What a boon that boy was in these early days of the occupation of the island! When Certain Events had taken place, thought the old man, he would bring over a governess from home for his Nannerl, and there would be other German children coming to live on Clerinel. But in the meantime how fortunate, how providential that there should be this trustworthy boy to keep the *liebchen* so contented.

'She makes progress, hein?' asked the General in careful genial English after submitting to a precipitous embrace from his granddaughter in the saddle. He patted the pony's neck kindly and looked inquiringly at the boy.

'Mam'zelle makes vairy good progress,' murmured the boy shyly, standing to attention quite correctly in the presence of his superiors. Really considerably better manners, the General remarked to himself, than one would have expected the English to have instilled into their servants.

'Excellent, excellent,' he repeated aloud. 'But' – he remembered the instructions he had received from Berlin – '*what* do I hear you calling this young lady? *What* is it that we now call all young ladies whom we serve?' His tone was heavily playful for he had no wish to make himself unpleasant to these poor barbarians who had had the misfortune to be born outside the Reich. The boy raised his downcast face.

'We call them "Fraulein",' he said impersonally, while Nannerl screamed with excitement and beat at both of them impartially with her riding stick. Her penny-bun cheeks were shining with health and her eyes glowed.

'He learns the German. I learn the English. I spik it more good than he the German spiks,' she bawled at the top of her voice. 'Say vat I 'ave you taught,' she commanded imperiously, banging Petit-Jean on the shoulder.

Petit-Jean obediently raised a blue-jerseyed arm, dropping the bridle at which his mentor made an agitated clutch. He clicked his heels together, drew himself up, thrust the arm out, almost hitting the General on the chest, and said in one breath, 'Morgenheilhitler'.

General Schleicher, under the sardonic eye of the pony, gravely acknowledged the salute. The boy really was most promising material – and what a relief it was to meet such docility instead of the usual stares of black hatred that greeted him when he drove to his headquarters through the crowded streets of Pol les Roches.

He sighed as he kissed his granddaughter again, and strolled away to the breakfast which awaited him in the house. He was a Bavarian-born soldier who had known a Germany kindlier than that under the present régime. Although steeped in the rigorous military discipline of the Party there were moments when he dared regret the extreme Prussian severity that Hitler's Reich saw fit to mete out to the conquered. However – he dismissed the unruly thought firmly and went into the sunny hall, hearing the faint sounds of Nannerl's riding lesson resumed in the distance.

General Schleicher might possibly have been considerably more disturbed if he could have seen further into the mind of his so-docile stable-boy. For an uneducated peasant lad who had spent all his days upon the island Petit-Jean had some quite odd traits. Perhaps one of his oddest was his intense curiosity. Despite his dreamy air of inattention very little passed Petit-Jean's ears unheard or unnoted. He was a great talker too. Although he could neither speak nor understand German he talked in his queer patois or in English to the German sentries posted round the grounds, he talked to the General's batman, a tough youth from the back streets of Dusseldorf, he talked to the two German girls who swept and cooked and kept an eye on Fraulein Nannerl. Luckily for Petit-Jean all the newcomers to the Point House spoke English of a kind, having been chosen to accompany the army of occupation for that very reason.

Altogether Petit-Jean, after his first few days in the General's service, was quite popular with the invaders. He slept over the stable in the loft since the house was on the full side. In his off-time he would sit in the dim light on the edge of the rough camp-bed with his elbows planted on his knees and his shoulders hunched, his square face solemnly staring into space, brooding, pondering. Sometimes he would walk up and down, up and down, thrusting his hands into his stubbly hair and frowning as though deeply troubled. If General Schleicher could have seen him in these moods he might well have instituted further inquiries into the history of his new stable-boy. He would have been even more perturbed if he could have deciphered the two words that appeared to be beaten into Petit-Jean's brain, hammering at his mind with every beat of the ponies' hooves, with every swish of the curry brush as he wielded it in the stable below. WEDNESDAY WEEK. WEDNESDAY WEEK.

For Nannerl the return of the English family's stable-boy was an unmixed blessing. She was a lonely small girl, and she clung to Petit-Jean with the persistence of a bluebottle, unrelenting in the attentions she demanded from him, and, in her heart, extremely grateful that here was one person on this queer, queer island, so different from Germany, who was ready to play with her. Every morning before *Frühstück* she tore into the stable to find Bellman waiting for her, and Petit-Jean ready to mount her and lead them both out into the big meadow for the morning riding lesson. She learned to make Bellman go where she wanted to go, to stop when she wanted to stop, and after only four days of Petit-Jean's tuition she could trot in a kind of awkward bounce. Nannerl began to live and dream 'ponies', much as her predecessors at the Point had done. She would follow Petit-Jean into the cool dark stable, and under his directions busily feed and water its three inmates, and learn how to bridle Bellman, how to slip the slender bit into his yawning mouth, how to test the saddle girths, and countless other lessons which Petit-Jean assured his pupil were all essential to the good rider.

When the work was done she would seat herself on an upturned bucket in the doorway while the stable-boy leaned lazily against the wall, carefully polishing a piece of leather to give a semblance of busyness. Her curiosity about the English childen, *die Engländer*, who had ridden the ponies right up to last week was intense. 'Tell me more,' she would cry, and Petit-Jean, with a queer smile playing about the corners of his mouth, would tell her long tales of Herr Mick and Fraulein Caro-lein, and the little Herr Thomas who rode her own pony.

'Tell me more,' she besought Petit-Jean, bouncing up

and down on the bucket much as she bounced in the saddle. Petit-Jean narrated long stories of the Pony Club in which the English children and their friends were the heroes and heroines. How gay it all sounded! What fun it must have been – the paper chases, the gymkhanas, the picnics, the secret meetings. Nannerl felt she knew all the members quite intimately. 'Oh, I do vish I to the Pony Club belonged,' she would sigh in her broken English, with lapses into excited German when her sentiments outpaced her vocabulary. 'I do vish they were not all gone to England.'

Her eyes grew wistful as she pictured herself sharing in all the busy activities of the Pony Club and galloping over the cliffs between Herr Mick and the young Fraulein Caro-lein. Nannerl was so certain Caro-lein would have been her friend. Indeed, Caroline Templeton and the Clerinel Pony Club became the theme-song of Nannerl Schleicher's little life. She even pinned on to her small person the cardboard badge with C.P.C. depicted in a hand-painted blue and scarlet monogram which she had found on Caroline Templeton's tweed riding-coat. It helped her to pretend that she had been elected a Junior Member of that gay company.

But Nannerl, too, would have been surprised if she could have peeped into Petit-Jean's mind and listened to the two words that beat like hammer on anvil – WEDNESDAY WEEK. WEDNESDAY WEEK.

*

And so the days went on. Across the cliffs where lived those good friends of the Reich, Monsieur Beaumarchais and his son, Caroline Templeton lay hidden in an attic, promenading after dusk on the deep-sunken lawn with her hosts. At the Martello Tower Karl Muller drilled and marched his soldiers, and stood sentry over the long sea-inlet with its secrets. In the old-fashioned Victorian Town Hall in Pol les Roches General Schleicher and his staff patiently sat day after day in conclave. At the Point House the General's granddaughter learned to canter and to absorb something of stable-management – and the stable-boy waited and watched, waited and watched, restlessness and the apprehension of failure filling his heart.

Thursday, Friday, Saturday passed. The sunny autumn weather broke into wild storms and gales. In the Town Hall the General, locked in conference with only his immediate subordinates, debated Certain Future Events. At the Point the stable-boy muttered despairingly, 'Only three more clear days before Wednesday.' At La Falaise the head of the house fatalistically spread his hands in a gesture and said to his refugee guest, 'Impossible anyway to sail in this gale. There is still a chance he will bring us the date. But they will bomb Tuesday night if he cannot confirm the new date.'

Monday passed. The stable-boy appeared so white-faced and gloomy at breakfast that Friedel, the fair-haired house-maid, produced a large bottle of castor-oil. On Monday night the wind dropped. Tuesday dawned in brilliant sunshine and showed a smooth sea on which even a sailing dinghy could have crossed to England. Suddenly, inexplicably, fate, in the guise of funny little Bellman, played into Petit-Jean's hands.

*

Nannerl awoke on Tuesday morning in a very cross mood indeed. She flounced out of bed and she glowered at poor Friedel, who was standing, her eyes swollen with homesick weeping, waiting to button the Fraulein into her jodhpurs and jersey. She stormed her way down to the dining-room where Grandfather sat peacefully over his rolls and coffee before the labours of the day commenced, and scandalized the punctilious old gentleman by upsetting her coffee cup and then stamping both feet on it as it rattled to the floor.

'She does indeed need the governess,' muttered the General as he hastily left his granddaughter roaring amid the wreckage and entered the staff-car to drive to his Headquarters.

At ten o'clock, when the entire household had been rendered nearly distraught by an enraged Nannerl bellowing with tantrum, she met her match in Petit-Jean.

'I vant to ride Dinah. I vant to ride Dinah.' This from the back of the placid Bellman with waving stick and feet kicking lustily.

'Fraulein Nannerl will ride Bellman.' Petit-Jean was feeling too desperate this fine Tuesday morning to pay more than lip-service to politeness.

'I vant to ride Dinah. I 'ate you. I vill not zis stupid leetle pony ride.' Yells of fury echoed round the stable-yard as Petit-Jean, unmoved, reached out for Bellman's bridle prior to leading him to the paddock. At the kitchen window two giggling maids clutched each other in ecstasy at the scene. At the gates the bored sentries shifted their rifles and grinned as the repercussions of the encounter floated down through the garden.

'*Schweinhund*,' screamed Nannerl.

'*Schweinhund* yourself with knobs on,' returned Petit-Jean tartly, too miserable to enact his part any longer.

Purple with temper Nannerl brought her stick down with a whack on Bellman's portly rump. It was a silly little stick, and the blow must have felt to Bellman like the tickle of a fly's leg. There was no excuse for a well-bred lawn-mower pony to behave so badly. For Bellman, née Tiny, offended beyond all control, raised his hind legs, and deposited the lady on the stable cobbles with a bang.

'Good old Bellman,' said Petit-Jean sourly.

In the ensuing confusion his exodus with Bellman passed unnoticed. He led the pony back into the stable, slammed the door shut with a well-aimed kick, and stood in Bellman's stall with his arms round the pony's neck and his face buried in Bellman's soft dark mane. 'I've failed, Bellman,' said Petit-Jean without a trace of island accent. 'I've let everybody down.' Bellman continued to look pretty well pleased with himself.

Outside the stable Nannerl's roars and shrieks mingled with the agitated clucking of the maids and the panting grunts of the sentries. These last, thinking that some spy was attempting an entry of their General's home, converged on to the yard at the double. They found the General's granddaughter sitting where she had fallen, with a bump the size of a pin's head rapidly rising on her forehead.

While the maids bore the screaming Nannerl into the house for butter and bandages and the sentries philosophically returned to the gates that nobody so much as wished to enter, Petit-Jean wearily took off Bellman's saddle and bridle, hung them on their pegs, and then seated himself on Nannerl's upturned bucket with his head in his hands.

Half an hour later Friedel, hurrying into the stable, nearly fell over the forlorn figure in the patched jersey, dejectedly gazing straight before it. 'It was not your fault,' she assured him anxiously. Friedel knew only too well how the best of servants could be blamed for such mishaps. 'It was the bad temper of Fraulein Nannerl,' the kind-hearted girl went on, patting Petit-Jean's shoulder consolingly. Friedel had run across with the good news that the child was not hurt – one little bruise, nothing more – so Petit-Jean could cheer himself quickly, quickly, for the Fraulein was almost recovered and had been laid on the sofa in the General's study, and now wished Petit-Jean to come and play with her.

'Amuse her well,' Friedel implored the stable-boy as she followed him across the yard. 'We do not wish for more scenes like this morning, Heidi and I. Gott, if my parents had the upbringing of that little one!' Friedel threw her hands up to heaven, the tears welling into her eyes at the thought of her mother in the tiny painted cottage in the Austrian mountains.

Petit-Jean said nothing. He appeared sunk in depression.

His face brightened slightly, however, as he clumped into the General's study where Nannerl reclined on the cretonne-covered sofa, an important bandage swathed round her flaxen head. It seemed like a lifetime since Petit-Jean had been last in that sunny octagonal room with the wide bay window encompassing the whole sweep of the hills in their descent to the sea.

Very little had been altered, his quick eye noticed, since the change of ownership. Where the bookshelf had once stood there were now two heavy steel filing-cabinets. The piano had been pushed back against the wall to make room for a plain deal table, and upon the wall there now hung a large-scale coloured map of Clerinel. Otherwise pictures and furniture remained in much the same positions as in the days of the English family's residence. The tired troubled eyes of the Templeton's late stable-hand wandered from the photo of Caroline Templeton on the mantelpiece to the virulently-coloured drawing of the house perpetrated by Thomas Templeton as a birthday present to his father. The last had been removed to the top shelf of the writing-desk, to make room for the piles and piles of letters and papers still awaiting filing.

The meditations of the stable-boy were promptly interrupted by a shriek of pleasure from the invalid, whose fall had at any rate served to improve her temper. She was lying surrounded by a litter of paints, tracing-paper, and old-fashioned catalogues, busily cutting out and painting the models in crude brilliant colours.

'You come and paint *mit*.' She summoned Petit-Jean to her side with a beckon of a paint-smeared hand. With the other hand she unloaded on to his lap, as he seated himself on a stool by the sofa, the whole bundle of slips of tracing-paper and the water-pot. Playing with Nannerl, Petit-Jean speedily learned, entailed no exercise whatever of the intelligence but required simply a capacity for holding whatever material the Fraulein elected to play with and handing it to her at the right moment.

Petit-Jean sat balancing the paraphernalia on his knees. Nannerl had so obviously forgotten their recent contretemps and was painting away with such furious concentration that he forbore to remind her of the episode by inquiring after the poor head. Her whole small being was totally absorbed in the line of fashionable Paris ladies who were beginning to lean limply against the back of the sofa. Every time Nannerl shifted her position, which was not seldom, the line swayed drunkenly and collapsed, and it was left to Petit-Jean to rearrange them in the intervals of passing Nannerl the slips of tracing-paper each time her brush poised itself over a new model in the tattered catalogue.

We Couldn't Leave Dinah

For another hour there was silence. Through the closed door came the busy household sounds – Friedel polishing the staircase and singing like a canary, Heidi clashing the pans in the kitchen in her vigorous preparations for the midday meal. Inside the study the only sound was Nannerl's heavy breathing as she laboriously snipped and painted. Petit-Jean sat in a dream, the pile of tracing-papers diminishing as Nannerl acquired more skill and worked faster and faster. The bandage on her head slipped off, the line of paper ladies elongated down the back of the sofa, the paint-water turned into an inky nauseating liquor with all the colours commingled. Still Nannerl concentrated her energies on this new ploy. The peace was unusual and the household acknowledged it gratefully.

Suddenly Petit-Jean, lost in his own musings, realized that the pile on his lap had diminished almost to nothing. He looked down and then glanced apprehensively at the industrious Nannerl. Only one more piece of tracing-paper, and that a crumpled bit with pencil marks already upon its yellow cracked surface. He sighed and wondered whether he could possibly cope with Nannerl's annoyance and frustration when she realized that her occupation was arriving at an enforced end. He cast his eye round the room for some more paper. Then he turned the last piece left over in his fingers and glanced idly at it. Nannerl was painting with swift scrubby strokes at an auburn-haired beauty in a pink and green evening creation. He opened his mouth to spoil her happy absorption by telling her he had run out of paper. Then something made him examine that last piece more closely – and again more closely still.

The room was very silent. Petit-Jean's fingers slowly and noiselessly folded the last slip of tracing-paper, pencil-marks and all – smaller, smaller. A minute square lay concealed in the palm of his hand. The room must have been very hot for at that moment the Schleichers' stable-boy put his hand to his mouth in an uncontrollable yawn and then into his trouser-pocket as though ashamed of his lack of drawing-room manners.

'Fraulein Nannerl,' he said in a quiet, expressionless

voice, 'there is no more paper.' He spread his empty hands out in a helpless gesture.

Nannerl raised her head. '*Hein?*' she said in annoyed tones.

'From where did the Fraulein obtain the paper she has been using?' inquired Petit-Jean in the same monotonous voice.

'From the grandfather's desk.' Nannerl's countenance turned rather red. She knew very well she was not supposed to touch her grandfather's desk. Although all military papers were at the Town Hall many letters and papers relating to the General's private affairs in Germany remained at his residence as yet unsorted.

Petit-Jean said nothing in reply, but managed to convey an impression of such disapproval that Nannerl wriggled uncomfortably and hummed an airy little tune in her embarrassment. The tiresome thing, from her point of view, was that there was still a plentiful amount of tracing-paper upon the desk. Was it worth while braving Petit-Jean, the one person whose respect she demanded, to filch it for more paper ladies? It was a debatable matter.

Luckily for Nannerl at that very moment when she was eyeing her companion in an attempt to gauge the extent of his disapproval the bell rang out in the dining-room to tell her that midday dinner was ready. Nannerl slid thankfully off the sofa, all invalidism forgotten. She seized the row of paper ladies in one hand, snatched up her paints, and ran out of the study.

Petit-Jean followed hard upon her heels, carrying the water-pot and the scissors. His eyes were thoughtful.

*

Two hours later silence reigned at the Point House. Upstairs with the blinds half-drawn the granddaughter of the house, clad only in a petticoat, lay on her bed, resting after the heavy *Mittagessen* upon which Germany nourishes young and old. Out in the kitchen Friedel sat nid-nodding over her letter home to Germany, resentfully picturing the gay afternoon Heidi would be spending in the town. The

We Couldn't Leave Dinah

General had telephoned to say he would not be home until supper-time as the town was seething with islanders come to register for ration-cards, and the military might be called out. His nephew Karl was coming in later in his off-time, but that would not be yet. Friedel considered herself as distinctly off duty and slept and wrote in snatches. Out in the road and up on the hillside the sentries yawned and bitterly wished they were back popping away at the Maginot Line instead of lounging about on this *verdammte* island.

Only Petit-Jean, the stable-boy, seemed to be completely wide awake, and even he appeared to be behaving in a somewhat mysterious manner. For instead of spending his free afternoon either in Pol visiting his relatives, or sitting reading in his bedroom-loft, he had crept, stealthily and with many backward glances, into the General's study – where he certainly had no right to be.

There he was deftly inserting a tiny slip of tracing-paper back among a whole pile of new tracing-paper on the General's desk. Then he moved to the telephone. 'It's not what they want,' he murmured. 'But they ought to have it.' Carefully, quietly he dialled a number.

The telephone gave a tiny click.

'Caroline?' Petit-Jean scarcely even breathed down the mouthpiece.

The telephone gave a startled, affirmatory click.

'Send here at once,' whispered the Schleichers' stable-boy down the mouthpiece.

Chapter 16

The Pony Club Elects a Member

Caroline slowly put the telephone receiver back on the stand. She stood for a moment with bent head and the sun shining through the landing-window on to her pigtails, feeling that she would remember this moment all her life. After all these days of enforced sickening inactivity and suspense it had happened at last! That was undoubtedly Mick's voice and he had said, 'Send here at once.' Send here at once! It could mean only one thing – that at the very last moment, just when she and Peter and M. Beaumarchais had all but given up hope, Mick had really pulled it off. Caroline's heart raced and her pulses tingled, as she made a leap for the stairs to tell her hosts that the end of their long, long wait was in sight, and that one of them must go off to the Point at once to help Mick.

She dashed down the wide shallow staircase, taking the last two steps at a bound and tore into the La Falaise drawing-room. And it was only as she pulled up on the threshold with the excited words dying on her lips that she remembered. There was nobody to send to the Point House! It was Food Registration Day on Clerinel, and the Beaumarchais would be away for the next hour.

Caroline clung to the door-handle paralysed and with a curious empty sensation inside. For an awful moment her mind panicked in a circle and became a blank. This *would* happen during the one hour in all that long fortnight when both Peter and his father were inaccessible. The order from the Food Control had arrived only that morning, commanding them to register with the other Bs at three o'clock that afternoon. M. Beaumarchais had shaken a gloomy head when Peter had suggested remaining behind just in case anything happened. 'It would only invite inquiries,' he had replied. Besides, nobody had expected Mick to phone. He had been instructed to get himself to La Falaise somehow with his information, and now – golly goodness, what was she to do? There was absolutely nobody – or – at least –

Caroline shied away from the obvious solution like a frightened pony. There was one person who could go. Then quite suddenly she gave one terrified glance round the comfortable drawing-room, took a deep breath and darted hurriedly through the french windows before she felt too frightened to move at all. From the time the telephone bell had rung to the moment of her decision to go to the Point herself four minutes had elapsed.

On the far side of the tree-shadowed lawn the one other individual who could be trusted in this household was lethargically putting in an afternoon's work on the hydrangea bushes. Caroline slipped like a shadow across the grass. Old Denis, the Beaumarchais' gardener, straightened up, touched his battered straw hat, and regarded the breathless, agitated mademoiselle with bright knowing eyes.

'Denis,' said Caroline in an undertone, 'tell Monsieur Beaumarchais my brother telephoned for us to – to fetch something from where he is. Tell him I've gone and that I'll be back as quickly as possible.'

Old Denis looked quizzically at the flushed face. '*Bon*,' he said curtly and bent again over an errant branch of hydrangea. What went on in the house was none of his business. Nevertheless he spat vigorously into the next bush at the thought of the Nazi invaders who were, he strongly suspected, the cause of the young mademoiselle's distraction.

Caroline picked up her skirt and ran in long strides along the little woodland path up which she and Dinah had galloped on Carnival afternoon. Given any luck she ought to be able to get into the Point House garden unobserved if she came down through the upper gate from the hillside.

As she emerged on to the open cliff at the top of the wood she found herself uneasily wondering why Mick could not have come to La Falaise as they had arranged. I do hope, she thought apprehensively, that he's not got to stay on at the Point for any reason. These last twelve days had been for her one long nightmare of fears and torments about what was happening to Mick shut up among the Nazis at their old home. She cheered herself on with the idea that now that Mick had done what he had set out to do M. Beaumarchais would never allow him to stay with the Schleichers another moment. But somehow the uneasiness persisted and kept flickering across her thoughts as she dashed along the Green Ride.

The cliffs were, as usual, deserted. The invaders had evidently seen no reason to patrol these great empty wastes of dying bracken and heather. Save for the detachment commanded by Cousin Karl that guarded the Tower and the camp M. Beaumarchais assured her was concealed above the inlet there were very few Germans quartered immediately in the neighbourhood. The officers had preferred to billet their men on the outlying villages, and, of course, the majority were concentrated near the aerodrome on the other side of the island and in Pol les Roches itself. Peter had come back from his excursions into Pol muttering angrily about the grey-clad soldiery who strutted up and down the streets and paid for what they bought in worthless money.

Caroline crossed the junction of the tracks and ran lightly down the home path. The nearer she came to her home the more her fears seemed to be calming themselves. As she rounded the last bend her spirits were soaring. There was the gate through which she and Mick had come back to the Point that memorable morning after the night on the quayside in Pol. But the landscape did not look quite the same on this occasion – Caroline pulled up dead and backed into the bushes. Blocking the gateway, mercifully with broad back to her, was a large German sentry with steel helmet, grey overcoat, and rifle. He was leaning over the gate and gazing earnestly down into the garden below.

In the undergrowth Caroline considered the position with firm-set jaw and gleaming eye. It had taken just the sight of that Nazi leaning familiarly upon their gate to chase away the last remnants of fear. 'If that man thinks he's going to keep me out of my own home he's jolly well wrong,' she said truculently to herself as she skirted the fence on all fours to where she knew there had once been a loose paling. Aha! here it was. The Nazis for all their boasted efficiency had not discovered Thomas's secret exit from the Point garden. With vindictive satisfaction she inserted herself in the aperture and edged herself gingerly through. Sucks to Hitler!

Caroline wriggled a cautious passage down the hill toward the study windows. There was about a hundred and fifty yards of undergrowth to be covered, and from years of scouting games played with Mick and Thomas and the Pony Club she knew she could make the whole course completely hidden. If only Mick were in the study! He was, she guessed, almost certain to be there since it was from there he had telephoned.

When she emerged right up under the house wall her whole person was covered with large black smears from her snakelike passage among the leaves and twigs and earth-mould. She wriggled flat on her front along the wall and then raised her head. Yes, there was old Mick ensconced behind the study curtains anxiously watching for the messenger from La Falaise. Caroline cast a glance round the landscape before lifting a grimy hand. Then she waved her arm to and fro until Mick should look that way. Even in that tense moment when his questing eyes finally fixed on it and he swung the french windows open Caroline noticed how tired and dispirited was the set of his shoulders, how drawn-looking his face.

'I wasn't expecting it would be you.' Mick automatically warded off his sister's bearlike hug as she slid into the study.

'There wasn't anyone else. They've gone to register in Pol,' said Caroline breathlessly, still clutching Mick as though he might disappear in smoke the next minute. 'O Mick, I *am* so glad to see you. Are you all right? Has it been absolutely awful?' He looked terribly thin, Caroline thought, and not a bit like a boy who had just baffled the whole German invasion plan.

'I'm all right. No, not awful. Look Caroline, there's no time to talk. You must get back quickly.'

'But you're coming too, aren't you? Mick, you can't stay

here. I won't go back without you,' interrupted Caroline, her secret apprehensions once more rearing their ugly little heads.

'I've got to stay. You don't understand.' Mick suddenly looked pinched and desperate. 'What I've found out isn't what they want at all. It's something quite different that I thought they ought to know about. But there's still a chance for me to get the real thing. It's only Tuesday afternoon, and the R.A.F. won't bomb the inlet until late tonight.'

Caroline's heart ached for her brother. This *sickening* war! It was no good, she knew, trying to gainsay Mick in this mood. If he'd made up his mind to stay, even though in his heart he knew it was hopeless, stay he would. 'I wish you'd come,' she said miserably, watching Mick extracting a slip of tracing-paper from his trouser pocket. But Mick's thoughts were already elsewhere.

'Look,' he said in low tones, moving nearer to Caroline, 'can you hide it somewhere? It's for M. Beaumarchais. It's some sort of rough sketch of the island, and those crosses and queer marks on the other side of the island may mean anything, gun emplacements or something. He'll know if it's any use. Tell him the original was among a whole lot of bits of tracing-paper. I think it was a trial sketch they forgot to tear up. Anyway, I've copied it and put the original back on the General's desk.'

Caroline eyed the slip of yellow waxy paper as though it might blow up. Then she bent down and ripped about five threads ruthlessly apart in the large clumsily-sewn hem of her peasant skirt. 'It'll be quite safe tucked in here,' she said, pushing the folded slip well into the hem. The skirt hung a trifle stiffly where the paper lay, but Caroline whirled round on her axis two or three times under Mick's critical eye, and he finally pronounced his satisfaction.

'I don't suppose it's anything very important,' said Mick pessimistically, 'but you'd better get it into M. Beaumarchais' hands as soon as he's back from Pol.'

As he spoke he turned back towards the window – and it was at that moment that disaster overtook the Templetons. Caroline was on the point of reassuring him that she would go straight back, and that there really was no danger at all of her being caught when something – she never knew what – warned her. She swung round and stared at the door. Her ears pricked. Was that a footfall outside in the hall? Mick had evidently no doubts. He gave one leap through the window, expecting Caroline to follow on his heels. But Caroline stood rooted to the spot. The door-handle was slowly turning – the door was opening.

Nobody ever knew who was the more startled – Cousin Karl at seeing a small frightened-looking peasant girl standing guiltily in the middle of his uncle's study, or the peasant girl at seeing Cousin Karl on the threshold, stout and spotty and very official-looking with blond hair brushed stiffly upward and rubicund countenance.

'*Gott in Himmel*,' said Cousin Karl, his pale eyes bulging.

'Gosh,' said the peasant child.

Cousin Karl pulled himself together. He had not received his promotion long enough to have become used to possessing authority, and he still found it necessary to shout a great deal. He was not a pleasant young man. '*Was tun sie hier?*' he barked ferociously. A vacant expression appeared on the child's face. Cousin Karl made an effort, 'What do you do here?' He advanced threateningly down the room, feeling rather silly. Bearing down upon a small girl in a private house was not quite the same thing as bullying scared Belgian refugees along the muddy Flanders roads in the great Battle of France.

Caroline blinked at the fat, stupid face of Cousin Karl. Cousin Karl at close quarters turned out to be surprisingly unfrightening and nothing like such a bogey as she had imagined from his earlier sinister appearances. Still, she was in a nasty jam.

'I came –' she said, praying for inspiration, 'I came – monsieur – er, to see the General. I am the sister of Petit-Jean. I wish to ask if I can work here.' To her own ears the story sounded extraordinarily unconvincing. She scarcely dared even glance at Cousin Karl's face. But to her surprise his piggy eyes lost their look of suspicion. He sauntered across to the sofa and threw himself on it. Caroline noticed that the springs gave vent to an agonized squeak as Cousin Karl's portly form settled itself comfortably among the cushions left by Nannerl that morning.

'Ach,' he said, 'so.' He looked meditatively at her. Caroline did not realize that the young man was feeling that he had made a fool of himself. For one glorious moment Karl Muller had thought upon entering the study that he had caught an English spy red-handed. And it was only one of these wretched islanders come to see about work! Cousin Karl's expression was glum.

'I'd better go to the kitchen,' said the peasant child brightly, edging nearer the door. 'Perhaps I ought not to have come here but – er, er, – but Monsieur Templeton, he was always here in this room.' She nodded round the study with what she hoped was a convincing smile.

Alas, alas for a good idea gone wrong! Alas for Caroline's plan of escape! Sorely had she underestimated Cousin Karl. As she backed past the mantelpiece in her effort at self-dismissal, as she opened her mouth to bid *adieu* to the gentleman with an accompanying little curtsey, she saw, to her horror, Cousin Karl's rather blank expression change suddenly. His pale-blue eyes widened, his mouth hung open. Caroline swung round and followed his gaze. Her heart sank. Of all places to choose to stand and make a farewell speech!

She turned back and looked hopelessly at Cousin Karl. She realized that the game was up. Cousin Karl, with his neck slowly turning a deep purple, was looking from her photograph on the mantelpiece to her and back at the photograph. The likeness could not possibly have escaped any one even more unintelligent than this young Nazi officer. Caroline waited for the storm to break.

'You – you –'

Caroline thought he looked like an angry Piggy Porker. She took a deep breath and gazed up into his infuriated face.

'All right.' She interrupted Cousin Karl's imprecations. 'All right,' she said. 'You needn't go on like this.' The sooner they got down to business the better. 'If you want to know I *am* Caroline and I got left behind by mistake when we evacuated 'cos you were coming, and I've been living in a cave ever since and now it's too cold to go on and I want to go back to England anyway, and I came to see the General and tell him all about it and ask if I need be interned but couldn't he get me off. That's what I was waiting for. *See?*'

Cousin Karl stood towering over her. He didn't know what to think. He didn't know what to do. This plausible English brat! He didn't want to make a fool of himself by arresting her. A German officer did not arrest children. And yet the English were enemies. . . . He looked helplessly at the child who stared hostilely back at him. What was he to do? He moved over to the telephone. At any rate he could ring up his uncle in Pol and shift it all on to him. Keeping one would-be ferocious eye on Caroline he dialled the military headquarters of the Nazi-occupied protectorate of Clerinel.

''Allo. 'Allo.'

Followed a brisk and staccato dialogue in German which Caroline could not follow. From the frequent mopping of a moistening brow and the queer mottled colour Cousin Karl was turning she surmised that he was not being too popular with his busy uncle.

Caroline was not far out in this guess. General Schleicher, interrupted at the final staff-meeting before Certain Operations were carried out, was scarcely interested in his nephew's garbled account of an English child stranded on the island. 'Use your wits, boy, use your wits,' he thundered down the receiver to the amusement of his staff. 'I'll be back at seven. Well, if you're going on duty lock the girl in the larder or the stable.' He slammed down the receiver muttering, '*Himmel,* these young men . . .'

Cousin Karl also put the telephone down with an angry bang. He glared at Caroline who stood on one foot and glared back. 'You will come with me, please,' said Cousin Karl, putting a hand heavily on Caroline's shoulder in an effort to propel her towards the study door.

Caroline more furious than frightened, tried to twitch her shoulder free. At any rate, she consoled herself, the quite odious Karl had not yet connected her with General Schleicher's stable-boy. Further, she still had the secret map hidden in the hem of her skirt: Two points in her favour – and if she was going to be locked up anywhere about the house it would be a poor show after all these years of living at the Point if she couldn't scramble out of some window or make some sort of getaway somehow.

She felt slightly less confident as Cousin Karl marched her across the hall and out of the front door. If she was going to accompany her captor back to his beastly Tower she was indeed sunk. She'd never escape from the Martello Tower, and the R.A.F. would bomb her along with the barges when they flew over that night. 'Where are we going?' Caroline screwed her head round in some anxiety and looked up at Cousin Karl, who looked back at her with distaste.

'Leetle girls should not ask the questions,' replied Cousin Karl hatefully, as they swung round the corner of the house in a frog-march.

Leetle girl! Wounded to the quick, Caroline almost burst with suppressed outrage. She gathered herself together as Cousin Karl thrust her inside the stable and locked the door on her. Whirling round, she stooped down to the keyhole and shouted after his retreating figure, 'I'd have you know that our form's collected fifteen and ninepence towards a Spitfire.'

Then she turned round with her back to the stable-door and reviewed the situation while Cousin Karl's heavy footsteps were dying away in the distance. She was in a fine fix now, she said to herself. There was absolutely no way out of the stable other than through the locked door. Her one hope now lay in Mick.

A movement in the gloom of the stable startled her. Gracious, she thought with a shock of surprise, there's Dinah. Well, one wish of hers at any rate had been granted. She'd pictured herself over and over again during the dreary sojourn in the Cave being granted the opportunity of bidding a romantic farewell to Dinah. It was now five o'clock. She could say good-bye to Dinah for some two hours before the General came to intern her! Somehow the prospect did not allure her. She was much more concerned with getting Mick's message through to the Beaumarchais.

If only Mick knew where she was! Surely, surely he'd had the wits to hide in the garden and watch her fate. Or had Cousin Karl gone straight off and arrested Mick too? He was certain sooner or later to tumble to the obvious connexion between the Templetons' late stable-boy and the appearance of Caroline Templeton at the Point. She only hoped he wouldn't notice the likeness between her and the stable-boy! Caroline absently stroked Dinah's nose, too preoccupied to do any romantic farewell-ing to her pony. She walked out of Dinah's stall and paced up and down, while the three ponies watched her interestedly. There was no chance of escape. The only light came from a high window with bars crossing the glass on the outside wall. There was no exodus from the stable-loft. In any case the ladder was not in the stable. Her heart sank to her shoes. There was absolutely nothing she could do, except wait.

Half an hour passed. Caroline was too upset to sit quietly down and compose herself. She strode up and down, up and down the dim stable. She was so busy striding that she did not hear the fumbling, the faint cautious thrusting of key into lock on the outside of the door. As she turned at the far end of the stable in her restless passage she suddenly saw a chink of light stealing down the door, widening, widening. She stood stock-still for a second, her heart beating in terrific thumps. Mick had found her! She leapt forward. The door swung open. A rush of daylight and fresh air dazzled her. In the entrance the small figure of Nannerl confronted her.

'Oh,' said Caroline flatly.

Nannerl beamed and carefully closed the door behind her, shutting herself and Caroline into the stable atmosphere, heavy with the smell of horse. Neither said anything for a moment. Then Nannerl took a step forward and politely held out her hand with a little bow. Solemnly the pair shook hands. Caroline was feeling quite sick with disappointment.

'I saw you mit my Cousin Karl,' Nannerl was saying. ''E is not nice – Caro-lein.'

'No,' said Caroline with feeling.

Nannerl stared up at her with frank curiosity. 'I did not know,' she went on, 'zat you were Caro-lein when I spoke wiz you zat day. You did not tell me. Petit-Johann 'e did not tell me either.' She was speaking in a hoarse whisper, evidently as little anxious as Caroline that this dialogue should be overheard.

'He did not want people to know I was still on Clerinel,' Caroline replied, wondering in a confused rush of ideas how best she could exonerate Mick in the eyes of the General's granddaughter and whether it would be practicable to bash Nannerl over the head and make a run for it.

'I am very pleased to see you Caro-lein,' went on Nannerl. 'I 'ave so moch about your Pony Club learnt. I 'ave too your badge.' She indicated Caroline's blue and gold badge pinned across her fat little chest. 'I do so vish you were going to stay on zis island and that we could have ze Pony Club again.' She sighed wistfully, and looked from Caroline to the three ponies in their stalls as though she were picturing all the wonderful things they would do if the Clerinel Pony Club were still in action.

'I probably am staying on zis – I mean, this – island,' said Caroline grimly. This queer meeting in the Point House stable was quite fantastic, and Nannerl was behaving as though she were royalty receiving in Buckingham Palace.

'You do not vish to stay?' Nannerl's eyes were shrewd. 'You did not like Cousin Karl to lock you in here? You vant to go, yes? Vhere you go, *hein*?' She peppered Caroline with a string of questions. Caroline stared down at her, her brain whirling.

'Why –' Caroline stammered 'I – no, I don't want to stay shut up on the island. I – I could go to England. I'd meant to go to England. What d'you mean?'

'I would like you to stay here wiz me,' said Nannerl. 'But I do not like Cousin Karl to shut you up. 'E is now gone back to 'is tower out on ze cliffs. 'E vill not know if you go now. Vy do you not go, Caro-lein?' She waved a hand at the door and stood, looking expectedly up at Caroline.

'Go?' said Caroline slowly, a wild hope dawning in her. 'Do you mean – just *go*?'

Nannerl nodded. 'You 'ad better go quick. I vill lend you Gretchen to go mit. She goes quicker than your feet. You cre-e-ep out of the garden and I ride up past Heinrich Schmidt who stands all day at our gate. He vill not mind me. He vill be surprised that I ride alone. But zat is all. You can wait for me and I vill give you Gretchen. You can perhaps arrange that she comes back?'

There was no doubt that Nannerl Schleicher had her head screwed on the right way, thought Caroline dazedly as she helped Nannerl saddle and bridle Dinah. 'But what will your grandfather say if I'm not here when he comes back?' she asked.

Nannerl butted Dinah's flank energetically with her head and dragged a girth tighter before replying. ''E vill not mind,' she panted confidently, face red with her exertions. ''E is a vairy kind person, Caro-lein. 'E vould onderstand zat you could not hurt Germany and 'e vould not 'ave shut you up like Cousin Karl.' Here Nannerl very regretfully spat on the ground. Dinah looked mildly disapproving. 'It is the good business,' she chuckled, 'that Cousin Karl is gone back to 'is work and zat 'e cannot see you now.'

'It is indeed,' agreed Caroline, giving Nannerl a leg up on to Dinah and wondering at the same time if Mick would, by any stroke of fortune, see her departure and know that everything was going to be all right after all.

Nannerl was eyeing Dinah's ears nervously. 'I 'ave nevair ridden Gretchen alone before,' she said apprehensively.

Caroline firmly led Dinah toward the door. 'Bend well down as you go through,' she commanded Nannerl. 'You needn't worry about Dinah. She won't hurt a fly. All you've got to do is to walk her quite slowly up the path. She knows the way perfectly well. Here, what are you doing?'

Nannerl was fumbling with the Pony Club badge. She held it out to Caroline. 'Zis is yours,' she said sadly. 'You most 'ave it to take to England.'

Caroline looked at the little badge as it lay on the palm of Nannerl's broad, stumpy hand. Suddenly she had an inspiration. There was just one thing she could do for the small German girl who had rendered her so great a service.

'You keep it,' she said generously. 'You keep that, Nannerl. And I'll tell you what. There's a boy on this island called Peter Beaumarchais. He used to be President of the Pony Club when we were all here. You find him and tell him Caroline Templeton made you a Junior Member of the Pony Club and gave you her badge. He – he'll remember me.'

After all, Peter had delegated her authority to elect members to the new London branch of the Pony Club. She knew he wouldn't mind, considering what they all of them owed to Nannerl, this election of Nannerl to membership of the parent club.

She felt more than rewarded by the sight of Nannerl's expression of incredulous ecstasy as she pinned the badge back on to her jersey. 'There,' she said, giving Nannerl's shoulder a friendly little pat, 'there you are. Now you're a Junior Member, same as my brother, Thomas. You make Peter show you Headquarters. You can help him to dust them.' She nearly added 'until we all come back,' and then remembered it wasn't a very tactful addition.

'I do vish you were staying, Caro-lein,' said Nannerl, torn between delight at so glorious an occurrence and anguish at the imminent departure of this wonderful new friend.

'Never mind,' said Caroline, busily dragging the heavy door open for Nannerl to ride through, 'we'll meet again. Perhaps you could come to London after the war.'

Nannerl beamed and nodded her head up and down so vigorously that Dinah's ears twitched in sympathy. '*Ja, ja*,' she said enthusiastically, 'Breetish Museum.'

'Olympia,' breathed Caroline raptly.

'Tower of Lon-don,' sang Nannerl.

'Lyons' Corner House,' capped Caroline, envisaging the increasing possibilities of Knickerbocker Glories now that escape was once more imminent. She pulled herself out of the happy daydream. 'Go on,' she said, and gave Dinah a gentle tap. Dinah walked out of the stable into the evening sunlight.

Caroline remained in the dark stable for five more minutes to give Nannerl time to get past the sentry at the upper gate. Then she slipped out into the yard. There was nobody about. Friedel was busy cooking the dinner, for a delicious whiff of *Wienerschnitzel* greeted Caroline's nostrils as she ran on tiptoe round the house. There were no signs of Mick anywhere.

She slid under the nearest hydrangea bush and began her long snakelike trek up the hillside toward the loose paling. Everything, after all, was going to come out all right.

Chapter 17

Good-bye, the Island

Dinah flew noiselessly over the close-cropped turf. Her ears lay flat to her head, and her nostrils were wide to the salt wind that blew up from the sea. The bracken stalks swayed across the old track, parting before her hooves, as she tore down the Green Ride. If ever pony expressed pleasure it was Dinah with her blowy little snorts of delight.

After an agonized moment of bumping Caroline hit on the idea of hitching the bulky skirt well up over her knee-caps. By the time they had crossed the junction where the home-track joined the Green Ride, she had settled herself easily in the saddle, her eyes watchful and her hands low and light on the reins as Dinah fled along the winding path. The sun was setting over the sea in a riot of gold and azure, and the glory of the west had transfigured sea, sky, and cliffs to a golden world. The withered heather tops were tipped to flame across the hills, and the shadows in the clefts and gulleys to wine-purple. Clerinel would never be lovelier than for Caroline's last unexpected ride on Dinah.

As far as Caroline herself was concerned all danger was really over. Cousin Karl Blue Feather was safely goose-stepping at the Tower, the General was still closeted in his room at Headquarters, and, back at the Point House, the latest recruit to the Pony Club proudly treasured the secret of a captive's escape.

Caroline's heart sang with a rapture that made her feel as though she would burst. For the first time since she had watched the *Queen of Clerinel* sailing away without her she was completely happy and at peace. Every now and then she clutched the hem of her skirt to make quite sure that Mick's slip of paper still reposed safely in its hiding-place.

Even Mick's assurance that it was not the real secret failed to depress her. She was buoyed up with the conviction that somehow the whole thing was going to turn out perfectly all right.

She slackened Dinah to a fast canter, the little mare instantly responding to her touch. It was marvellous, thought Caroline, as Dinah steadied her pace, how the things she and Mick had done with the Pony Club in the past had come in useful during this last exciting fortnight. Whatever, to begin with, would they have done without the new Headquarters? What about their hot, weary labours upon the ancient smugglers' way – weren't they more than justified, now that a Club member was tearing down the Green Ride on business even more urgent than that of those earlier travellers? And then the ponies – hadn't the ponies themselves been co-opted into the whole business too? They would never have managed to get to the Cave, nor she to Pol les Roches that dreadful foggy night, without patient, reliable little Punch. Caroline was now ready to admit that Dinah would never have done those particular jobs so well as Punch. But this evening Dinah had come into her own too. Even though she, Caroline, could have run back to La Falaise on her two feet, it had expedited her return more than she and Mick would ever realize to ride across the hills on Dinah. Punch could not have raced like a bit of flame down the Green Ride. Even comic Bellman had been apparently the indirect cause of Mick finding his piece of tracing-paper. Caroline smiled to herself at the thought of Bellman, and wondered if he would go back to being the lawn-mower pony when Nannerl started to ride Dinah.

The soft sea-wind blew across Caroline's face as Dinah quickened her pace for the last lap before turning off to La Falaise. The sun was sinking fast over the horizon, and the uplands were taking on a darkened, remote aspect as the shadows crept along the lower slopes. Clerinel was slowly settling itself for another night. Alone in the landscape, Caroline felt she would like tonight to ride on and on to the edge of the world. Her happiness rose like a fountain of spray inside her. When Dinah rounded the last corner she let out a glad yell, regardless of any possible listeners. A thin, dark figure, silhouetted against the evening sky, had risen out of the bracken by the La Falaise fork. She drew rein, and Dinah slowed to a trot and came to a standstill, panting with the long non-stop ride.

Peter stepped forward and took the bridle as Caroline slid out of the saddle. 'We got your message,' he said briefly. 'I thought you'd be almost certain to come back this way, though I didn't expect to see you flying along on Dinah. However did you get her?'

Caroline quickly told him about her escape from Cousin Karl through Nannerl's intervention.

'Good work,' commented Peter. 'Now you'd better go straight on home. Father's waiting for you. I'll ride Dinah over to Trois Chênes Farm and borrow a bike to come back on. The Trois Chênes people can hide her tonight, take her back to the Point tomorrow, and say they found her wandering about. I don't suppose Nannerl'll get into a row with the General, even if her share in the affair is discovered. She seems more than able to take care of herself. See you later, Caroline.'

He swung into the saddle as he spoke, checking Dinah, who was eager to be off again, until he had finished his conversation with Caroline. Then he grinned conspiratorially at her, wheeled Dinah round, and, leaving the track, galloped off through the bracken and heather.

'Good-bye, Dinah, good-bye,' called Caroline. She stood knee-deep in the heather with one hand shading her eyes, watching until Dinah's flying form disappeared between the hills.

There had been no time to bid the romantic tearful farewell to Dinah. But it didn't matter, thought Caroline, not feeling at all tearful. It didn't seem so bad leaving Dinah behind on the island this time. After all, Nannerl seemed a fair hand with ponies, and Mick had probably taught her a good deal about stable-management. Dinah would be well cared for, and would be there when she and the family came trooping back after the war.

So, for that matter, would the island still be there.

Caroline blushed as she remembered her distress at leaving Clerinel. All that somehow seemed feeble and sentimental now, just like her feelings about Dinah. She broke into a run as she reached the outskirts of the Beaumarchais' wood. It was beginning to get quite dark, and the silver radiance of the crescent moon was already illuminating trees and under-growth. The little path down beneath the thickets was like a dark tunnel. Through the trees on the lawn below she could see M. Beaumarchais, a solitary figure pacing to and fro between the patches of moonlight and shadow. She sped round the last bend of the path, and skipped nimbly across the lawn to meet him as he turned beneath the overshadowing chestnuts.

When he saw the small form in the all-enveloping skirt M. Beaumarchais' face lighted up with a relieved expression. He hurried forward with outstretched hands. '*Ma chère* Caroline,' he began, but Caroline waved him off.

'Wait a shake,' she said importantly, fishing in the hem of her skirt. 'Mick says he's frightfully sorry, but this isn't really what you want. It's a side-line he discovered and thought you ought to have – but –' she passed him the slip of paper – 'are you quite sure it isn't? Oh, do make quite, quite sure before *you* say it isn't,' she begged eagerly. Up on the hills she had felt so confident, despite Mick's gloomy doubts, that the long-sought secret lay in their hands, but as she handed it to M. Beaumarchais her bright certainty wavered a trifle.

'Tell me what happened to you. Where is Mick? Is he on his way here?' M. Beaumarchais unfolded the slip of paper as he spoke.

But it was too dark in the sunken garden to decipher Mick's faint pencil drawing. He moved towards the house, with Caroline trotting at his elbow, narrating her adventures with Cousin Karl. 'And Mick did say he was going to stay and have another shot,' she finished doubtfully. 'But I should think now that he'll realize the General's almost bound to connect him with me. I expect he'll come straight here tonight, don't you?'

'Yes,' said M. Beaumarchais absently. 'We'll try and get

you both away as soon as possible. The island will be no health-resort for you two children.' He entered the porch, pushed open the front-door, and went into the lighted house. It was clear that his thoughts were centred on the slip of tracing-paper that Caroline had handed into his keeping.

Caroline, sensing his preoccupation, turned back into the garden. It was so gorgeous a night that she was reluctant to shut herself up indoors. She felt she must work off some of her excitement by walking round and round the garden until M. Beaumarchais returned to tell her what Mick had discovered. The autumn moon was now riding in triumph through the sky, and the stars were beginning to twinkle. The night-wind had dropped completely in this silent garden in the hollow of the hills. Caroline was just stepping on to the lawn when her eye was caught by a movement in the shadows on the far side of the lawn. Her hand flew up to her mouth, and she caught her breath. Was Cousin Karl lurking there in the dark undergrowth? Even as the thought crossed her mind it was dispelled. A figure emerged from where the chestnut boughs swept the grass. It walked out into the moonlight and started to trudge to the house – a small, stocky figure with a listless droop to its shoulders.

Caroline had no doubts about the identity of the figure. She hurled herself upon it in one terrific leap. 'O Mick,' she said, 'I'm so thankful you've come. I thought you would. Did anybody see you leave?'

Mick plodded steadily across the moonlit grass to the house. Beyond a weary grin at his sister he seemed singularly unresponsive. 'Where's M. Beaumarchais?' was the only answer he made to Caroline's inquiries.

In the moonlight Caroline could see that he was covered with dust and very untidy. 'He's in the house reading your map-thing,' she replied. 'Mick, how did you get here?'

'Bike. Coast-road,' replied Mick tersely. 'I hid the beastly thing in a bush a couple of miles back so that they couldn't track me here, and walked on.'

'Caroline.' M. Beaumarchais reappeared on the porch, searching the darkened garden with his eyes.

'Mick's come, M. Beaumarchais,' called Caroline joyfully as the pair came up to the porch.

M. Beaumarchais shepherded both children into the hall and shut the heavy front-door behind them. The sudden light made both Mick and Caroline blink. Before he could say a word to welcome the new arrival Mick had stepped forward.

'I'm awfully sorry, sir,' he said in flat tones, 'I couldn't get the information you wanted. I meant to stay and have another shot, but when the General's nephew got hold of Caroline I knew sooner or later there'd be inquiries. I thought I'd better quit. I'm awfully sorry.'

There was a pause. Mick stood his ground, weary but dignified in his failure. Caroline's eyes went from him to M. Beaumarchais. Then M. Beaumarchais spoke. 'But Michael,' he said, 'you have not failed. Indeed you have not. The little map you have so carefully drawn for me is the very information for which we have been waiting.'

Both children stood open-mouthed, staring up at him.

'I – I don't understand,' said Mick at last. 'There was nothing about a date on it. It was the change of invasion-date you wanted.'

M. Beaumarchais regarded his dishevelled guest with a smile. '*Non*, Michael,' he said, 'it is not *date*, it is *place* that matters.'

Caroline sat down on the lowest stair as though it were all too much for her. Mick continued to stand, gazing at M. Beaumarchais like an untidy little owl.

'The messages that our agents in Berlin intercepted, both about a date for the invasion and a change of date, were blinds. They were meant to distract the attention of our men and cause them to concentrate upon discovering the new *date*,' M. Beaumarchais explained.

'But I still don't see,' put in Caroline, clutching her head in her bewilderment, 'what were our agents meant to be distracted *from*?'

'From the *place* where the barges were hidden. We were given to understand that the Tower inlet was the base for these invading barges and supply ships. They gave me to understand that even when they requested me to formulate some strategy for taking the Tower. It was one of the most elaborate bluffs ever staged by Germany. Only a few, a handful of men in the High Command, knew the truth. The barges are not in that base at all. They are in the less good but less obvious bases – the inlets on the other side of the island. Those markings on Mick's map, in conjunction with other scraps of information we have collected but have been unable to understand, confirm this beyond a doubt. It is the most incredible good fortune that that bit of tracing-paper got in among the unused slips – and the most incredible piece of carelessness upon the part of somebody at Headquarters. It is only a rough sketch, and was probably meant to be destroyed. If the markings on it are really as faint as Mick has copied them it is no wonder that the paper was mistaken for a clean piece. That yellow waxed paper is very deceptive.'

'But – but –' stuttered Mick, 'the barges *are* in the Tower inlet. You told us definitely they were.'

'False barges are there. They knew our reconnaissance planes would be over. There is only a mere showing of anti-aircraft fire round the Tower. The real barges, probably very heavily camouflaged, are on the east side of the island. The code-signs for barge concentrations on your map are quite unmistakable, Mick. The Nazis are now simply waiting for the R.A.F. to make up its mind to bomb the concentration on the *west* side by the Tower. Then, on the appointed invasion-date, the fleet will sail, unharmed, from the real bases. I knew all along Germany could not afford to go on losing barges at the rate of the past few months. It is all very, very clever – but we are even cleverer,' finished M. Beaumarchais calmly.

'Oh,' shrieked Caroline, unable to keep quiet any longer. She had been fidgeting for some minutes while M. Beaumarchais was speaking. 'Don't for goodness' sake, stand talking to us any longer. Can't you do something about it? The R.A.F.'ll start bombing the wrong place. Can't you get in touch with them right away?' She danced up and down in an agony on the staircase.

M. Beaumarchais began to laugh. 'It is all right, *mes enfants*,' he said. 'What is your phrase? – keep your hair on. The English Secret Service knows all about it, and so by now does the Bomber Command. Mick, Caroline will be able to tell you that our communications with England during the past week have improved beyond recognition. We are no longer completely dependent upon a cork and an oilskin wallet. We now have our little portable pocket wireless for morse transmission. Generally I set it up on the hills if I have a message to send, to avoid having the transmission tracked back to La Falaise. But tonight I risked it. While you children were in the garden I sent the information through. I rather fancy that by tomorrow morning most of that particular invasion fleet will be strewing the coast with its wreckage, thanks to Mick and yourself.'

'Oooh, not *me*. It was all Mick.'

'Gosh, not *me*. It was absolutely accident.'

'*Both* of you,' affirmed M. Beaumarchais stoutly, leading the way into the dining-room. 'It was good teamwork between the pair of you. Now, there is need of much haste. You must be off the island before the R.A.F. put in an appearance this evening. Food first, and then Peter and I will conduct you down to the beach.'

*

An hour later the little party of four stood for the last time on the famous ledge outside the Pony Club Headquarters. It was, M. Beaumarchais remarked, not the best kind of night for a secret embarkation, since the whole landscape was flooded with bright moonlight.

The supper, which they had eaten before leaving the house, had turned into the most hilarious celebration, with everybody in the highest possible spirits and inclined to giggling and general over-excitement. Peter had come racing down the drive on a ramshackle borrowed bike in the nick of time, and had ransacked the La Falaise larder for food that bore even the faintest resemblance to party fare. He cleverly managed to produce a box of crackers and paper streamers left over from the famous Carnival, so that the scene speedily became positively festive with paper-caps and toast-drinking and coloured ribbons festooned round all the furniture. Everybody enjoyed themselves the more because M. Beaumarchais, beaming from under a brigadier-general's paper hat, assured them that the danger really was over.

Nobody, he said, would ever connect Mick with the leakage about the invasion barges, since he had so carefully put the original map back among the other papers, and since Nannerl was extremely unlikely to confess to having borrowed the pile of tracing-paper for her own uses. The General would merely think that Petit-Jean had helped Caroline to run away and had then run away himself. Probably, added M. Beaumarchais, there would be a hue and cry for them, but the Nazis would never be able to trace them to La Falaise. He did not see fit to tell the party that it would be necessary for him tomorrow to cover up their tracks considerably more skilfully than they had done themselves.

In the middle of all the excitement Caroline had found time to draw Peter aside and tell him about the enrolling of Nannerl as a Junior Member. 'Could you keep an eye on her?' she urged him, as they left the house after supper and made their way over the cliffs towards the beach. 'You see, she'll be so awfully sick about Petit-Jean disappearing, and she's got no one to ride with except that horrible Cousin Karl.'

'I will,' promised Peter, and added that he could see no reason why, when the children of other Nazi officials joined their parents on the island, the Pony Club should not be restarted. 'You and Mick wouldn't mind us carrying the show on, would you?' he asked.

'Goodness, no, not a scrap,' answered Caroline cheerfully, clinging to Peter's elbow as she scrambled down the cliff path. 'We shall be frantically busy getting the London branch started, and coping with Hubert and Penelope. It'll be marvellous thinking of you sweating away on Clerinel teaching little Nazis to ride. Couldn't you make Nannerl secretary, or is she too young?'

Peter laughed, but would not commit himself. They joined Mick and M. Beaumarchais on the ledge and stood in a line peering across the moonlit bay.

'Listen!' M. Beaumarchais raised a hand. 'There he is – to the minute we arranged.' The low, muffled sound of oars rose to the children's ears from the water below. Peter turned on his heel and led the little cavalcade down to the shore, with Caroline and M. Beaumarchais bringing up the rear, the former shivering with excitement. As they reached the water's edge a boat, manned by ratings, loomed up out of the darkness, and a dark figure jumped out into the shallow water with a slight splash.

'This my party?' whispered a voice that sounded more accustomed to booming across the decks of a capital ship. A short stout naval officer with a cheerful face shook hands all round as M. Beaumarchais in a low voice performed the introductions. Caroline could barely distinguish his features in the moonlight, but she knew in an instant that she was going to like him and would enjoy travelling to England in his company.

'You seem to have done some pretty good work,' said Commander Seymour to Mick as M. Beaumarchais propelled the hero of the party forward. 'I want to hear all about it. In fact, there are several people in London who are anxious to hear the whole story, and say a polite thank you.' He drew M. Beaumarchais aside for a few words, while the boat bobbed up and down on the miniature waves like a float.

While the grown-ups talked the three children gathered in a little group on the wet ribbed sand by the water's edge. They stood first on one leg, then on the other. There was nothing left to say. Caroline felt vaguely that these last precious moments should be filled with memorable sayings that each would treasure in his innermost heart until they all met again after the war. But they had talked themselves tired. Their throats were dry and their brains were blanks.

'Now then, you two, hop in.' Commander Seymour, followed by M. Beaumarchais, returned briskly across the sand from his private confabulation. 'If we're to get clear before the fun begins we must set sail. She's a lot safer than she appears, Caroline, so you needn't look so dismayed.'

'I thought we were going by destroyer,' wailed Caroline, 'not in a thing like that.'

The other four burst into a roar of laughter, quickly hushed by M. Beaumarchais. 'She's out in the bay all right, my dear,' chuckled Commander Seymour; 'even she draws too much water for these shallows, you know.'

Caroline turned scarlet, and flung herself into the arms of M. Beaumarchais and planted a large kiss on his moustache. 'Good-bye, good-bye,' she said. 'Thank you most awfully for having us, and do take care of yourself and not get caught.' She had forgotten for ever how she and Mick had once detested the funny little Frenchman. She crept gingerly into the boat with Mick after her. Commander Seymour took his place and the ratings pushed off.

'Good-bye, good-bye.'

'Good-bye, Mick. Good-bye, Caroline.'

'See you after the war, Peter.'

'Good-bye, and good luck.'

The farewell whispers floated over the widening strip of silver water that separated the little boat-load from Clerinel.

Huddled in the bows Caroline strained her eyes for a last sight of the beloved island. But Clerinel was already hidden in the darkness. Anyway, she thought, it didn't much matter. Like the ponies, Clerinel would be there after the war. It was the same thought with which she had comforted herself up on the cliffs earlier in the evening. Funny, even that last ride over the hills on Dinah was already beginning to seem like a dream. She settled herself more comfortably. 'I've got plenty of rugs and coats aboard the *Ibex*,' said the Commander, as the boat shot across the bay towards the open sea.

For some minutes nobody spoke. Suddenly there was a low murmuring among the men and a word of command. Oars were shipped, and the boat lost way until it floated idly on the calm, silver sea.

'What's happened?'

'Somebody seen us?'

Both children started from their respective reveries and shot the questions at the Commander. Then – 'It's all right,' said Caroline, reassured. 'Look, Mick, he doesn't think there's anything wrong.' She dug her brother in the ribs and indicated the still figure of the Commander, as he threw back his head and listened intently. The ratings, too, had raised their heads.

'But what is it?' asked Mick, leaning forward.

'Listen!' said the Commander.

At first with their less-trained ears they could hear nothing. Then, from far over the horizon, came the hum of distant engines, nearer, nearer.

'What are they?' whispered Caroline, remembering the last time, standing on the quayside in Pol les Roches, that she had heard those great engines sweeping across the sky.

In the moonlight she saw Commander Seymour shake his head at her sudden apprehensions. There was a note of triumph in his voice. 'No,' he said, 'not Nazis this time. That's the first wave of British bombers coming to attack the invasion fleet on the east coast of Clerinel. There's more to come.'

'Have we really stopped the invasion?' said Caroline, awestruck.

The Commander smiled. 'They'll try again,' he said. 'They'll go on trying. But we shall always beat them. Don't you worry.'

He gave the order to return to ship. The children sat with their heads flung back, scanning the sky as the drone of the first wave of planes died away in the distance. A minute later the tall bows of the *Ibex* rose up almost above the boat in the moonlight.